SOMETHING NEW

A Novel

By

Angie D. Lee

ISBN 978-1-7328641-2-2 (paperback)
ISBN 978-1-7328641-3-9 (ebook)

www.angiedlee.com

To every woman who chooses vulnerability, authenticity, and fearlessness. You are embraced.

CHAPTER

1

Mama named me Serenity because she said I was a peaceful child, unlike my older brothers, James and Ellis, who were always rambunctious as hell. She said I was a free-spirited soul, one who followed the beat of my own drum, who brought a sense of calmness to her life. When Mama was married to my dad, he used to abuse her, including while she was pregnant with me.

My dad used to hit my mom so hard it'd knock the wind out of her. She often contemplated aborting me because she didn't want the reminder of how much he hurt her. She wasn't sure if she or I would survive the pregnancy. My dad would strangle her so hard she was sure she'd die. Despite this abuse, Mama said she couldn't get rid of me. She said I came to her in a dream, and she could see my hazel eyes, curly hair, and smile. She loved me then, and my mama's love was like no other.

My fortieth birthday was quickly, yet dreadfully, approaching this weekend. The last few years, I'd typically been in a somber mood on this day. Mama passed away three years ago on my thirty-seventh birthday, and ever since then, I hadn't really been myself. I became stoic; I lost my zeal for life. I felt like time stood still, and I just couldn't come to terms with this hole in my heart.

Her death affected every part of me, including my marriage. Dave, my ex-husband, could only hang on for so long, and I couldn't blame him. I was no longer the same person he knew after Mama passed.

I used to be a thriving yoga instructor at one of the top yoga studios in Sedona, Arizona. I led some outstanding yoga retreats three times a year that brought people together from all walks of life. We didn't have children and never really felt that was a priority for us; we just enjoyed each other's company and felt children would disrupt that. We held weekly potlucks and mindfulness sessions at our home, traveled often, and lived and explored life together. I would fly Mama out to Phoenix all the time to hang with us. The look in her eyes always held a lot of pride. She understood me.

As a child, I loved quiet time, poetry, being in tune with others, and following my own path. My big brothers often called me weird, but Mama always protected me and said I was otherworldly, an anomaly of some sort. Her love for me gave me so much confidence.

People always told me, for a black girl, I had a very exotic look and could be a model or an actress, but none of that ever appealed to me. Mama always encouraged my thoughts and goals. She would say, "Serenity, you wanna join the circus? Go right ahead. You wanna hang out with animals for a living? Well, be the best goddamn vet you can be. You wanna join an ashram? I will buy your ticket and get you settled." She loved me so much and honored the explorer in me.

When Mama died, I lost a piece of myself, and there was nothing Dave could do about it. I've always respected the choices people make, and I felt no different about Dave's decision to end our marriage. I had to let him go in peace because I, too, was on a journey and didn't know if I would come back to him the way he'd hoped.

For the past three years, I just couldn't seem to connect with anyone on the deep, spiritual level I yearned for. Mama was always the catalyst for that in my life. She was my rock and the one I would go to for guidance. Because of her, I felt I was able to connect with myself and others.

I rarely got to see my friends anymore. Cynthia, my girl from my hometown and NYU, was living in New York, and Jeanette had been on mission trips for the past year and a half. Thank God for Dave's alimony checks; they allowed me the freedom to visit them whenever my heart desired, but I rarely even made the effort.

I guessed, technically, I would be considered depressed, but I didn't believe that. I felt it was completely normal to grieve my mom. Yes, there were days where it was hard for me to get out of bed, and honestly, my appetite did wane a bit, but I still went to work and taught yoga classes. I typically spent my free time in the library reading, and occasionally, I would go to the movies. I was still grieving, but I knew deep down inside it would eventually turn around. I would never force anyone to wait on me during this time, but I also didn't believe I needed to rush the process; I gave myself permission to do just that. I decided to call Cynthia because talking to her always made me feel better.

"I swear, Serenity, you always seem to call me when I am literally thinking about picking up the phone. I don't know how you do it, but it's like you have super powers or something. But now that I think about it, your mom was the same way."

"For some reason, you're the only person that can mention my mom without bringing me to tears. Now, how do you that?"

Cynthia and I met in our sophomore year of college. We were two city girls from Baltimore, broke as hell, trying to make it at NYU as sociology majors. I was always excited to learn about people, relationships, and human activity. However, as much as Cynthia tried, sociology just wasn't her thing. Cynthia thrived in the corporate world. She loved calling the shots and was career driven, so she switched her major junior year to Leadership and Management Studies and later on became an investment banker. To say we were like night and day was an understatement, but we were extremely close, and she loved Mama, which brought us even closer.

In college, I would attend underground poetry sets or research vegetarian lifestyle or meditation. I also wasn't into committed relationships with men; I was more into free love. I believed people should not feel stifled by "settling" with one person. I guessed that was why it came as such a shock when Dave and I married, but at the time, he seriously swept me off of my feet.

Cynthia was all about status and loved to shop. In an effort to support her spending habit, she actually worked as a high-class call girl for a couple of years while we were in college. Cynthia wasn't too much of a party animal, though. She was always working toward her business and making money. What attracted me to Cynthia was her heart of gold. She loved hard and was genuine. I even lived with Cynthia for about a year when I was struggling financially, prior to meeting and marrying Dave. She was barely home, as she traveled often for work, but she was there for me during a time I needed her most and was there in ways most people wouldn't have been when Mama died. I would always love her for that.

"Well, your mom was amazing, and I will always honor her because she birthed you. I love you, Serenity, and I miss you so much! We haven't seen each other in, like, a year. We've got to do better."

Cynthia knew how much I had been struggling with Mama over the past three years, and there were many times she tried reaching out to me. I had a difficult time reaching back, but Cynthia always kept trying; it was just in her nature. She didn't take no for an answer and was always very strategic about it. I guessed that was the result of all those years of being an investment banker and knowing how to convince businesses to entrust her with their accounts. With time, her clients grew to love her because they would witness their returns. Cynthia was definitely a friend I trusted with my life. She had my back, and I knew anything she did was with a pure heart.

"I know, Cynthia. I've been doing better, though. I'm getting out more, getting back into activities I love. I went to an art gallery last night. It was pretty cool, until I saw a painting that reminded me of Mama, and I had to step away. I felt like it took me back a few steps."

"When was the last time you saw your therapist?" Cynthia asked, concerned.

"It's been a few months. For a while, I felt like I was making progress, and then I just had a moment when I realized none of this is going to bring Mama back." I was fighting back the tears as I said this.

"I know, honey, but therapy is there to help you come to terms with the world you now live in without your mom and how to navigate in that space." Cynthia's voice was warm and soothing, as if counseling a teen dealing with self-esteem issues and feelings of inadequacy.

"I guess I'll start going back. It's just hard sometimes; it really is."

"I really do empathize with you, Serenity. That's why I booked a flight to Phoenix for two weeks. I'm coming to see you next month. I'm so excited!"

"Oh my God, seriously? How in the hell were you able to skip work for two whole weeks?"

"Look, don't worry about that. You know I've got this! Just know I'm coming to see my Poodah and that's final."

I loved how Cynthia did her own thing, no questions asked. No one could tell her what to do, but this never made her seem cocky. She used her wealth and flexible schedule for good and was coming to see me. She used Poodah as a term of endearment for me. Cynthia was only a few months older than me but treated me like a younger sister. She was territorial over me, but I liked having someone fill the older sister role, as I'd only grown up with brothers.

"I can't wait! Thanks, Cynthia, I kind of need this time with you."

"Girl, well, you've got me for a whole two weeks now. We gon' kick it, and maybe we'll find you a man."

"Look, you know I'm not really into that right now."

"So, you saying you into women now? I can help you find a girlfriend too! You know you've always been a free spirit." Cynthia chuckled.

"Look, neither. I haven't had sex since Dave and I split a year and a half ago. I've been content with arriving on my own," I said confidently.

"Hmm, see, that could very well be the problem. Getting yourself off can get old. With my busy lifestyle, that was a regular occurrence until Rob and I hooked up again. I didn't realize how much I craved a man's hands on my body and the comfort I would get from that. Yeah, toys are cool and all, but it doesn't replace human touch."

I knew Cynthia was right, but all I could think about was the time and effort it would take to meet someone, build a connection, and let them into my space. Quite honestly, I didn't feel like getting all dolled up, shaving, and taking a much-needed trip to the salon for a new look.

"Cynthia, I hear everything you're saying."

"Yeah, I know what that means. You hear me, but you ain't listening."

We giggled like school girls because Cynthia knew me so well.

"But seriously, I'm so glad you're coming out to see me next month. I can't wait. This time of year is tough for me. While my birthday is right around the corner, it's also the anniversary of Mama's death. Even years after she finally decided to pack up and move us away from my father, his abuse loomed over my mom, and sometimes, I wonder if the stress and hurt of her escape is what caused her stroke. Even after she heard about him passing away, she always appeared on edge, as if she thought he would come back from the dead or something."

"That's heavy stuff, sis. All the more reason to go back to therapy, you know? You owe that to yourself."

"I know. I'm doing the best I can."

"I know you are. I just want to remind you that you have support."

"Cynthia, God, I miss you, and I can't wait to reconnect."

"Same here, Poodah. I'll talk to you soon, okay?"

"Okay, hun."

Hearing Cynthia's voice and knowing she was coming to town had me excited and boosted my energy. I needed to connect with my girl, and I always appreciated her persistence. Lord knew I needed that in my life right now. I was really fortunate to have her as my friend.

As I sat down on my fraying sofa with its sunken pillows and faded blue fabric, I smiled. It was the first piece of furniture Mama bought for our apartment when she left my dad. She was working two jobs in order to keep us afloat without his financial support. When she earned her first two paychecks, I distinctly remember her writing a check for the rent and then ordering a new sofa from the neighborhood furniture store. She was so proud of that couch. We spent many birthdays, holidays, and house parties on those cushions, and when I got my first apartment after college, I told her I wanted it. Mama smiled and said, "You know, I was just about to get rid of this thing. I can actually afford something better now."

That sofa meant so much to me because, when I was a kid, my dad punched Mama in the face and blood began to gush out of her nose onto our old sofa. I cried as if I could feel the sting of that same blow within my own nostrils. She tried so hard to get that stain out of the sofa, but it was always there. She never knew I saw them that night, and she never told us about that blotch. She made it seem as if someone had spilled something on it or that she couldn't remember how it had gotten there. At times, she would try to camouflage it with a throw pillow or a slipcover, but my dad would always get angry with her and tell her to arrange the sofa back to the way it was because he liked its original color. Sometimes when she sat on that sofa, she would rub the blood-stained fabric profusely, get angry and cry when she thought no one was looking. She was extremely broken, and even as a little girl, I could feel her imbalance and despair.

Mama was determined to make a fresh start when we finally broke free of my dad's destructive hold. She didn't even bother buying beds or a coffee table. I wasn't surprised the first piece of furniture she bought was a new sofa. Mama didn't want any reminders of the pain she endured. I never questioned her about it because I knew why. When the sofa arrived at our house, Mama enveloped herself in it, as if she had never experienced anything new in her life before. She started rubbing the sofa like she used to when she would think about the blood stain, but I guessed when she realized she was no longer living in that world, she broke into a sob that scared my brothers. They kept asking her what was wrong, and I quietly sat down next to her and held her without saying a word. At that moment, I could tell Mama knew I understood.

So, my collapsing sofa that I was sitting on right now meant the world to me because it meant the world to her. Dave always felt the couch wasn't a good fit for our home, but that was one non-negotiable thing for me and probably would always be.

*****

It was my fortieth birthday and the three-year anniversary of Mama's death. I dreaded my birthday these days. Over the past couple years, I would seclude, lie in bed, and just cry all day. Rarely would I pick up the phone and allow anyone to formally wish me a happy birthday. I would typically send a text back with a dry *thanks*, thinking that was acceptable enough, as if I had some major plans going on at the time. I just couldn't pull it together.

I remember Dave trying to throw me a party two years ago on the anniversary of Mama's death. All I could think about was how insensitive he was for thinking I would want to party on that day. I was furious and said things to him I could never take back. I'd seen how couples experienced the death of a close family member or friend and how they would lash out at one another, but somehow, they would survive such challenging times. Dave and I just couldn't weather that storm, I guessed.

Sometimes, I wondered if I was ever really in my marriage for the long haul to begin with. Dave and I were only married five years and those years were great, but we didn't deal with our problems. I was attracted to his spontaneity and carefree lifestyle, but I wasn't sure we ever really connected. He was actually seven years younger than me but had such an old soul.

Dave had created an app while attending college that helped students keep track of their grades and GPA. He hit the jackpot with that one and ended up dropping out of school and moving to Silicon Valley. He was only twenty-one years old at the time. Then there was my bum ass, who took a quick trip to California with Cynthia and Jeanette, despite not having a dime to my name. Even though I couldn't contribute anything, Cynthia loved having me around. For some reason, she never felt weird about helping me out. Cynthia had high standards—she didn't hang around no bums, but she never made me feel bad about my situation and even paid for my trip to California. That was where I met Dave.

Dave was a lanky twenty-one-year-old, but he approached me as if he were older. He was tall and scrawny chested, but the outline of his package in his pants was impressive; he was obviously well endowed. He was easygoing and respectful. I was worried he'd feel entitled to everything, including a free-spirited, bohemian black girl like myself. I appreciated that this wasn't the case. He was intelligent and respectful—even with my 36C perkies staring him in the face.

Dave was Jewish, but we had similar backgrounds. He too had grown up in an abusive household, but for some reason, Dave just didn't seem as broken as me. Maybe he had his shit together, even at twenty-one years old. We had sex the same night, making love to me as if he knew me in another life, and when I would refer to what turned me on, he was so eager to please. I think Dave loved me from the moment he saw me.

We kept in touch for years even though we lived in different states. I was trying to get my life together, and I wasn't exactly sold on the idea of a long-distance relationship at the time. I was a tad bit stressed because I couldn't find a job to save my life with a sociology degree. A friend suggested I take up yoga to relax my mind. Before I knew it, I was doing yoga every day. I saw an ad at one of my classes regarding getting certified to become a yoga instructor, so I figured I'd give it a try. I didn't have anything to lose. I ended up loving it and began teaching yoga part time while waiting tables at night.

As much as I appreciated Cynthia for allowing me a space in her home, I was tired of the cold weather and wanted a change of scenery. I thought California was so expensive, but I loved the weather and was determined to live there. When I told Dave I was moving to California and that I was looking for recommendations of where to live, he said, "Why don't you come live with me? You can have your own space. I won't bother you. You'll still pay a portion of the rent and bills. I just want to help you out."

I took Dave up on his offer, and as much as we tried to just be "roommates," it turned into something much more. We didn't really want to see other people, but anytime we wanted to explore outside of our relationship, we were honest with each other. Dave's business continued to take off, and he felt that Arizona was a good move for him. I figured that was the beginning of the end for us, but then he asked me if I'd want to move with him. I said yes, then he asked me to be his wife.

Dave was a good guy. Because of his job and lifestyle, we were able to travel the world. We saw everything, from the Taj Mahal and the Great Barrier Reef to the Great Wall of China. Dave knew how much I loved the outdoors and how I connected with nature, so he made sure we traveled the world.

But when Mama died, I couldn't get a grip on anything. My job, my friendships, my relationship with my brothers, and even my willingness to explore life felt like it was slipping through my fingers. Dave was as attentive as he could be; even with a busy schedule, he made time for me. He rearranged meetings to sit quietly with me while I cried and attempted to respond sensitively to my moods. He also offered to teach a few of my yoga classes when I just couldn't get out of bed. He'd mastered a lot of the poses, and watching him do each brought a smile to my face.

When grief took hold of me, it was like nothing mattered. It had gotten to a point where I felt Dave couldn't say or do anything right. I even made a comment to him one day that he was too young and inexperienced to handle a woman who had been through so much. I would never forget the look on his face when I said that. It was as if I diminished who he was and everything he'd been through in just a matter of seconds, and I couldn't take it back. For the first time, I saw tears swell in his eyes. I thought that was Dave's breaking point. I wish I could've taken it all back, but just like Mama's death, it was something I had no control over. I would never excuse my words and actions toward Dave, but he was the closest person to me at the time, so every emotion seeping from my pores, he essentially felt and had to endure.

The ring of my phone distracted me from my thoughts. Well, speak of the devil, sure enough, Dave was calling me.

"Happy birthday, Serenity."

"Thanks so much for calling, Dave. I was seriously just thinking about you…well, thinking about us."

"Us?"

"Well, not exactly *us*, but just what we've been through over the past couple years. Why do you sound surprised?"

"Well, it is your birthday and the anniversary of your mom's death. I know how difficult this time is for you, so I just figured I would've been the furthest thing from your mind. I'm actually shocked you answered the phone. I was about to leave you a message."

"Every day is a challenge, but I'm taking it day by day. I'm going to start seeing my therapist again," I said with a bit of lightness in my voice.

"That's…good to hear." I noted the hesitance in his voice and sighed.

"Look, Dave, I know you tried really hard to get me to be consistent with therapy, but please know you did everything you could, and I totally understand why you felt you had to end our marriage. Your own sanity and self-preservation were at stake. I have to respect that. I know how difficult it must've been for you to live with me, considering the depth of my grief. I'm just trying to find my way."

"You sound a lot better, Serenity, and I miss the hell out of you—if that's okay to say?"

I smiled. "I accept that."

Our laughter felt good, and when we settled down, he asked, "Hey, can I take you out to lunch? I mean, it is your birthday."

"I'm not sure if Melissa would be okay with that."

Melissa was a busty, brunette fitness model who used to be a member at the yoga studio I currently taught at. I did peep how she kept questioning me about Dave and when he would teach a class again. I politely set her ass straight and let her know Dave was *my* husband and was temporarily filling in for me. I never trusted her, and I hated feeling that way because being jealous was not me. It always seemed like she was plotting to get Dave, and after Mama passed away and I fell apart, she made her move. To my knowledge, he was always committed to me. I couldn't be mad that Melissa decided to shoot her shot at Dave after our divorce. He owned the juice bar in the same plaza as the yoga studio, so she was bound to run into him at some point.

"Melissa and I are dating, yes, but she's not exclusively my girlfriend, you know?"

"So, you all have a situation-ship is what you're saying?"

Dave's laugh always sounded like a hyena in heat, but I still loved him just the same. "You crack me up, Serenity."

"Dave, get with the times," I teased. "I'm older than you, and I'm hipper with the lingo than you are."

"Whatever, Serenity. So, are we gonna do lunch or what?"

"I would like that. Can I pick the place?"

"Of course! Whatever you want, I got you."

"Thanks so much, Dave. All jokes aside, I really needed this, so thank you for constantly reaching out, even when I didn't have the strength to reach back."

"Always. So, you mentioned you were thinking about us earlier. In what way?"

"How about we chat about that over lunch? I need to shower, and shaving my legs wouldn't be a bad idea as well."

"You know I don't care about that," he said. "I like when you're in your earthy space."

"All the more reason for me to shave."

"Serenity, are you trying to make yourself less attractive to me? Because you know that's just not possible."

This was an interesting position Dave and I were in. I knew he still loved me and, no doubt, I still loved him, but hell, he divorced me, not the other way around. I couldn't help but wonder where all this talk was headed. I tried not to think too hard about it and just enjoy my birthday for once.

"No, I just like to joke around with you. But let's meet up soon at—"

"Meet up?" Dave chuckled. "C'mon, you know I'll come get you. It's not like I don't know where you live."

"Okay, you've got a point. Give me about thirty minutes to get myself together."

"It always amazed me it never took you long to get ready. I guess that's how it goes when you're a natural beauty."

Dave never hesitated to compliment me while we were married, but for a divorced couple, he was laying it on pretty thick, and it was apparent us getting together today meant a little more to him than I expected. I was still dealing with a lot of emotions and had a lot to work through with my therapist, but I wanted this to be cool.

"Okay, Dave, I know it's my birthday, but you don't have to do all of that."

"One thing I've learned from being married to you is when you need space. So, we're just going to enjoy your day. I wouldn't want compliments to make you uncomfortable," Dave said.

"Thanks. You know I'm still dealing with a lot. I just don't want to get overwhelmed—"

"No need to explain at all, Serenity. I'll see you in about thirty minutes."

"Okay, cool."

When I hung up the phone. I couldn't really tell if Dave was disappointed or not. I guessed I would find out soon. It would've been easy getting swept up in feelings from the past like sharing cute compliments with one another and the excitement of going out on a date. I didn't want to fall into that trap because we were no longer together. We had only been divorced for about a year and a half, and we hadn't really spoken much since then, but it was apparent Dave had moved on and started dating. I just didn't feel the need to get tangled up in the nostalgia. I still loved Dave, but I couldn't help thinking his decision to get a divorce was for my own good, though Melissa did seem more like his type. I wasn't surprised to find out he was into her. She could've been my opposite—her appearance either surgically enhanced or achieved through a waist trainer. I was in pretty good shape myself due to yoga and a vegetarian lifestyle, and genetics had already blessed me with some curves, but it wasn't like I was interested in making sure the whole world knew it existed. I knew Dave had never been a shallow guy, but he was rich, young, in his prime, and tended to attract those type of women. Maybe it was only a matter of time. Then again, maybe I was still going through my own shit. One thing was for sure: I knew Dave always wanted me to be happy, and I would always love him for that.

I took a quick shower, ran some styling cream through my hair, and applied a little mascara on my lashes, highlighter on my cheeks, and gloss on my lips. When they said, "black don't crack," they weren't lying, because for a forty-year-old biracial beauty like myself, I was doing alright.

*****

"So, I see you decided to bring me to the very first restaurant we visited when we moved to Arizona," I said.

"Well, you were still undecided about where you wanted to go, and I know how much you loved this place. You love vegetarian food, and when we moved here, I wasn't able to tear you away from this place."

"Thanks, Dave, but you really didn't have to do this."

"I wanted to. What's wrong with doing something nice for you on your birthday?"

"There's nothing wrong with it. I just don't want you to feel like you have to go overboard today after everything. I'm not your wife anymore, remember?"

He hesitated before speaking, "I hope this doesn't come off sounding insensitive, but I don't feel bad about our divorce. I love you, Serenity, and I always will, but I still feel like it was the best decision for both of us. Just because we're not together doesn't mean I can't treat you to something nice on your special day. I know you're open to the kind of friendship we share even though I'm not your husband anymore. Even when we were married, you didn't try to define what we shared based off societal norms, so why define this? We'll always be connected no matter what. I will always acknowledge your birthday and will always be here for you."

I reached out and patted his hand. "I appreciate that, Dave." Even with no ring, his hand was just the same as it was. Maybe he was right; maybe we didn't need to define this. I never needed to before.

"You know," I started, drawing my hand back and lacing my fingers through the other, "I miss that." He raised a quizzical eyebrow, and I laughed. "Feeling free, I mean. Like I was before."

"And you will. It just takes time."

"I hear you, and I'm looking forward to going back to my therapist and sorting a lot of these things out."

"I'm really glad to hear that," he said. "Believe it or not, I've actually been seeing a therapist myself."

"Wow, really? What made you start going?"

"Well, when you met me, I was just a kid who just earned way more money than he knew how to handle, both economically and socially. My circle of friends changed, and it was kind of tough dealing with their jealousy or greed. My friends were the people I could really count on. I just really started to come to terms with that around the time of our divorce. Me telling you this is not to make you feel bad because I knew you needed time to grieve. I guess we could've just separated or gone to counseling together, but I felt like you needed to totally break free from me in order to heal."

"After all these years, I never knew you felt that way."

"All I can say is therapy helps. After talking it over with my therapist, I think maybe I let you go because I didn't want you to feel like you were being forced to stay. I think I also wanted to be the hero, and twistedly, I thought sacrificing our marriage would make you happy. I know it seems kind of confusing at first, but a lot of what she says makes sense to me."

"All that matters is that it makes sense to you." I still didn't quite grasp how divorcing me was supposed to be seen as some badge of honor, but we all have our perception on things.

"I'm really glad we can still talk like this. We've had a few conversations over the phone here and there, and we've maybe seen each other three times since our divorce, so it's nice we can still be cordial and have lunch."

"You know, Dave, we've never been the kind of people to have a lot of drama. I think people always assume you can never be friends or have some sort of respectful relationship with your ex, but I beg to differ."

"Yeah, I agree."

The silence we settled into was comfortable as we both sipped on our waters, perusing the menu, but there was a question gnawing at me I was dying to know.

"Well," I said, "since we're being so open, I always wanted to know if you and Melissa hooked up while we were together. I mean, seriously, Dave, she was after you way before we divorced."

"No, I promise you we didn't. I would be lying if I said I wasn't attracted to her, obviously, but I honestly wasn't interested at the time. I was so focused on helping you through your grief and maintaining my other businesses that I never gave her a second thought. After you returned to your classes, I only saw Melissa when she was at my juice bar.

"Yeah, I'm pretty sure once she figured out your schedule, she probably showed up at the same time on purpose." I could feel myself becoming uneasy, and it took much effort to keep from rolling my eyes.

His lips quirked up in amusement. "Now, I know we're not jealous, Ms. Serenity."

"*No*," I said. "I just know women and how we can be when we really want something. Ruthless comes to mind."

"Well, Melissa and I are just good friends. Nothing serious is really going on. We've been out a few times, but we've never even had sex," Dave said while nursing his stir fry. Dave wasn't really into vegetarian dishes. He would only eat it because he knew I liked it.

"Really?"

"It's nothing to be surprised about. She's just not holding my interest. I mean, she is driven and has lots of goals in life, which I can appreciate, but I feel like it's all so mechanical. When we talk, she seems interested but not really engaged. And let's be honest, Serenity, with all the money I have, being selective is not only a choice but a necessity for me.

"I can understand where you're coming from."

"Take us for instance. You never gave a damn about any of my money. You cared more about experiences, connecting with others and nature, more than any money."

I shrugged. "That's just me. I love the outdoors and seeing parts of the world I've never seen before."

"I know. You wouldn't even want to go to five-star hotels and resorts when we traveled. You wanted to be amongst the locals."

"That's the only way to travel."

"You really opened my eyes to that." He gestured to his dish. "I also enjoy vegetarian food and yoga because of you."

"Now, stop lying about that vegetarian food."

He chuckled. "Okay, you're right about that. It's not my favorite, but I like a few things." Dave smiled and grabbed both of my hands, slowly lifting them toward his face. He stared into my eyes for a few seconds then closed his and kissed my hands. I felt Dave's energy and the Arizona breeze through the restaurant. Both calmed me.

"What was that for?" I asked while gazing into Dave's eyes.

"I miss you, and I'm sorry for how we ended. I could've been a lot more patient while you grieved. I just didn't know how."

"Dave, let's just be in the moment."

"I am in the moment with you. That's why I'm talking like this. I'm just not censoring how I feel. I'm not putting any demands on you right now, and I have no expectations. I just want to know if you're feeling what I'm feeling right now."

"I am," I admitted, though I drew my hands back. "But I'm not exactly in the space I want to be in right now. This grief has taken over my life, and I feel like I'm finally starting to deal with it."

"And take all the time you need. Again, you won't get any pushback from me."

"But seriously, Dave, if it was all really so simple, why couldn't our marriage work? I'm just curious why you didn't feel this way before."

"Like I said, I didn't give you any pushback then. I thought I was being selfless by letting you go. I know it sounds mixed up, but that's what I thought at the time. I felt like I couldn't say anything right and couldn't relieve you of any of your pain. That broke me. I didn't know how to deal with that."

"I'm not accusing you. I just don't want us to get wrapped up in nostalgia and start making rash decisions based off of that."

His brows rose in surprise. "Wow, this is a different side of you I've never really seen before."

"What? Being responsible? Taking some accountability?"

"You don't have to say it like that. I'm just saying, typically, you're a bit more relaxed about things."

"Well, clearly, you seem to think my eclecticism means throwing caution to the wind. I'm still the same person; I just don't see the point in going down memory lane with you. If anything, I feel like the person I am today is pretty much the same person I was when you decided you wanted a divorce." I could feel the frustration rising up in me. "I didn't call you an idiot, I didn't yell at you or try to force you to stay, and I definitely didn't get down on myself like I had done something wrong. *You* wanted the divorce, and I didn't fight you on it. I could not predict my mother's death. I definitely didn't know I would respond to it the way the I did. But I accepted all of me during the process. I've accepted your actions as well. So please don't talk to me about being more relaxed about things."

"I was not trying to upset you, Serenity, I promise."

"And trust me, I'm not going to let you upset me. Just look at it this way: I will always love you. We will always be friends. We can even still hang out from time to time, but anything else like getting lost in the moment, little kisses here and there, and staring into each other's eyes is pretty much a wrap. I'm angry, but I feel like our paths intertwined for a reason. We were supposed to share a life together for a time, but a decision was made to end this, and it was not because of me. So I will always respect you for what you felt you needed to do, but I'm not going back, Dave. I do not want to be with anyone who chooses to leave me during one of the absolute hardest times in my life. Still, I refuse to hold a grudge against you for it, and that, my friend, is a true free spirit."

I could tell by Dave's demeanor that he felt he was put in his place. It was not my intention, but I felt he needed to be made aware of my true feelings. I felt like Mama's death solidified something in my life, I just didn't know what it was yet. I felt like I had a new attitude and outlook on life now, and Dave deciding to divorce me was a part of this.

"I've upset you, and that was not my intention. I just wanted to do something nice for you on your birthday. I'm sorry if this brought up any bad feelings."

"Honestly, it's the opposite. I'm feeling more like myself sitting here talking with you."

"So, telling me off is actually helping you?"

We both couldn't help but laugh. I knew Dave had a good heart and typically didn't let a lot of things upset him. I was always attracted to him because of that. Those feelings could've easily resurfaced, but I didn't want them to.

"It's all good. I know you mean well. Mama's death and the time it's been taking to heal has just been a real eye opener for me lately. I feel like something new is on the horizon. I'm not sure in what context, but I believe it'll reveal itself in time."

"You've always had that intuition." After a moment of hesitation, he continued, a note of fear in his voice, "Serenity, there's something I've been wanting to give you. I'm not sure if it's the right time."

"What is it? You're making me nervous."

"I'll be right back."

I watched from the window as Dave went to get a bag from his car.

"Happy birthday, Serenity. I hope you like my gift."

I looked inside the recycled shopping bag only to see a designer shoe box which I thought was odd; he knew I wasn't very materialistic. What would make Dave think I wanted a pair of shoes for my birthday? When I opened the box, I gasped. My lips began to quiver, and a warm tear streamed down the right side of my face. I thought I had lost them—a pair of heels I bought for Mama when I graduated college.

Seeing that she was a domestic worker, she rarely dressed up. Mama said, *You know what, Serenity? When you graduate from college, I'm going to wear a pair of heels for once. I'm going to put on a little makeup too. It's about time I do that for myself.* So, I surprised her by buying her a pair of black Donna Karan heels. I'll never forget how beautiful she looked at my graduation. When Mama passed away, I wanted the funeral director to clothe her in that same dress and heels, but when I was cleaning out Mama's closet, the heels couldn't be found. I ripped everything apart only to find myself grieving all over again. My brothers insisted I calm down and "let it go because it's just a pair of heels," but they weren't to me. When it came to Mama, symbolism meant so much, and I felt like those heels were the last opportunity I had to see her just the way I remembered her.

"Where the hell did you find these?" I said while sniffling and wiping my eyes. I was pretty sure the little mascara I applied on my lashes earlier was officially extinct.

"Actually, they were at my house in the basement. I guess when I moved out, I accidentally packed them with my things. I know there were a few things you said you kept after your mom passed, but I couldn't remember what those things were. I was doing some much needed cleaning the other day and figured these were your mom's. This was my little surprise for you."

"If you only knew how much this means to me. There's so much history in these shoes, and I know people might think I'm crazy, but—"

"Stop. Don't even utter those words. You're not crazy. More and more I've come to realize the deep connection you and your mom shared."

Dave reached over and hugged me, and this particular time, I felt him. I engaged in the moment and cried. I knew his shirt would be soaked, but this was one of those times the release of grief needed to happen. Dave held me tighter while rubbing my back. He finally understood.

2

"I'll be there in a minute!"

I was in the middle of cooking one of Mama's favorite dishes, shrimp scampi, and listening to The Jones Girls' "Nights Over Egypt," which was what Mama used to play every Saturday morning while cleaning. Who could possibly be at my door? I wasn't expecting any company and Cynthia wasn't due here for another week. I ran to the door on my heels to avoid messing up my toes I'd just painted.

When I opened my door, I saw a very beautiful couple with what looked to be a seven- month-old baby in a stroller. The symmetry and bone structure the two of them had was damn near perfect and truly an act of God.

"Hey, can I help you?" I asked curiously.

"Hi, we're the Torres'. My name is Imani, and this is my husband, Alex, and our daughter, Yaya. We just moved into the neighborhood about a month ago."

"Oh, cool, welcome to the community. My name is Serenity. This neighborhood is a really nice place to live. Everyone is super friendly around here, and there're actually quite a few families, so your little one will definitely grow up with kids as well," I said as I winked at baby Yaya.

"That's so great to hear. We've already been here a month, but we haven't really had an opportunity to meet our neighbors, as we've been rather busy adjusting to our new home and Alex has his new job, but we've seen you jogging and reading on the porch. We wanted to stop by and introduce ourselves."

"Aww, well, that makes me feel good. I'm glad I could be a pleasant face who welcomes you here."

The timer on my microwave started to beep, and I could hear the water boiling with the linguine noodles for my shrimp scampi.

"We're sorry to interrupt," Alex said in a very deep yet commanding voice. "It sounds and smells like you're cooking up something rather delicious in there. We just wanted to stop by and introduce ourselves."

I was taken aback by Alex's dark brown eyes, wavy hair, and bulging muscles peeping through his collared shirt. It was apparent Alex was of African descent but also Latin, as I could pick up on his accent right away. I would be lying if I said he wasn't sexy as hell, but Imani was pretty hot herself. I couldn't help but briefly wonder about them and their story.

"Oh, you're not a bother. Actually, why don't you all come on in? It's hot as hell out there."

"Seriously? We don't want to intrude," Imani said while rocking Yaya's stroller back and forth.

"Girl, it's no stress at all. I see Lil' Mama is not feeling this sun because she's whining, and I don't want to get on her bad side. Her face is an entire mood right now."

We all laughed as I welcomed the Torres' in my home.

"Thank you! You have such a lovely home. I'm still trying to get things in order at mine." Imani sounded a little disappointed, so I waved a hand at her.

"Honey, please. You all just moved in a month ago, and you have a little one. I'm just amazed you're taking the time to meet your neighbors. But thank you."

"Well, actually we've really only taken the time to meet you so far," Alex said.

"By any chance, do you all like seafood? I'm hooking up some shrimp scampi right now, and I'm almost positive I've made enough for thirty people. Come have a seat in the living room."

"Oh, wow! Are you expecting company?" Imani asked.

I laughed. "No, thirty is exaggerating, but I've always tended to cook large meals since I was a little girl. I grew up with older brothers who ate like gorillas, so it's kind of ingrained in me even though I live alone."

"Now, that's a surprise. I just figured you had some kids who were gonna come running downstairs. You seem very welcoming, and I could tell by the way you connected with Yaya she likes you already."

"Oh, that's sweet. But no, I don't have any children, and actually, I've been divorced for almost two years now. It's just me."

"Sorry to pry," Alex apologized, and I was pleased at how genuine he sounded. "We're not trying to get all up in your business. Imani is a straightforward woman, but that's one of the things I love about her." His smile was proud.

"As you should! I love bluntness, so, Imani, I believe you and I are going to get along just fine." We smiled at each other, then Yaya started cooing as well.

"Ha! I think that's Yaya's stamp of approval. And she's also tugging on my shirt, so you know what that means."

"Yep, lunch time." Imani and I laughed.

"See, you know babies." Imani winked at me as she began pulling out her milk-filled double D's to feed her growing baby.

"Baby, can you pass me the blanket, so I can cover myself while I feed Yaya?"

"Honestly, it's up to you to cover yourself. It doesn't offend me at all," I said comfortably.

"I really appreciate that. Yaya is getting so big, and she practically rips the blanket off of herself these days anyway when she's feeding."

"I can imagine," I said.

"So, Serenity, not to bring up the whole kid subject again, but you do seem to understand a lot about babies."

"Probably because when I was married, my husband and I always had family over to our house. Many of them lived out of town, so when they would visit, they would stay with us. My brothers have kids too. I would relieve them and their wives so they could enjoy a night out. But things have changed a lot since my mom passed away, so we don't really do that as much anymore."

"I'm sorry to hear that," Alex said, voice concerned.

"I really appreciate that. I was pretty out of it for a while. My mom passing took a huge toll on me and my marriage, hence our divorce. I'm getting stronger every day, though, and most importantly, I feel better. Honestly, this is the first time I've had any company over to my house since she died three years ago. One of my homegirls from New York is actually visiting in about a week, so I'm looking forward to that. But you all have been the first people I let step foot into my home in two years. I don't know what that's about because I'm a city girl; we don't just do that with people we don't know.

"Well, I've always been told people feel pretty comfortable around me, even though they barely know me," Imani said in a confirming tone.

"Imani has always had a keen sense about people. She's very intuitive," Alex said.

"I can tell. My mom was the same way, and I feel she passed that on to me." I began staring off into space.

"Why don't I help you finish cooking," Imani suggested. "Alex, you got Yaya for a second?"

It was cool how Imani offered to help me finish preparing the food. It felt like I was getting reacquainted with a friend I hadn't seen in a while.

"Yeah, babe, go right ahead. Your milk practically knocked her out anyway." Alex chuckled.

"Thanks, hun." Imani kissed Alex on the lips, and the soft look he gave her was so endearing. Even as she walked away, I could tell he valued her and thought she was sexy. Hell, I did too. Imani's curves were mesmerizing. She had a confidence about her that could draw anyone in. Even being a new mom of a seven-month-old, she didn't look disheveled. No, the snapback was not apparent, every hair was not in place, and there was a milk stain on her shirt, but she was still so beautiful. Her voluptuousness and the way she tended to Yaya was so comforting. The fact that she wanted to help me made me more drawn to her. Imani followed me into the kitchen and appeared excited about the aroma of the food.

"So, let's see what you got cooking up in here." Imani placed a hand on her hip.

"Well, like I said, shrimp scampi is on the menu. My mom always loved when I cooked that for her," I said proudly.

"I love the way you talk about your mom. She must've been an amazing woman."

"Amazing is an understatement. She'd been through a lot in life, but she was a warrior, you know? I'm not sure if I inherited that trait. I was always more tranquil, but she really loved that about me and praised me for it."

"I can sense that calmness in you as well. Alex says the same thing about me, even though I never really saw myself that way. He loves how I don't stress about too many things and how willing I am to try something new. I remember the time I told Alex I wanted a water birth with Yaya. I thought he was going to look at me like I had two heads because he comes from a conservative family, but he was all for it. And let me tell you, he was such a champ during the whole process."

"That sounds amazing! It's funny, I know we've only just met, but I can tell you guys have a great relationship." I then send her a teasing grin. "And from the way he keeps staring at you, I can tell he's into more than just your personality," I reassured Imani.

"Ha! That's too funny. Yeah, he's so drawn to this wagon I'm dragging back here. He never hesitates to grab this Georgia Peach of mine."

"Oh, cool, you're from Georgia?" I asked.

"Sure am! Born and raised in A-T-L."

"Yes! I love it. Atlanta is definitely a spot I loved to visit. The seafood nachos out there are the truth!"

"Girl, you ain't said nothing but a word, you hear me? I miss the south, but this is our home now."

"Is that where you guys lived before moving here?" I started wondering if I was asking too many questions, but I was so intrigued by Imani. It felt good to have a conversation with someone without feeling like I was going to have a complete meltdown.

"Yeah, well, actually I met Alex in college. I went to Spellman while he was attending Morehouse. Girl, I was like, who is this Latin papi who happens to be a Kappa too? I was dumbfounded and horny as hell when I saw him at a step show." We both laughed.

"Wow, did you pledge as well?

"Yeah, I'm a Delta, but girl, I ain't been active in years. I said I was gonna get more involved again once Yaya got a little older."

"Well, I'm a firm believer in being in the now, so take baby steps. If you want to take more of an active role in your sorority, you should go for it," I advised.

"That's a good point. I want to start getting out more. I don't want to lose myself to motherhood."

"I'm pretty sure you're doing just fine. It takes a little time to adjust to your new lifestyle."

I could tell Imani was enjoying our conversation. She seemed to be blushing a little. Cynthia and Jeanette were my closest friends, and I hadn't been close to any other women since college. This was the first time in a long time I felt connected. Talking to Imani made me feel hopeful about the future. It would be nice to hang out with her and Alex again. They seemed like a fun and laid-back couple. I was really glad she and Alex stopped by.

After we finished cooking, Imani and I laid the food out across the dining room table. Alex and Yaya joined us, and we all talked and laughed like we'd known each other for years. I was finding so much solace in the moment. I brought out some wine and turned on some '90s R&B music. My house began to feel like a home again, filled with laughter and conversation. Imani got excited as she said the music brought back memories. Alex grabbed Imani's arms and wrapped them around his neck as his hands slowly moved toward her waist. They were rocking back and forth in sync, as if their bodies were made for each other. They were in their own beautiful world, and I felt like an intruder. Maybe a voyeur was a better word because I gained a certain satisfaction from watching them. I decided to direct my attention to Yaya and played with her.

"Hey, Serenity, dance with Alex while I go and change Yaya."

I hesitated, but before I could decline, Imani grabbed my arm and pulled me to Alex. She took Yaya into the living room to change her.

I clammed up a bit. I felt myself perspiring, as I didn't understand why Imani was encouraging Alex and I to be in such close proximity. I was fine dancing with a tall, sexy man, but I hadn't ever been in a position where their wife was okay with it. I definitely wasn't going to decline, though. I may have been divorced, but I wasn't old; I allowed myself to live a little and be in the moment. Alex was clearly madly in love with his wife, so I didn't take it too seriously. When Alex held me, it felt really good. It could've been the wine kicking in too, but it was nice. I really didn't want to envision this man in a sexual nature because he was married, but it was hard not to. The rhythm in how he moved his hips was definitely a nice mix of his Latin heritage and his fraternity roots. Kappas were known for how they swayed when they danced.

God, where do they make men like this, and feel free to send me one, I thought.

Even though dancing with him felt extremely sensual, Alex still seemed to have eyes for Imani. He didn't look at me the way he looked at her. It just appeared that it was all in fun. There was no groping or inappropriate conversation going on while we danced.

"You're a pretty good dancer." Alex winked.

"Aww, thanks! You're too kind." I could feel myself blushing.

"No, seriously, you are. You look like you might have a little salsa in you too. You know how to salsa?" Alex asked with that damn accent, swaying his hips.

"Believe it or not, I do. I spent a couple of summers in Cuba after graduating from NYU. I may have picked up a few moves. I had quite a few friends in New York who exposed me to the Latin night life."

"Yeah, I can tell. I'm from Puerto Rico."

"Damn, you noticed that while we were dancing to an R&B song?"

"In Puerto Rico, we feel the same way about dancing as you guys do about sports."

I couldn't believe I was vibing with a married man, one who could get it, while his wife was in my living room, changing her baby's diaper. It seemed like Imani was offering her man temporarily to me, and I hoped I wasn't misinterpreting this and she would actually get jealous. My thoughts were racing.

"Hey, you two lovebirds. Yaya is getting pretty sleepy. We better get her home," Imani said, looking a little tired herself. I figured this was when the other shoe would drop.

"Here I come, babe. Let me get Yaya's stroller." He started packing up and getting ready to go. Alex was definitely devoted to his wife. Our little moment had ended, and rightfully so. Alex was not my husband.

"Aw, babe, you all were having such a great time, but you know baby duty calls. Serenity, I would love for us to hang with you again sometime— when your schedule allows, of course," Imani said, yawning.

"Oh my God, of course! I understand. It's getting late, so definitely get that beautiful baby home. Let me get your cell, and I'll call you when my girlfriend Cynthia comes into town next week. Maybe we can have a ladies' night out if you don't mind, Mr. Torres?" I was still trying to maintain a certain level of respect even though Imani and Alex seemed cool as hell.

"I'm definitely cool with that. Imani was just saying she wanted to meet some ladies to hang out with, so that's perfect."

"Most definitely, Serenity. I've been doing the stay-at-home mom thing, so it's always a pleasure to get out with other adults. Baby, can you get Serenity's number and plug it into my phone? It's in my back pocket." Imani held a sleeping Yaya in her arms.

Alex grabbed Imani's phone and her ass at the same time while winking. I just kept thinking, *goddamn*, did Alex have a brother? The passion that oozed from the both of them was seriously unquestionable.

Alex and I exchanged numbers, and I thanked them both for stopping by and hugged them both. Alex's smell lingered on my clothes for the rest of the night.

"It was a pleasure meeting you, Serenity. I can't wait to get together soon," Imani said.

"Yes, I'm looking forward to it."

After I closed the door behind Alex and Imani, I started cleaning up my dining room. God, it felt so good having them here. I hadn't danced and laughed like that in a long time. They seemed to be really genuine people. Imani was so sweet, and Alex…well, he was a gift from God. I started smiling to myself when I thought about the two of them dancing. The way Imani's body moved while Alex held her was nothing short of amazing. It was weird; I felt myself being attracted to the both of them, but I didn't try to figure it out. I just allowed myself to fantasize, and it was one damn good fantasy.

The next morning, I got up feeling refreshed and renewed. Alex and Imani were still on my mind. The past three years had been rough, but having them at my house last night seemed like such a healthy distraction. I was so intrigued by the both of them. Imani's confidence was so appealing to me. I liked how comfortable she was with herself as well as with Alex. The energy Alex exuded was strong yet soft and endearing. I liked that about them. I really wanted to get to know them more and didn't feel weird about that. Something about them stopping by yesterday seemed so mystical. The day I was actually able to cook one of Mama's favorite meals and finally listen to one of her favorite songs without breaking down in tears was the day they both showed up. For some reason, I didn't think that was a coincidence. Dave finding those heels I bought Mama and gifting me with them on my birthday didn't seem like a coincidence either. I wanted to bask in the feeling I was having all day long. I thought about going into my basement and lying across Mama's old sofa and even breaking out the old childhood photo albums, but I wasn't sure if I was quite ready for all of that yet. Besides, I needed to shower and get ready to teach my eleven o'clock yoga class at the studio.

Eventually, I got dressed and started heading to the studio. It was so hot outside, but I loved that about Arizona. Cynthia always joked about me liking the heat and said that came from the "white side" of my family. New York was brutally cold during my college years, which was why I fled to Cuba every chance I got during the summer. That was why Arizona was perfect for me.

The one thing I'd been itching to see more of, though, was diversity. I lived in Paradise Valley, which was a small affluent town about ten minutes from Scottsdale, but the majority of my neighbors were white. It was such a pleasant surprise meeting Alex and Imani. My neighbors were always cool, and I never felt disregarded or isolated by them, but I couldn't lie; it was nice being able to swap stories and experiences with people of color from time to time.

The house I was currently living in was the one Dave and I lived in together, but he let me keep it after our divorce. It was big, and often I considered finding a smaller spot, but I really did love this house and always thought maybe once I started to regain my footing, I would start entertaining again. Despite never having the desire for children of my own, I loved playing with my nieces and nephews in these halls and the backyard.

As I pulled up to the studio, I noticed Melissa, Dave's supposedly not girlfriend or whatever the hell they were, walking through the door. I hadn't seen her at the studio in a while and would've thought she had the decency to stay away, as she was dating my ex-husband. As long as she stayed in her own lane, we'd be fine.

"Oh, hey, Melissa, I haven't seen you around here in a while," I said, polite but curt.

"Yes, I know. I've actually been back and forth out of town. My modeling career is really taking off. It's been great, but I've also been skimping out on some of my workouts, which is not cool considering my looks are what makes me money." Melissa giggled incessantly.

I didn't know what Dave saw in her, and even if he said there was no real chemistry, he was still hanging out with Ms. Busty Brunette.

"Well, that's phenomenal news. I'm excited for you," I replied dryly with a fake smile.

"Thank you, hun. So, what are you up to these days?"

Why was she still talking to me like we were friends? I was really confused by this. While I didn't want Dave back, I felt no connection to Melissa, so this conversation needed to end.

"Just taking it one day at a time. I'm so glad I have yoga. It keeps me centered. I hate to cut this conversation short, but my class is about to start. It's so unprofessional to have my students waiting." I started walking toward my class.

"Oh, okay. Well, maybe we can have dinner this evening, or maybe even lunch tomorrow. I noticed you weren't on the schedule to teach a class."

So now she was checking my schedule? She was starting to get too close for comfort.

"Melissa, I actually I have plans this evening so—"

"That's okay, what about tomorrow?" Melissa cut me off before I could come up with a lame excuse like blow drying my hair or something. My brow furrowed. She genuinely seemed like she wanted to hang out with me.

"Well, okay, maybe seven tomorrow evening?"

"Perfect! I wanted to pick your brain about some things. I'm excited!" Melissa squealed. I wondered what could she possibly want to pick my brain about.

"Sure, we can check out that sushi spot on 90th Street. They have some good vegetarian options there."

"Sounds great! Thank you so much, Serenity!"

She seemed really excited, but I couldn't imagine what she wanted to talk about. We didn't have much in common. Melissa was a twenty-seven-year-old woman who still listened to N'Sync, for God's sake. Her idea of a good time was probably Instagramming her life and googling how to make and keep friends. This was a judgmental side of me I didn't like. I always tried to keep an open mind and befriend people from all walks of life. It was crazy how I felt so good this morning, but after seeing Melissa, I became a Debbie Downer. I was glad I was seeing my therapist that evening because it had been a long time, and judging by my thoughts, it was time for a real pick-me-up.

Stretching with my class helped. If it wasn't for yoga, I probably would've completely lost it. As much as I wanted yoga to heal the pain I'd had for the past three years, it could only do so much. I was overdue for some time with my therapist. I was glad I'd started feeling a little better, though. If meeting Alex and Imani was a glimpse at what was on the horizon for my life, I really wanted to work on getting back to myself.

It sucked always being so relaxed, open minded, and willing to try anything then suddenly experiencing a deep loss. It felt like the rug had been pulled from underneath me with no warning. I was forced to just deal with it. I was angry on Mother's Day, Thanksgiving, Christmas, and every holiday because I no longer had my ride-or-die. Because everyone was used to me being a bright light—someone that lived life on her own terms and made no apologies for it—I felt like I was letting everyone down by not being that person anymore. Only God knew how much I wanted that Serenity back.

I stood in one of the empty studio rooms, awaiting my eager students, staring at my body in the mirror. From head to toe, I took inventory of myself. My hair was tossed in a bun but looked fuller than it had been, my makeup-free face was void of blemishes, I'd gained back the weight I'd lost while grieving, and I looked visibly stronger.

"Don't be so hard on yourself, Serenity," I said to myself. "It's taking some time, but you're getting there."

*****

"It feels good to be back, Dr. Wilson. I love how your office always caters to us earthy folks. Being able to sit criss-cross applesauce on a yoga mat while talking to you always does wonders for me," I said.

"I'm glad you feel that way. During our last session, you told me about your father and how you blamed him for your mother's death. Are you ready to talk more about that this time?"

Dr. Wilson was a very straightforward therapist and did not allow any excuses in her office. She called me out on everything, but with a calm tone and warm smile. She was like the older, white, bohemian version of Iyanla Vanzant.

"See, Dr. Wilson, what had happened was…" I laughed, trying to make a joke out of it.

"Uh-uh, don't do that. This right here is not a joking matter. There are parts of you that are still shattered. Don't think you can bust out of my office, not return any of my calls, and then waltz back in here months later and joke about any of this. Remember, I see you, Serenity. You're here for a specific purpose, and that's to heal. Please don't come here and try to make light of your situation by cracking jokes, thinking this one-hour session is going to get you back to where you want to be. I need your full commitment on this. Do you understand?" Dr. Wilson asked sternly.

"Yes, ma'am." I felt that same nervousness when I got lectured by my mom for acting out as a teen.

"Now that we've gotten that out of the way, we can proceed," she said with the most welcoming smile and stretching her arms wide.

Dr. Wilson wasn't your typical therapist. She was more like a spiritual advisor and she would always give me a hug at the beginning of our sessions. Our hugs always lasted about thirty seconds, which provided us with enough time to embrace each other deeply while including at least three deep breaths. Our chests were close, so we could feel each other's heartbeat.

Dr. Wilson stated it was important for her to integrate some form of touch with her clients, even though it was considered taboo or unconventional in her line of work. Dr. Wilson said all humans needed to be touched and feel trust and non-sexual intimacy on a regular basis, especially her grieving clients who experienced a significant loss in their lives. She compared it to exercising or even vomiting because when we lost lots of fluids during the process, we had to replenish ourselves. Dr. Wilson said when people experienced grief or any other traumatic experience, the soul was running on empty, and trying to function in that state was damn near impossible, so physical touch was the fuel, and therapy was actually putting ourselves in motion to getting on the right track. From there, we could become more deeply connected with our spirit.

"I feel so much better after that hug."

She smiled. "I know."

"So, Dr. Wilson, I wanted to tell you about—"

"Remember, before we jump right in, we have to connect with our spirits first," she said. "I always want to ensure both of our hearts are in the right place before we proceed. There are no guarantees you will be open to this process, but I always want to set the stage for guidance, openness, and a willing spirit. We need to first release any toxicity such as worry, doubt, and confusion. Let's begin by holding hands. No words, we just meditate for two minutes straight and then begin." Dr. Wilson closed her eyes.

I had to admit this was the part I hated when I first started seeing Dr. Wilson. The pain I felt when Mama died was so unbearable that sitting quietly with my thoughts felt like a cruel and unusual punishment. It was hard for me to learn how to release that energy, so I really struggled with the meditation piece. Now, I was more open.

When I opened my eyes after meditating, I felt reinvigorated. The aromatherapy lingered, and the myriad of colors such as yellows, blues, purples and oranges that graced Dr. Wilson's office awakened my senses. The low volume of the nature sounds that played throughout Dr. Wilson's office, along with the natural light that peeped through her windows and the plants, provided a healing quality that enhanced the space.

"How are you feeling, darling?"

"Well, considering I haven't felt the warmth of an embrace in I don't know how long and haven't meditated even longer, I feel so much lighter."

"Good, that's what I like to hear. So, you were going to tell me something before I interrupted."

"Oh, yes. I had an opportunity to meet with my ex-husband, Dave. He actually took me out on my birthday."

"Wow, that was a nice gesture. You seem really excited about that."

"Believe it or not, I wasn't really sold on the idea at first when he extended the invitation, but I chose to go anyway."

"Let's explore that. Dave obviously has played a very integral part in your journey, but he asked for a divorce at a major turning point in your life—when you were grieving your mom. Last time we talked, you didn't really seem too angry with Dave, but he wasn't exactly one of your favorite people at the time either, which is understandable. What made you have lunch with him? Not only did he take you out on your birthday, but that was the anniversary of your mom's death."

"I'm not sure."

"Take your time and dig deep. I want you to really connect with your thoughts and your feelings. Think about how you were feeling when Dave asked to take you out to lunch," Dr. Wilson said calmly.

"I guess I was feeling a sense that he genuinely cared, and I was tired of feeling lonely and crying all damn day on my birthday. I needed to do something different."

"Good, and when you decided to change the narrative of feeling hopeless and in despair, you allowed Dave to express his genuine love and concern for you. What happened next?"

"He took me to one of my favorite restaurants, and we talked about our divorce and a woman he's been dating."

"And what feeling accompanied that?"

"I guess…relief, clarity maybe? I always wondered why he wanted the divorce. He said he failed because he felt helpless and didn't think he could make me happy again. He wanted me to be happy so badly that he sacrificed our marriage, thinking that would give me what I needed to heal."

"The Superman complex."

"Exactly!"

"From how you described Dave before, he is very driven by results, especially in his line of work as an entrepreneur. His goal is to bear the risk in order to reap the reward. That's an entrepreneur at heart. They will risk it all in order to produce something great. They solve problems. That is how they thrive. Think about how Dave came into your life when you didn't have a job or any assets to your name. He was your Superman."

"But I never asked that of him. That was not my aim."

"I know that, and you know that, but his need to do that was his identity, not yours. It sounds like you all were both dealing with some inner soul work that needed to be addressed."

"He mentioned that he'd started seeing a therapist."

"I'm glad to hear that, but there's something that came out of the meeting with you and Dave that put a smile on your face. What was that?"

I told her about how he found Mama's shoes.

"I can tell that meant so much to you."

"It sure did. I couldn't even describe to him in words how much it meant to me. When I began to cry, he held me for quite some time, and for some reason I felt relief, I felt understood, and I genuinely felt loved. As long as we'd been together, I had never felt that kind of love from him. That was the love I felt I needed from him when Mama died."

"At that moment, were you angry with him at all for showing you that kind of love a little too late?"

"Believe it or not, Dr. Wilson, not at all. I actually felt somewhat free and ready for the next chapter in my life."

"And that, my friend, tells me something new is on the horizon for you. Be aware and pay attention to the synchronicities. You're being guided every step of the way. These are signs you're reconnecting with who you truly are. We're going to revisit those feelings of hurt you felt with your dad at our next session.

"I'm still intrigued by the joy you felt when you met up with Dave. There's a reason that was the first thought you had when you entered my office today, and I felt that needed to be explored. Now I see why. Do you see how that encounter with Dave lead back to your mom and the sense of comfort you felt? When you were ready to shift your consciousness, this is what occurred. It's all connected if you allow yourself to dig deep."

"Dr. Wilson, you are one bad sista," I said with a finger snap.

"Well, I can't take all the credit for that. It's truly God-given."

I chuckled. "Thank God for you then. Now give *me* a hug."

Dr. Wilson willingly obliged. I was happy to have her and her guidance. I felt like this was truly helping me.

3

"Cynthia!" I greeted my college friend at the airport. She had already retrieved her luggage, but she dropped it to throw her arms around me in a hug. We hadn't seen each other since Mama passed, which made us hold onto each other even longer. Cynthia attempted many times to visit, but I didn't feel like myself and really didn't want her or Jeanette to see me that way.

"God, you look beautiful, Poodah! But then again, you always have. When we would talk on the phone, you made it seem like you were now toothless and looking like Skeletor. I was trying to prepare myself to see you, so you've got some explaining to do, honey, because you look amazing!"

"For a minute, I did lose quite a bit of weight, but I've been getting back on track," I said proudly.

"Well, you're doing more than getting back on track. Your skin is glowing, your hair is so full, and is that an ass I see back there? You always had a nice shape, but that butt looks like you've been eating some collard greens on the low."

We both laughed while walking to my car. Cynthia was also breathtaking. She was a vixen with curves in all the right places and a tiny waist. It looked like Cynthia ditched the wigs and weaves and opted for her natural tresses these days. I was utterly envious of the exotic twist- out she donned. Cynthia, no doubt, was always hot, but she was smart as hell and could run circles around anyone who thought she was just a big butt and a smile.

We buckled our seatbelts and headed back to my house. I knew Cynthia could feel how excited I was to have her in Arizona with me. I loved her so much and knew how much she loved me.

"So, tell me, honey, what are we going to do while I'm here for the next two weeks?"

"That's a good question. I haven't really planned much. I figured we could play it by ear."

"That's totally fine by me. You've had a lot going on. I'm glad I was able to visit you. I really wanted Jeanette to come too, but I think she's in Indonesia right now on a mission trip."

"She sure is. She actually sent me an email the other day with pics and everything. She seems so happy. I'm glad she's doing what she's always wanted to do. So, what's been going on with you?"

"My job keeps me extremely busy so I'm always on the go, but you will not believe who I ran into when I was in Miami for business."

"Who?"

"Do you remember Lewis Cutter?"

"I sure do! He was so sexy!"

"You won't believe this. He actually ended up marrying that Kelly Kapowski-looking girl who was in our sociology class."

"Wait, you're talking about Jenny? Wow, he married a white woman? He was so into pro- blackness he felt like he couldn't even sit by our white classmates, talking about how we need to do away with integration."

"Girl, those be the main ones with his hotep ass. He was the president of the black student union, didn't eat pork, and was greeting everyone on campus with an *As-salamu alaykum* but was screwing every chick in sight. But he still fine, honey, whew!"

"But his ass went to a white school!"

"You know he was confused—sexy as hell but confused. But enough about him, what's been going on with you?"

I was still driving, but I could feel Cynthia's gaze; typically, the look with her one eyebrow up and lips cocked to the side as if she knew there were some juicy details for me to disclose about my life, but I had nothing.

"We're almost at my house, so I'll fill you in when we get there."

"Oh, it's like that? This sounds like it's about to be good."

"Don't get your hopes up. I doubt it's anything fascinating."

As we drove up to my driveway, Alex was going for a run and began slowing down once he saw my car. I rolled down my window.

"Hey, Alex. You're actually running out here in this heat?"

"Aww, it ain't too bad, Mami. I won't be out here too long, plus I'm going for a quick swim later. Imani took Yaya on a playdate, so I'm solo right now. I'm just trying to enjoy this weekend before it ends. I have a pretty busy work week ahead." Alex was jogging in place next to my car.

"I totally understand. Well, tell Imani I said hi. I was gonna call her anyway this week because I wanted to go out with her now that my homegirl is in town."

"Oh, cool, you must be Cynthia. I'm Alex."

Cynthia leaned over me, happy to greet Alex. I couldn't believe Cynthia was really leaning lower to show her boobs. This woman was too much. I had to laugh at how obvious Cynthia's flirting was. "I didn't realize anyone knew me out here in these Paradise Valley streets."

"Well, when Serenity mentioned her best friend was coming into town, I couldn't help but tell how excited she was. Your reputation precedes you." Alex flashed that million-dollar smile, and I was pretty sure Cynthia was going to melt like butter.

"Now that's what I like to hear." Cynthia was laying it on thick.

"Hey, Serenity, why don't I let you park so I can help with Cynthia's bags?"

"Okay, cool. Thanks so much, Alex."

"Thank *you*, Alex." Cynthia winked at Alex.

"You're being quite extra, don't you think?" I whispered to Cynthia.

"Girl, please. I'm just having a little fun," Cynthia whispered back.

While we were whispering to each other at the door like middle school girls, Alex was carrying Cynthia's bags into my house.

"So, Alex, you live in the neighborhood?" Cynthia was acting like she hadn't had any action in years, but I knew that wasn't the case. She had just gotten back together with Rob, and even if she hadn't, she traveled so much and met men left and right.

"Yep, my wife and I moved here about a couple of months ago."

"Oh, so you're married?" Cynthia asked, intrigued.

"Sure am. We have a little girl too." I loved how proud Alex was of his family. He always exuded a genuine happiness when he talked about them.

"Well, Alex, we don't want to keep you from your run, especially because it's going to get even warmer out there. Enjoy your day." As happy as I was about Alex being so comfortable around me, I still felt too strongly about being around him without Imani present.

"You do the same, Serenity. And I'll be sure to let Imani know I ran into you and tell her you'll call her."

"Thanks so much. I appreciate that. And kiss little Miss Yaya for me." I smiled.

"I sure will. Oh, and that yellow sundress looks really nice on you. You look beautiful."

"Oh, thanks," I said shyly.

Alex closed the door behind him, and Cynthia gave me a look like I was withholding classified secret information.

"Um, why are you giving me that look?" I asked, confused.

"*Um,* don't act dumb with me. What the hell was that?"

"What?"

"Oh, so we're going to act like your new neighbor ain't sexy as fuck? He was looking at you like he wanted to see what Serenity was working with."

"Girl, *please.* That man is married. Like hella married. Like Beyoncé and Jay-Z married. Like Will Smith and Jada Pinkett-Smith married. You should see the way he looks at her." "You just named two couples whose marriages are questionable."

"Get off of that. Alex is a very charming and confident man. I'm not going to assume he's interested in me. Trust me, if you saw the way he looks at his wife, you wouldn't think he was interested in me."

"Well, how does his old lady look?"

"She's drop-dead gorgeous. Even with a baby, she's still got it!"

"Aight, whatever, Serenity. But why does he seem so comfortable around you already?"

"Alex and his wife stopped by my house a few weeks ago to introduce themselves because they'd just moved into the neighborhood, and we hit it off instantly."

"Little Ms. Baltimore letting strangers into her house now?"

"Honestly, I surprised myself with that, but I don't know why. I just vibed with the both of them from the jump."

"You did always have that intuition like your mom. But, damn, that Alex can get it all day, every day!" Cynthia said.

"So, what about Rob?" I asked to help Cynthia get back on the subject of her own man.

"Okay, I see what you're doing. C'mon, you know I'm just admiring the view. I haven't forgotten about Rob. But there's nothing wrong with seeing what else is on the menu while I'm out here. Rob doesn't own me, and he doesn't need to know what I'm up to."

"Listen, I'm all about admiring the view as well, but even while Dave and I were together, I never cheated on him. I just believe if you're going to have multiple partners, that's something all parties have to be on board with, and for some reason, Rob does not strike me as the sharing type."

"Girl, he ain't the *nothing* type," Cynthia said with disappointment.

"Oh, no, what's going on?"

"It really ain't nothing to get all pressed about. I'm just tired of these men awakening something in me and then it falls flat. Rob and I were seriously just kicking it, you know? I put no demands on him. Hell, I didn't want any demands put on me. Plus, you know my work schedule; I felt no need to get serious. My career was pretty much my boyfriend, so I wasn't tripping. He was the one who kept saying he wanted something more. I should've gone with my intuition and just kept him as a good friend-with-good-ass-benefits, but then I start thinking I should settle down because I'm damn near forty. Come to find out, he had a whole baby mama he was seeing back in Baltimore. Girl, I just ain't got time for this shit."

"Damn, I didn't know."

"No worries, I'm truly okay. It just sucks sometimes. Don't get me wrong, I love my life. I have an amazing career, I make a shitload of money, I travel the world, I have great family and friends, but I ain't gonna lie, it gets lonely at times. The vibrator shit only works for so long. I want companionship, and dammit, I like men with money. I took a chance on Rob's broke ass because I was trying to switch things up and not seem so high maintenance. I've realized, though, that's me—I'm high maintenance as fuck and always have been. I just can't get with that whole broke mentality, still fucking the baby mama and shit."

"I know, honey," I said while rubbing Cynthia's back.

"I mean, maybe I should take a cue from you and marry up. I know what you're going to say; it wasn't about the money with you two. Hell, I know that because you've always been a minimalist and the earthy type so that was never your motive. He was good to you, Serenity."

"Up until the time he left, at least. The lesson I learned from that is this: Dave is an amazing man and always will be, but we were only supposed to be together for a specific season, and that's okay. We loved and shared. I had the opportunity to experience another human being in its purest form and will always appreciate that."

"See, you're good. You've always been able to see the glass half full. I'm struggling with that right now."

"Just keep living and appreciate the beauty of life. The guy you're supposed to meet will show up when it's time."

"See, I'm over here supposed to be comforting you, and you're trying to help me. That's why I love you, Poodah."

"I love you too, boo. I don't know, I'm just feeling hopeful these days. Don't get me wrong; I still have my moments, but I'm taking it one day at a time. After seeing Dave and meeting Alex and Imani—I don't know—that just put me in a very serene space."

"Wait a minute, you met with Dave? What was that like?"

"See, that's what I wanted to talk to you about before we got distracted by Alex."

"Oh, yeah, his fine ass. Okay, spill the tea on Dave, and please tell me some more about Alex because I think you're holding back."

I told Cynthia about Dave's lunch date on my birthday and the details about the time Alex and Imani came over.

"So, you were trying to act like ain't nothing been going on with you, but all this sounds like a lot to me. Dave is back in your life, and Alex definitely seems interested in you. I don't care what you say, he is," Cynthia said.

"Whatever. If given the opportunity, I think Dave would like to give it another shot, but honestly, I'm just not into him anymore. I just believe we had our time, but it's over now. Listen, I'm not holding a grudge, but he left during a very low point in my life. That speaks volumes to me."

"Well, you're right about that. At least he left you with this big-ass house. A nice one, I might add. You definitely switched some things up around here. I don't know how many plants a girl can have, but I get it. I know how you want to feel like you're out in the forest somewhere in your own home."

"Girl, shut up," I said jokingly while tossing a throw pillow at Cynthia.

"But seriously, it's nice to see your smile again. Now, be honest: Alex has a little to do with that, right?"

"Okay, maybe a little, but I really like his wife. We clicked right away, and she was so comfortable in her own skin and didn't seem insecure when Alex expressed himself around me. I don't know, I just get really laid-back vibes from both of them, like me."

"Yeah, must be something because I wouldn't be letting a man like Alex out of my sight. I bet he makes himself jealous just by looking in the mirror every damn day."

I chuckle. "Let's not give the man that much credit."

"You're right about that 'cause these men will start feeling themselves too much. If we're honest, I just get the sense he's into you, Serenity. He probably won't step out if he's like you described, but if he was given permission to, I think he would."

"That's funny; given permission like an open marriage? Swingers?"

"Yeah, don't act surprised. You should know how people get down."

"Yes, this I know, especially with my circle of friends, but I'm not sure about that one. I'm not getting the open marriage vibe from them, and definitely not the swingers vibe. I will say they do seem a little more open than the average married couple. Oh, well! Whatever makes them happy, that should be their priority."

"You're right about that. But damn, Serenity, will I ever have the whole marriage and kids thing, like seriously?"

"Is that what you truly want?"

"I mean, yeah, I guess?"

"You don't sound too sure."

"I just feel like maybe I should be doing more."

"Girl, go start a business, jump out of a plane, or go scuba diving. You don't have to get married and have babies."

"You've got that right."

"I'm just saying. I did the marriage thing, but I never had an interest in having children."

"Now, that's something I find very interesting about you. I've seen you with kids, and you seem like a natural to me."

"Imani said the same thing when we first met."

"Really? After knowing you for two seconds?" She nodded in approval. "I have to meet this chick."

"Well, you'll get a chance. I was hoping the three of us could go out for dinner and drinks."

"Okay, cool. Set that up, Serenity. I need to get out of these clothes and take a much- needed shower."

"Okay, honey, you know where the guest bedroom is. Go help yourself."

"Which one? You know you've got so many damn rooms in this house." Cynthia laughed.

"Ha, whatever. The one on the right."

"Okay, gotcha."

As Cynthia walked upstairs, it completely slipped my mind that I was supposed to call Melissa back with my availability to meet. She had to reschedule our dinner, and I seriously didn't understand why she would want to meet with me. None of it made any sense. I guessed I'd find out once I talked to her.

I turned on some music and danced in my kitchen. The picture on the counter of my mom and her sister at the beach when they were kids always made me smile. It also made me think about my brothers and how I should give them a call. Maybe it was time to get back to our traditional family gatherings at my house. I did miss them, or at least I should say I missed my nieces and nephews.

Thoughts of family always led me back to my mom. God, I missed her. I missed her smile, her scent, the way her voice calmed me. I was coming to terms with the fact I would always have this hole in my heart when it came to losing her, but maybe it was time for me to start making new memories. I thought she would want that for me.

*****

"It's been a minute since I've had sushi. I'm glad you picked this place." Melissa was sitting across from me, smiling, while looking at her menu. Typically, I liked dining alone anytime I went to Hiro Sushi in Scottsdale. Whenever I would leave work and needed time to unwind before heading home, I would stop here. Even Dave knew this was my "me-time" spot. I hadn't been here in a while, and when Melissa said she wanted to talk with me, I figured I'd better have my comfort food just in case she said something that would irritate me.

"Yes, this is definitely one of my favorite sushi places, especially because of their vegetarian menu."

"Ugh, you're so good when it comes to how you eat. With my hectic schedule, I haven't been eating the best lately. When I was on a private jet to Europe for a photoshoot, I had this steak and potatoes that was amazing! The additional two inches I gained in my waistline was not," Melissa said sadly.

I wasn't sure whether I was supposed to agree or ignore everything she said. She was so privileged and didn't even know it. Then again, I lucked up and married a millionaire myself, so who was I to judge?

"Well, my vegetarian lifestyle really sparked in college when a friend of mine started going on mission trips and talked about animal cruelty. I had kind of flirted with the idea of becoming a vegetarian, but after reading about the health benefits of it, I decided it was the way to go for me. On my dad's side, there's a history of hypertension and cardiovascular disease, so it was kind of a no-brainer for me."

"Wow, it's amazing you're so conscious about your health. I must admit, I'm a little more concerned about my weight but should consider how a lot of foods affect me in other areas. I know everyone says I'm like the ideal size, but when I get a lot older, like in my mid-thirties, I know I won't always bounce back as easily."

Okay, Lord knew I was trying with her, but why did everything that came out of her mouth make her sound like a long-lost Kardashian? I prayed I wouldn't say anything sarcastic or condescending and hurt her feelings.

"Well, this restaurant is the ideal place. You don't have to worry about a thing," I said with another forced smile.

There was an awkward silence for a few moments until she cleared her throat and started with, "So…"

I wanted her to just get to the point.

"The real reason I wanted to meet with you is because I have some exciting news. I recently scored a two-year contract with Wilhelmina Fitness, so I'll be doing some extensive traveling and was booked to be a model for all the press of that festival that's coming up in Bali next year."

"Oh, the Vitality Fest?"

"Yes! That's the one!"

Melissa was extremely excited, and I could honestly say I was happy for her but couldn't help but wonder why she made it a point to share her good news with me. It humbled me for a minute because I was honored but still confused.

"That's an amazing festival that brings out thousands of hand-picked attendees. I've always admired the organizers for putting together an event that really seems to make health a priority and not just a gimmick. Obviously, there's been so much going on with me the past few years, but I think I'm going to make it my mission to attend in a couple of years."

"Well, how about next year? I know it's only a few months away, and it doesn't really give you a whole lot of time to plan, but I think you'll be fine."

Now I was really confused.

"Melissa, I'm not sure I follow. I have a full schedule at the yoga studio. I'm not sure if I want to rearrange my whole life right now for a trip," I said.

"No, I'm not just talking about you going as an attendee. My agent's wife is one of the co-founders of the Vitality Fest. Her team is looking for an experienced yoga instructor to lead the wellness retreat part of the fest.

She's very particular about who's hired to come on board and said she was looking for someone who has experience, preferably leading yoga retreats, and I thought about you!" Melissa was beaming with excitement. I couldn't comprehend what was happening. The woman my ex-husband was supposedly dating was offering me an amazing opportunity.

"I—I don't know what to say."

"Say yes! You're perfect for the job. I'm actually glad I waited to tell you this because she actually had someone else in mind, but that fell through, and she's looking for someone ASAP. And just being honest, my agent's wife is seriously connected, so if I get in good with her, she might not be so hard on me. Right now, I think she thinks her husband is attracted to me. The way she's feeling could cost me a damn good agent."

"That's cute," I said. "She does know that representing beautiful women is his job, right?"

"Yes, but I think they've had some issues in their marriage recently with infidelity, but if you come on board, she might not be as cold toward me. This is my big shot," Melissa said eagerly.

It was an amazing opportunity even though Melissa was pretty much doing it for herself, but it could really open up some incredible doors for me.

"Okay, count me in!"

"Great! I'm going to text you her information now, and please don't forget to tell her I referred you. Her name is Lisa Fletcher." I could hear the youthfulness in Melissa at that moment.

"Okay, I've got it. I'll definitely give her a call tomorrow. It's getting kind of late now and my friend is here visiting from New York."

"Oh, I'm so sorry to pull you away from your friend," Melissa apologized sweetly.

"Trust me, it's okay. Cynthia's a big girl. She's probably already lining up our night for when I get home." I chuckled.

"Oh, cool. Are you hanging out tonight?"

I didn't want Melissa to invite herself out with us, so I said, "Well, I'm not sure yet. Anyway, I'll keep you posted about when I call Lisa tomorrow."

"Thank you so much, Serenity. You're the best!"

"Well, I appreciate you for even thinking of me. Let's finally dig into this food. I'm starving."

Melissa smiled. "Same here."

What an interesting connection to make. Who would've thought Dave's new love interest would offer me an opportunity like this?

*****

"You look hot!"

Cynthia was standing in the living room with a fitted, red mini cocktail dress on, leaning a little to the side, trying to put her earring in. To say Cynthia was blessed when God was handing out the perfect physique was an understatement. She knew this and made no apologies for her curvaceous figure. I always loved her confidence.

"Thank you, Poodah. I try." Cynthia jiggled her hips, and we both couldn't help but laugh.

"Girl, I'm beat." I plopped down on the couch and rubbed my hand on the upholstery, back and forth, and all of a sudden, flashbacks of my mom began hitting me like a ton of bricks.

I knew this feeling all too well. Anxiety was making its arrival out of nowhere without my permission. I got a feeling in the pit of my stomach, an indescribable exhaustion, and the feeling I was I going to cry. I couldn't fight it, but what was I hiding from? It was just Cynthia. We were just about to go out and kick it, and I didn't want her to regret coming to visit me.

"Poodah, what's wrong? You're shaking," Cynthia said with worry in her voice.

I couldn't get the words out. I started rocking back and forth, then the doorbell rang. "Cynthia, can you get that?" I barely mustered up the words.

"The hell? You want me to answer the door at a time like this? Have you lost your mind?"

"Please, just answer the damn door. It's probably Imani. We're all riding together tonight," I said while trying to catch my breath.

"You're having a meltdown and you're trying to go out and kick it?" I could tell Cynthia was losing patience but was also confused with what was going on with me. She was scared and had every right to be.

"I'm begging you, Cynthia, please just answer the door," I said while still gasping for air. I was having a full-blown panic attack at this point.

Immediately, Imani walked in, dropped her purse to the floor, and ran to my kitchen to get me a cup of water. She sat down next to me and cupped my face in her hands.

"Listen, Serenity, you've got this."

Then Imani grabbed my hands, looked me in the eye, and told me to take a few deep breaths. She began doing breathing exercises with me. I could barely see Cynthia in my peripheral vision, but I couldn't focus on that right now. I needed to see this breathing exercise through. I was yearning to just feel better, to return to my normal self. I didn't know what was my normal these days and thinking about that had me getting worked up all over again.

"Okay, Serenity, I need you to take those deep breaths. You're allowing your frustration with this to upset you. You're going to be okay, but I really need you to breathe."

I started all over again, breathing with Imani. I felt defeated and sad. Then came what felt like a flood of tears that wouldn't stop. All of a sudden, Imani lifted my head up and stared into my eyes for what felt like eternity before she held me. I felt extremely vulnerable, but in some weird way, I felt comforted. Our chests were so close that our hearts started beating to a syncopated rhythm. It was so quiet in my house I could literally hear a pin drop. Imani's embrace was warm and so soothing. Her dress was now covered with my tears and snot, but it was working. I felt my heart rate returning to normal. I stopped shaking and allowed Imani to comfort me. I thought about nothing else but how I felt at that moment. I truly felt loved unconditionally and felt the presence of my mom.

"So, does anyone care to tell me what just happened?"

I could tell Cynthia was upset, as if I'd kept a huge secret from her. In some ways, I guess I had. I had my first panic attack about a year ago, and Dr. Wilson discussed some options with me on how to deal with it. Of course, I was opposed to taking medication, so we went with a more holistic approach. Dr. Wilson made it very clear to me that I needed to identify a point person who could get to me right away if I were to have an attack. I really didn't want anyone to know I suffered from anxiety, though. When I met Imani and realized how we connected, I knew immediately I wanted to share that with her. It didn't scare her off or anything. She said she was honored I would ask her, so I went over the things she needed to know in order to help me.

Thankfully, she'd never witnessed me having an attack until tonight. She helped me through it like a champ, just like I knew she would. The only thing was, I didn't know how I was supposed to explain this to Cynthia, the one person who'd been through so much with me.

"I'm so sorry I kept this from you. It's not something I really like talking about. I started having panic attacks about a year ago, but I promise this was only the third one. I was embarrassed and didn't want to worry you. Dr. Wilson told me to make sure there was someone who could help me in the event I had an attack, but she said it needed to be someone that could respond to me right away and with you living so far…"

"I find that very interesting, Serenity. I get the whole distance thing, but we're still friends. I would have at least appreciated you letting me in on this part of your life." I could tell Cynthia was upset because she rarely called me Serenity.

Imani glanced between us before getting up. "I'm going to leave you two ladies. I'll go into the den," she said quietly while trying to tiptoe to the other room.

"No, Imani, you don't have to go anywhere because clearly you're more aware of what's going on with my best friend than I am." Cynthia's words were direct, and she seemed more irritated.

"If it's okay to say this, Cynthia, can we just try to calm down, because I don't want Serenity to get upset and have another attack," Imani said.

"And I'm going to respectfully say, who the fuck are you? Don't get me wrong; Poodah has spoken highly of you, and I was looking forward to finally meeting you tonight, but I have been through some dark times with this chick right here. This is my sister, and I really don't need anyone telling me to calm the fuck down about my best friend. I didn't say a word when you were helping her through her attack, but I need answers now."

Cynthia has always been very direct and to the point. I really didn't expect anything different from her. I knew she was upset and had a right to be, but I wasn't in the mood to see the two of them go toe to toe on their first encounter.

"Cynthia, out of respect for Serenity and the current situation, I will not go back and forth with you. But just remember, don't ever talk to me like that again. I know I was calm when I was helping Serenity, but please don't get it twisted. I can go just like you can," Imani's tone was also direct, which demanded Cynthia's attention.

"Sis, I'm sorry. I'm just really hurt and was nervous as hell when I saw what was going on with my Poodah, that's all. I sincerely apologize." Cynthia was far from timid but recognized Imani wasn't going to be intimidated by anyone.

"It's all good. Like I said before, I'll be in the den." I could tell Imani was not feeling Cynthia at the moment but was trying to remain cool. I began telling Cynthia about my panic attacks and how they seemed to always be connected with thoughts about my mom.

"You could have told me that, honey. Why did you feel like you couldn't talk to me? You know I'd move Heaven and Earth when it comes to you. I'm on a plane in a heartbeat if you need anything!"

"And I know that. But when I'm in the moment of an attack, I can't wait for your plane to land for you to help me. I need someone that's close," I said sincerely.

Cynthia looked disappointed. "You're right about that. I know I can't be there quickly."

"I don't want to make you feel bad, but Imani has been real cool and she lives much closer, so it just made more sense for her to be that point of contact."

"I get that. What I just don't understand is why you never even told me. That's foul, Poodah, and you know it. I'm not trying to upset you, but we've been friends forever. You've always told me everything."

"I know, but this is still very hard for me. This is just fucking embarrassing. I thought I was moving forward and then out of the blue, I started getting panic attacks, and this grief shit gets on my nerves too because it pops up at the most random times. I was pretty tired when I got in the house but knew once I took a shower and changed, I would be ready to kick it with my girls tonight. And now I'm a mess!"

"You're not a mess, honey. You've lost your mom. I understand that. By the looks of it, Imani really understands that as well and in a short period of time. I'm here for you and promise I'm not trying to make this about me, but it's hard to understand what's going on when a stranger is helping you through a really tough time in your life and I have no clue what's going on. Tonight really scared me."

Cynthia's concern was heartfelt. Tears formed in my eyes, "I hear you. I really do. I'm sorry."

"No, don't you dare apologize to me. Come here." Cynthia held me close. It wasn't exactly the same warmth I felt with Imani, but I knew Cynthia meant well, and I loved her for it.

"Imani!" Cynthia called. Imani walked in, confused, which made me chuckle.

"What's got you all giggly, little miss tickle-me Elmo?" Cynthia asked me sarcastically.

"The two of you are so funny. I honestly thought it was about to be an all-out war in here. I know both of you don't take shit, so I was just hoping y'all would work out whatever was brewing between the two of you."

"I know I said sorry before, but Imani, I sincerely apologize for coming at you like that. I have to respect you for how you clapped back at me the way you did. I was thinking like, *shit*, Imani got that gangsta in her." Cynthia chuckled.

"Well, it is what it is. I'm from Bankhead, so I don't know any other way to be when being confronted," Imani said proudly.

"I totally respect you for that. I'm glad you were here for my friend."

"Oh my God, my girls are getting along. You all scared me for a minute," I said jokingly.

"It's all good. Emotions were just running high, and we both care about you, Serenity," Imani said as the voice of reason while looking down as if she was trying to figure out how to remove the wet marks from her dress.

"I have to admit, Imani, you look great in that dress, honey! Poodah kind of messed it up, though."

We all laughed.

"Whatever. Can we still go out tonight, ladies? I know you all were worried about me, and I really appreciate that, but I think going out would do me some good right now."

"You sure?" Cynthia and Imani said in unison.

I laughed. "You are definitely more alike than you think."

"As long as you think you can handle it," Imani said, though tentatively.

"I really want to go. Please?"

"Aight, girl," Cynthia said. "Get dressed so we can go."

"And let me just run home and change my dress," Imani added.

"Okay, cool. Let's be ready to leave in twenty minutes," I said with excitement.

"I swear, I don't know how this chick gets ready so fast and still looks put together, but that's my Poodah."

I kissed her cheek. "And I love you too, Cynthia."

I raced upstairs with a huge smile on my face. Not that long ago, I felt depleted and downright in despair, but I had my girls and they loved me for who I was. I felt Mama's presence; she was with me.

CHAPTER

4

"Cynthia!" I screamed from the bottom of my stairs.

"Yeah, what up!" Cynthia yelled with just as much force.

"I have a quick meeting this morning, but I'll be back in a couple of hours, and then we can do brunch."

"Okay, hun, I'll be laid up in this bed for a minute, but I promise to be ready when you get back," Cynthia said. She sounded a little preoccupied, so she must be checking her work emails or something.

"Cool, love you!"

"Love you too, Poodah."

I raced out the door to my car. I was running a little bit behind to meet Lisa about that amazing opportunity in Bali. She was in town for only one day and really wanted to meet with me in person. This gig would not only put me on the map, but they were willing to pay all of my expenses, including airfare, hotel stay, food, drinks, and a $1500 stipend per day. This was definitely a big deal. I wasn't as drawn to the pay as I was to the opportunity of connecting with so many fresh faces and being around so many people who valued health and wellness. There was so much going on, and honestly, that panic attack frightened me a little bit. I should've checked in with Dr. Wilson, but I was so consumed with Cynthia and Imani that I totally forgot. I was starting to feel a bit of anxiety as I was preparing for this meeting with Lisa, so I thought it would be best to give Dr. Wilson a call on my way there.

"Hello." Dr. Wilson's voice alone was so calming and soothing.

"Hi, it's Serenity. Did I catch you at a bad time?" I asked.

"Not at all, my dear. It's good to hear from you. You have an appointment coming up soon. Is everything okay?" She never sounded alarmed, but she seemed as if she could feel my emotions even though I wasn't in the office with her.

"Um…not really," I said hesitantly.

"Now, no need to brush off anything you're feeling. Remember to speak your truth. I'll ask you again: is everything okay?"

I sigh. "No. The other night, I had a panic attack, and even though it was in front of my friends, I still feel a little embarrassed about it and feel bad my friend, Cynthia, who's visiting me from New York, had to see it. She wasn't aware I even have panic attacks because I didn't tell her."

"First, Serenity, you have to remember you are not obligated to tell anyone about your panic attacks. It's a good rule of thumb to inform at least one person in the case of an emergency, and you have identified that person. Cynthia does not live here, which makes it more difficult for her to respond in a timely manner."

"I know, but she was pretty upset I didn't tell her. I mean she said she's good now, but I just didn't want to alarm her. I knew I had you and Imani if anything happened, so that's why I didn't tell her."

"That's totally fine and acceptable, no more explanation needed. Remember this healing process works from the inside out. You listened to your inner voice of what you felt was best. How Cynthia or anyone else chooses to respond to your choices is their responsibility, not yours. If you let external things or people dictate how you should feel, you're going to find yourself often disappointed. It's time to release that guilt about Cynthia and move on. Real friendship survives these kinds of things."

Dr. Wilson had a way of putting everything into perspective, and I knew she was right. I felt like I used to think like her, but losing my mom put me in a fragile and vulnerable state.

"You're so right."

"It sounds like you're driving. I don't want to distract you while you're on the road. Did you want to stop by for a few minutes to finish our conversation?'

"See, that's what I love about you; you always make time for me. I would love to stop by, but I'm on my way to an important meeting. I was offered an opportunity to lead a yoga retreat in Bali, and what's even more interesting is Dave's girlfriend is the one who referred me!"

"That is a pretty big deal, and I'm extremely happy for you. Dave's girlfriend referring you is surprising but amazing. Just when we think what's happening to us is going to tear our world apart, we see that light at the end of the tunnel. I'm glad you're following your heart and staying true to what you enjoy, which is yoga. I can't wait to hear all about it in our next session."

"Thanks, Dr. Wilson. I'll see you soon!"

Even though our conversation was brief, it was the pick-me-up I needed to get through this meeting because I was previously feeling overwhelmed. Lisa sounded like she could be a bit tough according to Melissa, but I was going to go in there, give it my best, and get this job.

As I was pulling up to the office, I saw Alex walking out.

"Hey, Alex!" I may have been a little too eager while greeting him.

"Hey, beautiful! What are you doing here?" Alex asked while giving me a hug.

"I have a meeting here regarding a great opportunity to be a yoga instructor for a major retreat in Bali," I said proudly.

"Oh, yeah, Imani told me about that. Congrats. You're doing big things!"

"I'd like to think so."

"Well, you are. I know your meeting is going to result in something amazing. I'm really happy for you. We've got to celebrate. I'll see if Imani wants to go out for dinner tonight. Maybe we can toast to your success."

"Oh my God, I would love that. You two are amazing. I really appreciate that."

"Well, I appreciate you, Serenity. You've really welcomed us since we've moved here, and Imani doesn't stop talking about you. You've been a really great friend to her, and it makes me happy to see my wife happy."

"That feeling is mutual. Imani has been a God-send, seriously," I said.

"Yeah, she mentioned the panic attack. I hope it's okay she told me."

"I can't lie, it is rather uncomfortable to talk about. It puts me in a vulnerable position, but I understand why she told you. I mean, you *are* her husband. The past few years have been kind of rough, and I haven't really let anyone in, but thank you for your concern."

"Anytime. Well, I don't want to keep you. You've got business to handle. I actually work in this building, but I have to run to a meeting with a client. I'll talk with Imani so we can discuss dinner tonight, if that works with your schedule?"

"That'll be great. Are you open to one more guest? Cynthia is in town one more night."

"Of course! It'll be great to have her, and it's a cool way for her to spend her last night here."

"Most definitely. I can't wait!"

"Me too." Alex smiled, and I couldn't help but think him looking like that should be totally illegal.

"Okay, go get that paper, and I'll see you tonight."

*****

I was beaming from ear to ear during the car ride home. All I could think about was how fortunate I was to be able to be a part of this yoga retreat. Lisa stated she was extremely impressed with my background and thought I was the perfect fit for position. Running into Alex didn't hurt either. I couldn't help but wonder about him and Imani. Both of them had been so open to the three of us bonding the way we had. I felt no jealousy from Imani when I was talking with Alex, and she really embraced me as a friend too, which I loved. Cynthia was in town, and despite my whole panic attack fiasco, it was so nice having her here. I was working through my grief with my therapist, and even Dave and I were on good terms. I felt like my life had taken an unusually positive turn since I'd met Alex and Imani. I couldn't put my finger on it, but something was so magnetizing about the two of them. I tried not to think too hard about it or even make sense of how easily we connected—I just let it happen.

While I found myself attracted to Alex, I also found myself drawn to Imani, but not initially sexual in nature. She was hot, and I could envision laying with her and holding her, but that wasn't what I was most drawn to.

She was such a beautiful woman inside and out, and I connected so much with her spirit. I'd never been so drawn to a couple like this, let alone a married one. Maybe as I healed, I was becoming more open to new experiences in life. I felt like if Mama were here, she would listen to me talk and never once judge me for my thoughts. Even as a loyal and dedicated wife, my mom understood how I viewed relationships and how I was more fluid. She would've loved Alex and Imani. Warmth came over me as I thought about Alex, Imani, my mom, and the many opportunities ahead. I hadn't felt so calm and at ease in such a long time.

Finally, I was home, and when I opened the door, Cynthia's luggage was packed and propped up by the couch.

"You don't leave until tomorrow morning. You're ready to bounce on me already?" I asked jokingly.

"I'm sorry, but one of my clients just had a major emergency regarding a hedge fund situation, and I'm the only person who can work this out. If I try to explain all the details to you, I'll confuse you."

"Wait a minute, so you're leaving today?" I asked, frowning.

"Yeah, unfortunately, Poodah. This is one of my newer clients, and building trust and giving them my time and attention is the name of the game. I mean, I knew in the back of my head that at any given moment my vacation could be cut short. Typically, my long-term clients are a little more independent and don't need me holding their hand anymore."

"I get it, but this sucks. I saw Alex right before my meeting, and he invited us out to dinner with him and Imani."

"Oh, really?" Cynthia perked up.

"Yeah, he said he wanted to celebrate my yoga retreat gig."

"First, let me just say I am so extremely proud of you too. I have witnessed you live your dreams for quite some time and know you've been dealing with a lot lately, but so much is starting to come around for you. I am so happy for you, Serenity."

"Thank you, boo, that means so much to me." I could feel the tears swelling in my eyes. Cynthia played such a huge role in my life and was the most amazing friend.

"But now, Serenity, something is up with Alex and Imani," Cynthia said seriously.

"What do you mean?"

"Okay, how do I say this? I'm not saying they're swingers or anything, but I think they are feeling you, and I mean *both of them.*" Cynthia punctuated each word with a clap to express how serious she was.

"Well, sometimes I get a vibe…"

"Honey, it's more than a vibe. Imani is gorgeous, and I can tell she really cares about you and your well-being. I just feel like she looks at you a little bit differently than I do."

"Well…"

"Are you saying you feel the same way about her? Him? Both of them?" Cynthia asked curiously.

"I mean, they are amazing people," I said while smiling.

"Okay, I'm not as open as you, so that's where I exit stage left, but I understand you see the world a little differently than I do. Just make sure to protect your heart and your pussy," Cynthia said with her hand on her protruding hip.

"Tell me how you really feel." I chuckled lightly. "I know you're just looking out for me, and that's why I love you so much. I hate you're going to miss dinner tonight. What time is your flight?"

"In three hours!"

"What? So, were you going to sneak out while I was at the meeting?"

"Hell naw. I just wanted to make sure I had all my things packed and was ready to go before calling you, but you made it in before I had to. I would love for you to take me to the airport, though. We can grab something to eat on the way there."

"Alright." I could feel myself sinking a little, but I was still so glad Cynthia was able to visit me because her work schedule could get crazy at times.

"C'mon, girl. You'll be alright. You can fill me in on how your meeting went in the car. After I leave, something tells me you will probably start getting a little more preoccupied." Cynthia smiled.

"See, there you go again. We may be overanalyzing this. They may just be really cool and relaxed people. They are probably not interested in me in any kind of way. At least not like how you're making it out to be."

"Poodah, you need to step up your intuitive game. If I can see what's happening with the three of you, you should *definitely* be able to recognize it."

"Whatever. Let's get you to the airport since you're leaving me and all."

"Yeah, I'm pretty salty about that because I would've loved going out to dinner with you all. You better still go."

"Oh, I am."

She raised an eyebrow at me. "See?"

"See what, Cynthia?" I asked with a little sass.

"I ain't got to say nothing. You'll see what I'm talking about with time," Cynthia said with a mischievous grin.

"Aight, whatever."

Cynthia and I both laughed and hugged each other extremely tight.

I needed her presence this past couple weeks. Cynthia being here had been a huge blessing and definitely a confidence booster. Her being here reminded me of how important my friendships and relationships were. I distanced myself from a lot of people when Mama died, but Cynthia never gave up on me. Now I felt my career moving again. I missed Mama still but felt good.

*****

I couldn't wait for tonight. I was abnormally excited about dinner with Alex and Imani, and my stomach fluttered. I couldn't remember the last time I felt like this. I was experiencing a youthful giddiness and possibly even a bit of nervousness. Imani told me she was excited too, as she and Alex hadn't really been out in a while. Imani's mom was in town for the next few days, so they were going to make the most of it. It was perfect timing that I had something to celebrate while they were free from parenting duties for a little while.

Imani's mom had gotten into town last night, and her and Alex booked a room at the Montelucia Resort for the next few nights. Once I found that out, I insisted on rescheduling so they could have their time, but Imani insisted it was no big deal. She said there was an amazing five-star restaurant in the resort Alex wanted to try, and when he mentioned to her he had invited me out to celebrate, Imani was so excited. I was taken aback because it seemed like they had pretty elaborate plans they decided to include me in on. I was trying not to think too hard about what was transpiring and just live in the moment. I had no expectations other than to have good conversation and good food with friends.

The attire for the restaurant was fancy, so I decided to wear a little black dress with strappy heels. I also let my curls out instead of wearing my hair in a bun. I questioned whether or not my dress was a little too revealing but stopped and reminded myself to just live and have the boobs out while doing it.

When I approached the resort, I admired the mini cascading waterfall outside of the main entrance. December was such a beautiful time in Scottsdale. The weather boasted sixty-five to seventy-degree days, and the sunset over the mountains was breathtaking. I felt calm and was reminded why Mama named me Serenity. She loved the water and loved being in peaceful atmospheres. I felt like Mama was with me. I could hear her voice, and before I let the valet take my car, I had to sit there for a moment and feel her presence. A light tear streamed down my cheek, and I let it fall; I needed this, needed to feel her. I needed to let it out if I was going to have an enjoyable night. I didn't want to hold anything back. It was overwhelming, but it felt so good.

I blotted my eyes, checked my mascara, and let out a huge sigh. Dr. Wilson reminded me of those good cries. She mentioned that if at any given moment I felt like a cry was coming, to let it out even if I had to excuse myself from company to do so. I was doing that, and it was freeing. Something about that release made me more excited about dinner with Alex and Imani.

When the valet took my keys, I was greeted by Alex who took my hand and escorted me out of my car. He looked dapper in his black suit, sans tie, and his slightly unbuttoned shirt. He hugged me and said he was happy I was able to make it. His scent lingered, and I felt myself instantly aroused but kept my hormones at bay. We locked arms, and he smiled at me while we walked toward the lobby of the resort.

As we approached the sliding doors, I saw Imani standing in front of the concierge looking like a million bucks from head to toe. Her silhouette alone was dangerous, as she was wearing an off-the-shoulder, sweetheart-style dress, and I couldn't but stop my eyes from immediately staring at her voluptuous breasts. She turned and hugged me before whispering in my ear, "Thank you so much for coming. This means so much to both of us." She kissed me on my cheek.

I felt like there was more meaning behind that statement and kiss, but again, I tried to draw no conclusions. As Cynthia said, time would tell.

We walked inside the restaurant and were seated by our waiter.

"I'm so sorry Cynthia couldn't make it tonight," I said remorsefully.

"Please, no worries at all. Everything happens like it's supposed to," Imani said while smiling at Alex.

"We're just glad *you* were able to make it. Everything seemed to work out perfectly. We're relieved from parenting duties for a night, and you had something to celebrate," Alex said with an extremely sexy grin, or maybe I was just horny. I hadn't had good sex in some time, so us all sitting here, dressed up at an amazing resort, was getting me in some kind of mood.

"So, have you ever eaten here before?" Imani asked.

"Actually, I have, and I've stayed in this resort before too. When my mom would visit me, she never had to worry about staying in a hotel because she always stayed with me and my ex-husband. But there was this one time she visited us while the rest of my family was here too, and I could tell she needed a break. I booked her a room here. She didn't want to be completely by herself, so she asked me to stay with her. We had such an amazing time." I felt myself getting a little emotional.

"I love when you talk about your mom. I feel like I learn so much about her when you share stories." Imani grabbed my hand. She could always tell when I needed a little TLC.

"Yeah, she was amazing. I must admit, I had a bit of a moment when I was thinking about her in the car," I said, blotting my concealer under my eye.

"Was it too much for you to come here?" Alex asked with concern.

"Not at all. My therapist has been amazing at helping me understand how to feel all of these emotions I blocked out after my mom died. There were days I tried to cry, and it just wouldn't come out. I'm sorry we're talking about this right now," I apologized.

"No apologies necessary. This is a true friendship, and real friends are here for everything, not just the superficial stuff. Your mom was a huge part of your life, and we want to know about that because it's important to you," Imani said.

"Listen, I'm not sure what I did to deserve meeting you guys, but I'm so glad you took the time that day to introduce yourselves. I can't explain it, but I've been experiencing really great things since I met you two." I was hoping I wasn't being too transparent.

"I am so glad you said that because I feel like that confirms how we've been feeling too." Imani smiled while looking at Alex again.

"I am in agreement with Imani as well," Alex added.

Before we knew it, we had eaten and talked for almost three hours. Time was flying, but honestly, this was one of the best dates I had ever been on. We talked about our upbringings and college life. Alex and Imani talked about when they got married, and Imani gushed about motherhood but also kept it real about the challenges she'd experienced too. Imani discussed heading back to work and how nervous she was about that. Alex brought up how hard it was for his family financially growing up, which was why he'd been busting his ass ever since he was a kid to make sure he and his family were taken care of. We were all so vulnerable with each other, and I loved every minute of it.

"So, Serenity, there's no real way to sugarcoat what I'm about to say, so I'm just going to say it." Imani and Alex looked serious.

"Is everything okay? You two are making me a little nervous," I said hesitantly, but I felt like I was starting to get a sense of what was going on.

"I'm sorry to alarm you, Serenity. It's nothing bad, but I'm not sure how you will respond," Imani said, trying to smooth things over.

"Oh, okay, good. Don't scare me like that."

"So, what I was going to say is"—Imani paused— "we're really attracted to you, Serenity. And yes, I said *we*." Imani laughed, and Alex smiled while grabbing Imani's hand.

"Oh, wow," I said while sipping another glass of Merlot.

"If this conversation is making you feel uncomfortable in any way, please just say the word and we can move on from talking about this," Alex said with authority.

"No, not at all. The feeling is mutual. I just didn't want to make any assumptions about the nature of our relationship," I said calmly but was extremely excited.

"Okay, good. Please know, Serenity, from day one, I think we all connected. It's just that your spirit and energy are amazing. If it's okay to say, you are sexy as hell," Imani stared intensely into my eyes. At that moment, I saw a freakier side of Imani starting to come out. Now I could understand what Alex felt when I would catch him grabbing her ass.

"I could feel the chemistry you and Imani had from the beginning, and I could tell this was different for my wife. She has friends, but not like you," Alex chimed in.

"And I could tell how Alex looked at you too, Serenity. It was an interesting thing that was going on, but the two of us vowed to talk about everything when we got together. Alex knew I'd had one relationship with a woman in the past before we'd gotten married, but I was mainly attracted to men and still am. But there's so many things about you I am drawn to, and when you and Alex were dancing that night in your house, I found myself aroused. That shocked me a little bit because you're another woman." Imani was becoming more and more transparent, and I could tell she was feeling the buzz from her wine a little bit.

"And Serenity, this is pretty new for me as well. Even though I was attracted to you too, I didn't have plans of acting on that out of respect for my wife. But Imani caught me off guard one day and could tell I was into you. One thing I love about Imani is her bluntness, and she just asked me if I was interested in exploring a threesome with you, if you were open," Alex admitted.

"Wow, you guys are very uninhibited, but I'd love that. I too have experienced threesomes, more in my college years. It's definitely been a while. To be honest, I have found you both attractive in very unique ways. Alex, the sexiness you exude is something I've definitely fantasized about, and Imani, your beauty is something I can't even describe. You're like an amazing friend, but I also wouldn't mind exploring you a little more intimately as well," I said.

"I'm loving how adult we're being about all of this." Alex laughed while crossing his legs and sipping wine.

"Of course, says the man who's getting crazy attention from two beautiful women tonight," Imani said sarcastically. She then grabbed Alex's shirt and pulled him towards her and began tonguing him down, right at the table. Then I saw her slide her hand down Alex's leg and grab his dick. All I could think was how I could get in on this action, but the restaurant we were dining at didn't look like they were ready for a full-on porn flick.

"We have a very nice suite upstairs and would love for you to join us for the evening, if you want," Imani said seductively.

I gave Imani the same sultry stare she gave me. "I would love to."

Alex took care of the check, leaving a good tip, and we made our way to the room.

As soon as I walked in the door of Alex and Imani's suite, Imani pinned me up against the wall and began kissing my neck as she caressed my breasts at the same time. The softness of her lips and her skin was what I missed most about being with a woman. The sensuality and attention to detail was always something I enjoyed.

I happened to look up, and Alex and I locked eyes as he pulled down his pants and began to touch himself. His dick was clean shaven and thick, with some definite length and a bit of a curve. I imagined at times what Imani and Alex's sex life was like because they oozed passion whenever I was around them. Now I was experiencing the two of them in real life.

Imani walked me over to the bed where Alex was and gently positioned me over the king- size mattress so my back was arched upright. Alex then came behind me; he kissed me softly on my neck while holding my breasts. He definitely set the tone and prepared me to receive his manhood inside me. Imani was taking off her dress which revealed a nice, round ass and very full breasts. I fantasized about sucking them a time or two and finally got to while Alex was handling his business like a champ. Before I knew it, Alex was doing me ever so nicely from behind while I had my face buried in between Imani's legs.

We switched into various positions throughout our session, and even though I was considered the third, Alex and Imani were very giving and attentive to my needs as well.

I had the pleasure of watching Imani and Alex as they made love and seeing how he looked at her while having her legs in the air was probably the most beautiful sight ever.

Alex's stamina was freaking amazing, as he also made sure he gave me that same energy while Imani watched and moaned from the sidelines.

I wasn't sure how many times I climaxed that evening. The three of us laid in bed together, Alex in the middle. There were a few times I jumped on top of Imani and began kissing her again while Alex was dozing off to sleep. We couldn't help it; we got it in again. Our breasts touching and our pussies pulsating underneath the sheets, she sang in my ear a few times, causing me to giggle. Alex and Imani were amazing that night.

5

I couldn't believe my trip to the Vitality Fest was almost here. The studio was thriving, of course, and I was in a really good headspace. I hadn't seen Melissa in the studio, but I figured I'd see her soon at the fest. While she wasn't my favorite person, I was still very grateful for what she did. I talked to Dave about a week ago and told him Melissa was the one to make this connection for me. He was taken aback, and I was surprised Melissa hadn't told him yet. He mentioned she'd met another man on one of her photoshoots and decided to break off whatever they had. He didn't seem heartbroken but actually relieved. Dave shrugged his shoulders and continued talking about him and Melissa as if she was a nice distraction from work but nothing more. He had been tremendously busy with his businesses and was too exhausted to entertain anything serious. Dave mentioned I seemed really upbeat and in great spirits these days. Of course, I didn't tell him about my adventures with Alex and Imani, not because I felt he would judge me, but because I didn't feel it was any of his business. Plus, the last time he and I spoke, he was acting as if he wanted to revive our marriage and that sure as hell wasn't going to happen.

What I was experiencing with Alex and Imani was magical, and I didn't want anything to ruin it. We didn't just have amazing sex, we were forming a bond. We'd been out to dinner a few more times, taken Yaya to an amusement park, and went to the movies together. There were times we would engage in a threesome, then there were times Alex would come over on his lunch break and enjoy me. When Alex would work late, and Imani felt overwhelmed with taking care of Yaya, I would go over to their house and give Imani a quick break by playing with Yaya, giving her a bath, and then putting her to sleep. Then, I would slide in bed with Imani, give her some good loving, and put her to sleep as well.

We had been seeing each other for almost three months, and our dynamic worked so well because we were so open with each other. It was refreshing to be with people who were mature about what we were doing, but it was also comforting to feel like I was a part of their family. I enjoyed their company, both individually as well as together. Alex and Imani said they understood I was single and might meet and have sex with other people, so they didn't try to stifle me. Even though I wasn't interested in anyone else, I appreciated they understood the position I was in. I wasn't sure where it was going, but I was enjoying the ride.

I asked Alex and Imani if they wanted to go to Bali with me for the fest, but Alex said there was no way he could take off work for a whole week, so he insisted Imani go. He even arranged for Imani's mom to come back to Paradise Valley to help out with Yaya so Imani could enjoy a "real break."

I loved the way Alex treated Imani. He knew she'd been overwhelmed. Imani hadn't returned to work like she'd hoped because she just couldn't figure out what she wanted to do. She'd received her undergraduate degree in accounting like Alex, but she didn't have a desire to do that anymore. She had been interested in singing and wanted to pursue that, but trying to schedule gigs while having a toddler and a husband who worked full-time took its toll on her. I looked forward to spending quality time with her during the times I wasn't working the fest. She needed this, and I was so glad Alex encouraged her to go.

I felt so good about where things were headed in my life. My mental health, career, and relationship with Alex and Imani gave me a new lease on life. I noticed I sang more while I cooked, danced around the house, and felt Mama's presence all the time. There were less tears and more smiles when I thought about her. I imagined she would be so happy for me right now, especially with how my relationship with Alex and Imani was blossoming. No doubt, I loved Dave dearly, and we shared an incredible life together, but when Dave filed for a divorce, I saw it a blessing in disguise. With Mama's passing, I felt like I was losing myself, then going through an unexpected divorce, I was depleted and unrecognizable. I never thought I would feel the way I felt today.

My phone rang and interrupted my thoughts, but I didn't care because I always loved hearing from Dr. Wilson.

"Hey, I wasn't expecting to hear from you today. Our session is next Thursday, right?"

"You're fine, Serenity." Dr. Wilson didn't sound like herself. As a matter of fact, she sounded like *she* was the one needing a therapy session.

"Is everything okay? Something in your voice sounds—"

"There's no easy way to say this, Serenity, so I'll just come out and say it. My doctors have informed me they've spotted early signs of dementia, and I think I may need to retire a little earlier than I was anticipating. I know I'm already at retirement age anyway, but I didn't feel the need to step away just yet."

"So, why are you?" I was concerned but also felt combative.

"I'm really not surprised by this at all. My mother and aunt suffered from dementia, and lately, I've been misplacing a lot of things, having difficulty remembering dates, and been a little moody. My daughters were concerned and demanded I see my doctor, and dementia was the prognosis. It's okay. This is where I am in life right now."

"Why are you okay with this?" I felt myself growing angry.

"Listen, it's not about being okay; it's about being at peace. Things are changing with me. That's what happens when you get old, honey. Nothing lasts forever. I'm not giving up, but I'm tired, and my brain is responding to that. This is why I'm stepping away from doing therapy right now. I have to take care of myself. I can't turn a blind eye to what's going on with me. Who knows what the future holds? But right now, being in a denial is not going to do me any good. I want my last years to be enjoyable."

I was on the verge of tears. "But you're only sixty-eight, dammit!"

"Take a deep breath. I know this is hard for you right now, and I wouldn't dare tell you how to feel, so I understand you're frustrated. But remember, we're still in the present moment right now. I'm not dying. I just have dementia, but I wanted you to know. I hear your voice shaking and want to give you a big hug. I promise you're going to be okay. I know you care about me, but what you're mainly worried about is how you're going to continue on without our therapy sessions. Believe me, Serenity, you have all the tools within you. This is going to be a huge transition, but you'd be amazed at the people who have been placed in your life already, who have been there for you, and will help you moving forward."

I needed to really take heed of what Dr. Wilson was saying, but this was feeling like another loss I wasn't sure I could handle. There were days I felt so fragile, even with all my healing from Mama's death. There were days that were still so hard, and yes, I pushed through them, but I always knew I had Dr. Wilson in my back pocket if I needed support. I was scared. What if I went back into that black hole like I did when Mama passed? I couldn't go back there. My breathing quickened.

"Listen to me, Serenity, I need you to understand something: You've got this. You have grown so much, healed even more. Take it one day at a time. I want you to do your breathing exercises even when you think you don't need to. I want you to always be practicing so when life hits you, breathing deeply and counting silently will become your natural default setting. This takes time, and I need you to recognize there are going to be things that will come up that feel like they're knocking the wind out of you, but don't give up, especially seeing as you've made such great progress. Breathe, Serenity, breathe."

I closed my eyes and took a few deep breaths while meditating on what Dr. Wilson said. I began to sweat uncontrollably and could barely count to ten. I was mumbling, and I was so scared. *One. Two. Three. Four. Five.* I was counting silently and breathing deeply. I kept cuffing my hands together as I felt the sweat between my fingers. My foot tapped incessantly, and my heart pounded extremely hard. *One. Two. Three. Four. Five. I can do this. I can do this.* The tears started to fall as I tried to convince myself of that.

"Serenity, I will always be here for you—always. Your life is forever changed by your mom's transition, but I feel her presence and I think you do too. Just think about the last time your mom held you in her arms. Think about how much she adored you and loved how you took life by the horns and went for it. Your mom is right there with you. I know that was a huge loss and this news I'm sharing with you takes you to that lonely place, but it doesn't have to. Your mom is here in spirit, and I am here right now in the flesh. Take another deep breath, honey. You've got this."

The sound of Dr. Wilson's voice soothed me, and before I knew it, my foot stopped tapping and my body relaxed. I felt my body returning to normal after another panic attack. For some reason, I felt ashamed, like I did when Cynthia and Imani witnessed my attack before. Dr. Wilson could clearly tell even over the phone.

"I know you're feeling embarrassed, Serenity, but it's only because those panic attacks you've been having expose you and make you vulnerable. Don't let that feeling make you want to seclude and hide. These are raw emotions and reactions to a very difficult situation. Don't ever skip the process. Allow yourself to feel all of it just like you did today. This allows you to grow."

"I trust you, Dr. Wilson, I do," I said while holding back more tears.

"It's okay, let it out. I'm right here with you. I'm not going anywhere until you fully release," Dr. Wilson comforted.

I let the tears flow. I screamed, got angry, then was sad. Dr. Wilson continued to comfort me during the process of my release.

"I was just sitting here, thinking about all the amazing things that were happening in my life, and then—"

"I know, and then I called you with this news. But in spite of this, you will be okay," Dr. Wilson reassured me.

"Thank you. I just need a moment to lie down. I'll be okay."

"I know you will.

"I will, Dr. Wilson."

Hanging up, I then texted Imani to tell her I needed to see her then cried myself to sleep during the middle of the day.

I later woke to my doorbell. I had lost track of time after I talked to Dr. Wilson and attempted to clean up my face as much as possible before answering the door. It was Dave.

"Um, hey, Dave. What brings you by here unannounced?"

"Actually, I've been trying to call and text you for the past hour, letting you know I would be in the area. I was thinking we could get some dinner or something. Are you okay? You look pretty tired."

"Hasn't anyone told you to never tell a woman she looks tired? Anyway, I was taking a nap, so I didn't realize I missed your call."

"Oh, I'm sorry."

"It's okay, don't worry about it. I am a little out of it, though. I didn't realize I slept so long."

"Are you sure you're okay? You seem a little more than tired."

"Well, if you must know, my therapist has dementia and just told me she's retiring a lot earlier than I anticipated. So, what started out as a good day kind of turned into pretty rough one."

"Oh, wow, you're talking about Dr. Wilson? I'm sorry to hear that. I'm really sorry, Serenity."

I could tell by the look on Dave's face he really wanted to be there for me. I just wasn't really in the mood for him right now.

"I appreciate that, I really do. This just really set me back a little bit," I said, exhausted.

"I can imagine. Well, I can definitely give you the number of my therapist if you want to give her a call. I'm definitely okay with setting up—"

"Dave, honestly, I appreciate that, but I'm not really in the mood to discuss finding a new therapist right now."

"Okay, I'm sorry. I'm not trying to upset you."

Our conversation was interrupted by another person at my door. Imani shouldered past Dave to reel me in for a huge hug and a kiss on the lips, telling me everything was going to be okay. This left Dave caught off guard by Imani's display of affection.

"Oh, I'm sorry. I'm Imani." Imani stuck out her hand to shake. Dave's eyes were widened with curiosity.

"No worries, I'm Dave."

"Oh my God, this is your ex-husband, Dave?" Imani whispered to me.

Dave appeared a bit disturbed. "Yes, I'm Serenity's ex-husband. I'm surprised you've heard about me while I've never heard about you."

"Listen, Dave, you and I don't talk often, and I didn't feel like I owed you any explanation about what's going on in my life, but now that you're here, I will not sugarcoat anything: This is my partner, Imani. Her and her husband live in the community."

"What the—?"

"Dave, you can pick your jaw up off the floor. Yes, we are involved in a poly- relationship, a thruple, if you will. I get the best of everything, and they have a daughter, so we're one big happy fucking family."

Imani couldn't help but chuckle, which caused me to laugh a little bit too.

"I mean, damn, Serenity, I know we've had our share of free play in our marriage, but I didn't know this is what you had going on these days." I could tell Dave was looking for more information, but I wouldn't give it to him.

"And there was no reason for you to know. Can you stop staring at her titties for a second?"

"I didn't mean—"

"You're funny, Dave. I take no offense. Serenity used to look at them like that too when we first met." Imani smiled.

"Oh, you got jokes, huh?" I half smiled.

"But seriously, hun, I'm so sorry I'm just now getting your message. I had my phone on silent while Yaya was asleep. It must've died while her and I napped together. Are you okay?" Imani cupped my face in her hands. I held Imani's hands on my face and told her everything was okay.

"Dr. Wilson told me today she has dementia and is retiring. It threw me for a loop and I… how about we talk about it later?" I didn't feel the need to discuss what was going on with me in front of Dave.

"Oh, honey, I'm so sorry I wasn't here for you. It wasn't another panic attack, was it?" Imani was so caring, but her trying to whisper just did not work. I was pretty sure Dave heard her.

"You don't have to apologize; you had Yaya to worry about. Dr. Wilson ended up calming me down, and I went to sleep." I was trying the whole whispering approach as well, but I failed miserably.

"Wait a minute, what's this I hear about panic attacks? What's going on?" Dave looked overwhelmed with everything he was learning about me at once.

"Dave, I swear, you sure picked a fine time to pop over. As much as I want to tell you to mind your damn business, I know you are genuinely concerned about me."

I told Dave about my panic attacks, but I still didn't feel the need to go in depth about my relationship with Alex and Imani.

"This is all a lot to take in. I'm sorry, Imani, to have showed up unannounced like this. If I would've known Serenity was involved with someone, I wouldn't have just showed up like this. I'm sorry about that."

"No apologies necessary, Dave, but I really appreciate that," Imani said, and I could tell Dave's eyes were zoomed right into Imani's double-D's again.

"Dave was trying to take me out to dinner, which is why he showed up."

"I mean, like I said, I wasn't trying to be disrespectful," Dave said nervously.

"Why don't we all go?" Imani suggested happily.

"Are you sure?" Dave and I said in unison.

"I mean, why not? There's nothing to hide around here. Dave, you know about our relationship now, and I can clearly see you care about Serenity's well-being, which always makes me happy," Imani said while putting her arm around my waist.

"Oh, wow, I just didn't really think you would be comfortable, seeing as we used to be married."

"Dave, no offense, but Serenity can't get enough of all of this." Imani ran her hands across her body to accentuate her silhouette while smiling at Dave.

"Um…well, when you put it like that…" Dave was in a trance. It was like watching a pubescent boy look at porn for the first time.

"Earth to Dave, you are ridiculous," I said with a slight smirk. "I mean, I'm okay with us all going out if you all are. But what about Alex? We should probably let him know," I said to not exclude the third person in this equation.

"Well, he's home with Yaya, but we can totally bring her if you all want?" Imani offered.

"This is a different kind of situation." Dave blinked in bemusement. "Listen, I don't want to make things too complicated. As a man, I just don't think this is something you want to just spring on another man. Maybe you should talk to Alex before we all meet up for dinner. No hurry, though. I'm still just trying to wrap my brain around the fact that Serenity is pulling more beautiful women than me."

We couldn't all help but laugh. Dave's shoulders appeared more relaxed and his eyes were no longer as wide.

"Dave, I really appreciate you checking in and being concerned about me. I know we still have a genuine friendship, and I value that, even though we're divorced," I said with gratitude and reached to give Dave a hug.

"And I'm sincerely sorry to hear about what you're going through with your therapist. If you need anything, just let me know," Dave replied.

"Thank you, I will."

"It was a pleasure meeting you, Imani, and hopefully, this won't be our last encounter." Dave reached to hug Imani.

"Thanks, Dave, the pleasure is all mine," she said graciously.

Dave let himself out, and Imani and I talked about Dr. Wilson and how I was doing. Imani was attentive; she didn't interrupt and allowed me to speak freely about how I was feeling. For a split second, it felt like Alex wasn't part of the equation. Imani and I shared such a strong bond since the beginning, and at times, I felt she and I were more intimate than Alex and me. I wasn't sure what to make of that. Was it just the woman-to-woman dynamic? I had been involved in threesomes that were based on sex, as opposed to a relationship, so I must admit the situation was new for me, and one I wanted to navigate with care and compassion because of how I felt about both of them.

"Honey, what's on your mind? You look like you're deep in thought," Imani said while caressing my hair.

"I don't know. I was just thinking about us."

"What do you mean you were thinking about us? Is something wrong?"

"Lately, I've been getting the sense that you and I are more intimate at times than when Alex is with us. Don't get me wrong, I am so into the both of you, but I don't know, I get around you, and I feel we have a deeper connection. And God, I want to make love to you every single time I see you and find myself wanting to do that without Alex." I felt like I was dropping a bomb on Imani without forewarning.

Imani seemed stuck. "Oh, wow, I'm not sure what to say."

"I'm sorry for making you feel uncomfortable, and I definitely don't want us to keep any secrets in this relationship. I just feel like I can share more things with just you when Alex isn't around," I admitted.

"Well, believe it or not, there are times when I look forward to Alex working late because I know you'll come over and help with Yaya and give me that quality time I feel like I haven't been getting from him. Don't get me wrong, you know he is an amazing man who always makes sure I'm well taken care of, but when you're there, you're extremely attentive to my needs, and dare I say, I enjoy making love to you more than I do to him," Imani whispered as if my house was bugged.

"I didn't realize you felt that way too. Damn, Imani, we've got to talk to him about this. The only way this will work is if we're always honest with each other."

"I know, but for a minute, can I just hold you? You needed me earlier and now I'm here. I just want to hold you," Imani said in a passionate tone.

Imani held me and stroked my head before sliding her hand up and down my body. Then she kissed me softly. We continued to hold and touch one another. Imani slid her hands down my pants into my underwear and caressed me until I couldn't hold back anymore. We laid down on the couch together and began to pleasure each other until we were both panting and out of breath. Whenever we made love, it was extremely sensual, and we always wished time would stand still. But reality set in, and I thought to myself, *How the hell are we going to tell Alex?*

CHAPTER

6

I had just finished a really exhilarating day of yoga. All of my students had performed their poses effortlessly; my guidance was barely needed. Everyone truly bared their souls on the mat, myself included. The sweat, deep breathing, and tears were a beautiful thing. It was by far the best day I'd had at work ever.

I was gearing up for my trip to Bali in a few weeks. I was excited and looking forward to what the retreat would bring to me and the attendees. I couldn't lie. I was also excited about spending so much time with Imani on such a beautiful island. We both agreed we would talk with Alex about our feelings for one another after we returned from the trip. The selfish part of me didn't want him to get upset and try to convince Imani to stay home, and I definitely didn't want her to challenge Alex and cause a disruption within their family. I was starting to feel like I was a wedge coming in between the two of them. I knew Imani had one relationship with a woman previously, but was she really more attracted to women than men? Was their marriage bound to run into these problems even if I wasn't a part of their lives? I couldn't help but worry because the three of us worked so well. I always thought Alex was fine as hell, but Imani was attentive and nurturing, and she quenched my thirst for eroticism. I wanted to explore every part of her, and I wanted her to do the same with me. I couldn't help but be excessively drawn to her because of that. The three of us together were electrifying, but the two of us were spiritual.

"Hey, Serenity. You got a quick minute?" Lisa had interrupted my thoughts, but when the creator of the Vitality Fest called, you stopped daydreaming.

"Yeah, sure," I said, a bit nervous.

"Okay, great. I have a laundry list of things to review with you prior to Bali in a few weeks. There have been a few changes, and you're going to take an even more active role in the Fest than I anticipated. What's your schedule looking like later this evening for a conference call with the team?"

I couldn't imagine what "more of an active role" meant, and honestly, I didn't want to wear myself thin. I was already pretty booked for the retreat and really wanted some quality time with Imani, but I didn't want to thwart this amazing opportunity by not being accommodating.

"Just let me know what time, and you can count me in."

"Okay, great, that's what I like to hear. As soon as I align a few more things, I will text you with the specific time and conference info."

"Sounds like a plan. Thank you."

"No, thank you. Your commitment to your craft and what you've designed for the yoga retreat is top notch. I knew we picked the right person for the job. I have a quick meeting, but I'll be in touch soon."

I was flattered and excited at the same time to be recognized for my work in the field. I was never the type of person who was business or money driven. I was always motivated by living my truth and doing what I loved but being given this opportunity was really exciting. I had definitely been exposed to a lot, being married to Dave. We were always invited to the fanciest dinners, the most beautiful and elaborate yachts, and the most exclusive private parties, but it was because of Dave's career path and *his* influence. I was starting to feel like I was carving out a path of my own, and it felt damn good. The money alone from this opportunity was more than I'd ever made at one time. Being married to Dave definitely exposed me to the finer things in life, so I was no stranger to them, but I felt good because I was the one now making things happen. I felt like I could maybe spoil Imani a bit on this trip and just give her an experience of a lifetime. Thinking about that made me smile.

I thought Alex mentioned he was working from home today, so I knew he, Imani, and Yaya would be doing something as a family, and even though I could've totally invited myself, as they were always welcoming of me, I really wanted some alone time today. After today's yoga session, I was looking forward to a hot bath, aromatherapy, and some meditation and unwinding before my conference call this evening.

That was what I enjoyed a lot about this relationship. There was room to participate in their lives but also space for me to continue my pursuits without feeling obligated to them. I enjoyed my own space and was respectful of theirs. I loved spending time with them, but I also enjoyed spending time with myself. And even though I adored Yaya, I couldn't imagine having a child of my own 24/7, and that was why I loved spoiling Imani because I knew she needed that break from time to time. I could also tell she appreciated what I provided for her.

I'd never forget the time Alex was working late and she called me in a panic, asking to come over and help out with Yaya. When I showed up, she had actually tricked me and already put Yaya to bed. She had a candlelight dinner waiting for me, and we talked and enjoyed each other's company. I could tell she had a long day with Yaya, but she was still so beautiful. Her hair was naturally curly like mine, but she typically straightened hers more often than me. That evening, she just let it flow. She had on some jogging pants, a white t-shirt, no makeup on, and was dead-ass gorgeous. I almost felt bad for Alex because I could sense, at times, she wasn't always in the mood for him, but she was *always* in the mood for me. I loved her spontaneity even though she had been feeling overwhelmed with being a new mom. It was like whenever she saw me, she perked up and would hold me like she never wanted to let go.

I wondered where all of this was going. Maybe it was normal in three-way relationships to have a certain bond with each person separately. Hopefully, it didn't mean Alex would be booted out because that was not my intention. I kind of wanted to talk to Cynthia about what was going on, but I figured she wouldn't understand and just say, "Listen, I ain't down with that freaky shit, but it's whatever you wanna do."

She still didn't know about the relationship I had with both Alex and Imani. I never let her in on the details about the night we spent at the Montelucia. Part of me didn't want to open up about all of it. None of the threesomes I'd engaged in in the past, including the one with Dave, were ever a full-out poly relationship, so this was all new to me. But there was always something about Imani loving to hear stories about my mom that allowed me to not have any guards up with her, and I loved that.

I needed an outlet. I knew it was time for me to review the list of therapists Dr. Wilson forwarded to me, but I wasn't ready to open up to anyone new just yet. My brothers and I were cool but not as close as I would've liked. There was no bad blood between us, but a distance developed after Mama passed. Maybe it was time for me to reach out. My brothers weren't exactly the affectionate type. I was always the one who took the lead on that, so maybe this was one of those times I needed to do that again.

I continued to get lost in my thoughts while placing my foot into the hot bath water. The steam rose up my shin and onto my thigh. As I fully immersed my body in the water, my muscles relaxed, and I allowed my thoughts to eventually disappear until my mind was totally clear. The aromatherapy and calming spa music playing in the background made me feel like I was floating, and at that moment, nothing mattered. It was as if any worry I had was drifting away on a cloud.

Before I knew it, my eyes had closed, and I saw Mama smiling and reaching out to me as if she had only been gone a few months and was returning from a trip. Her embrace was warm and safe. She stroked my hair like she would always do, while kissing me on my forehead. She asked me about life and how work was going. I told her about my upcoming Bali trip, as well as Alex and Imani, and she beamed with excitement, knowing I was doing so well and was happy. All of a sudden, her face turned pale and she began shaking uncontrollably. I screamed, asking her what was wrong. I felt helpless; I couldn't do anything. I called for help, but no one came, as if we were the last people on Earth. I continued to scream as I held Mama in my arms and looked down. Her eyes closed slowly.

I almost completely jolted out of my bathtub from the nightmare. I wished I could say it was only a dream, but it really wasn't because Mama was still gone. Maybe it was time for me to go through that list of therapists from Dr. Wilson after all.

*****

Bali was breathtaking. I was excited to experience the rice paddies, coral reefs, sunsets, and vegetarian food. I couldn't wait to begin the yoga retreat.

I arrived a couple of days prior to the guests for a meeting with the team. We went over pertinent details before registration.

Imani decided to catch a later flight so she could spend a little more time with Alex and Yaya before heading out. We still hadn't talked with Alex about how close we'd been getting. We both agreed to save that discussion until after the trip. I couldn't wait for Imani to get here, though. I knew she needed this time away, and I was glad she was spending it with me. Ironically, the last time I was in Bali was my honeymoon.

Lisa mentioned during our phone conference that one of her past yoga instructors offered a nude yoga session and asked if I would be interested in conducting one. That was an easy *yes* for me. Honestly, if I could walk around naked all day, I would. I even tried to convince Lisa to attend that session just because I knew it would make her face turn red. She seemed to be a bit uptight most of the time, but surprisingly, she said she might. This trip could have some surprising twists after all.

When I arrived at the hotel, I still had a little bit of time before heading to the team meeting. My room was exquisite, and the view was heart-stopping. Every detail was immaculate, from the way the towels were folded into little doves on my bed to the tea and crumpets eloquently placed on a table on the balcony outside my room. All I had to do was stay in the present moment, doing what I loved and sharing my gift with others. It truly got no better than this.

I forgot I'd had my phone's ringer off, but I felt its vibration in my back pocket.

"Hey, love." Imani's voice sounded so soothing on the other end of the phone.

"Hey, beautiful. I can't wait to see you tomorrow evening. You're going to love our room," I said with much excitement.

"I don't doubt that for one moment. You know how much I need this break. And I can't wait to see you in your element. I know you're going to rock that yoga retreat. Thanks for making sure I have tickets to your sessions as well. I'm going to definitely take full advantage."

"As you should. But seriously, I just want you to do whatever your heart desires on this trip. If you feel like attending a session or two, you know I'd love to have you, but if you want to go sightseeing, shopping, or whatever while I'm working, you know I'm here for it, just as long as we get some alone time to take it all in and feel each other's presence."

"Serenity, I would love that. I can't wait. My bags are literally packed and waiting by the door. This is a little different for me, though. Yaya and I haven't been apart for such a significant amount of time since her birth, especially for a whole week. I know my mom is a champ and will take care of everything, but it's going to be hard." Imani sounded a bit solemn.

"I know, hun, but it'll be fine. You sound a bit more upset, though, like something else is wrong," I said concerned.

Imani sighed. "Well, Alex and I had a bit of an argument a little while ago."

"What were you all arguing about?"

"All of a sudden, he said he was a little uncomfortable with me going away for so long and complaining about how hard it was going to be for him to work and handle Yaya, then he mentioned I still breastfed and was confused about how that was going to work. He just kept going on and on and about stuff that didn't make any sense." Imani's voice was shaking.

"Babe, please don't cry. I'm kind of confused by all of this as well. I mean, your mom is gonna be there the entire time helping with Yaya, and as far as breastfeeding, didn't he realize you stopped two weeks ago? Now, that's one thing I do know since I like playing with the girls." I laughed to lighten the mood.

"That's exactly the problem. Him and I haven't had sex since the last time all three of us were together," Imani said.

"Um, Imani, that was like three weeks ago. What's going on?"

"Can we just drop it for now? This is gonna make me sad all over again, and I just want to be in a better space when I head out tomorrow." I could hear Imani sniffling in the background.

"Okay, babe. I know it's pretty late there, so get some rest. I can't wait to see you tomorrow."

"Okay," Imani mumbled.

I could tell Imani was struggling, and even though all three of us were in this together, I still felt like it wouldn't be my place to talk with Alex about Imani. Even though both of them invited me into their relationship, at times, I felt like Alex didn't always see me as a full partner. We definitely talked and had conversations, mainly with Imani present, but even when he and I were alone, it felt like a quick release on his part, mostly physical, and nothing too serious. I chalked it up to him being a man and not being as expressive as Imani. I didn't know what his deal was, but I was ready to pull out all the stops for Imani when she arrived.

I was confused by Alex, but in a marriage, it was expected to have ups and downs. It didn't matter how free and forward-thinking a couple was, there would always be something that had to be worked through, ironed out, and made crystal clear. Having Yaya in the mix was just another part of their marriage that required added attention.

I thought that was why I'd never wanted children. I loved kids, but I knew how much stress it could place on a person and a couple. I also saw how much my mom sacrificed and endured for my brothers and I to keep our family together. I never wanted that, and it was nice being married to a man like Dave who also didn't want kids. But deep down inside, I felt like Dave would get that itch one day to be a dad. He was still young, and even though he and I were married, our relationship wasn't a prison sentence. We didn't put the typical restraints on each other many marriages seemed to have. Maybe if he were to meet a woman down the line he really loved, he may want the whole family thing. I wondered if that was why our marriage ended.

I hated that Alex and Imani were at odds, but I thought once Imani got away and had her "me time," she was going to be okay. Alex was one of the coolest men I'd been involved with, but he was still a man and men did dumb shit sometimes.

I was glad I could be there for Imani in a lot of ways. She and I were genuinely friends, so we could talk for hours and listen to one another. We just happened to be attracted to each other sexually. I actually liked serving her. Doing that brought me so much joy. When I met her, I knew there was something special about her but in a different way than I was used to. She always loved hearing me talk about my mom. She never got bored or frustrated with that, and it created a strong intimacy between the two of us because of how much I loved and missed my mom. I felt like I could tell Imani anything, and she didn't judge me at all. That made me want to give so much to her. I decided to grab a quick bite to eat to take with me to the meeting and get ready for an exciting and unforgettable week.

*****

Imani had finally arrived, but I was in the middle of helping Lisa with some registration details surrounding the yoga retreat, so I wasn't able to greet her in the room. The good thing was, once we were done meeting, I would pretty much have the rest of the afternoon and evening to myself before becoming busy over the next few days. It worked out perfectly for Imani to check herself in; as she mentioned, she was going to take a bath and get some much-needed rest before I headed back to our room.

I couldn't even describe the excitement I had knowing I was going to have Imani all to myself for one whole week. I couldn't wait to see her, talk to her, hold her, and of course, make love to her. We weren't going to be interrupted by Yaya crying or Alex calling to ask where he left his tie or his files. She could be free and not give a damn about anything. I was anxious to see her in a state of relaxation. I was seriously going to fuck the shit out of her all around our room, on that balcony, and in the shower. I would make her feel like the beautiful woman she was. Imani never held back either. She was always a very giving partner in bed. The orgasms we shared with one another were so intense. We never had these defined roles either, like who'd take the masculine or feminine role. That seemed juvenile to the both of us. We just expressed how we felt and didn't limit ourselves.

Even though I was still struggling with the death of my mom, I was glad I didn't feel like I had for the past three years. I had an out-of-body experience where I was watching myself recluse and confine myself to the four walls of my home. I struggled to get up and go to work, enjoy a great meal with a friend, or even delight in the simplicity of watching a cool flick at home. I was slipping away, which was out of character because I valued everything in life, even watching a bird peck at its food. I was drowning, but little by little, I began to feel like myself. Dr. Wilson played such a huge role in me finding my center again. I just felt incredibly blessed to be in the current space I was in. I didn't take any of it for granted and didn't take meeting Alex and Imani for granted. Them coming into my life was truly what I needed. For a while, I'd accepted that maybe I wouldn't find a deep connection with anyone—then they popped up on my doorstep. I found myself smiling.

"Serenity, can you hand me those registration cards?" Lisa asked hurriedly. "We're going to be wrapping up in a minute. I know you mentioned a friend of yours would be arriving soon, so I'm sure you want to catch up with her before this week gets started."

Lisa Fletcher was this amazon of a woman, standing at six foot one with broad shoulders and light blonde hair. Lisa was very fit; her physique boasted of her body building days. She strongly advocated for a healthy lifestyle and was not only the creator of the Vitality Fest but owner of many fitness studios, as well as wellness centers. She was truly a walking billboard of health. Her skin glowed, her hair was full, and she had the stamina of a teen track star. She supported anything health related, so she was willing to provide me with anything I needed to make the yoga retreat a success. Money was not an issue at this event—the budget was set at ten million dollars—and she spared no expense.

I liked Lisa. She could be pretty uptight most of the time, but I could tell that was the entrepreneur side of her. I remembered Dave's business friends having a stance a lot like Lisa's. The only difference was Lisa was a woman and was extremely badass when it came to business. It was hard for people to accept that a woman could be a force in the entrepreneurial world, and she didn't take any shit from anyone.

"Yeah, I'm really excited to see her. Imani is actually my girlfriend, so you'll see me loving on her throughout this trip, but no need to worry at all; I am the consummate professional. I won't be dipping off when I'm supposed to be working." I liked talking to Lisa like this because I could tell she liked knowing she didn't have to be so conventional around me.

"Oh, I'm not worried about that at all. Melissa gets on my damn nerves most of the time, but she got one thing right, which was referring you to me." She smiled then sighed, as if she really wanted to let her hair down and not be so professional all the time. I was surprised she said that about Melissa, though, because she didn't know our connection.

"Serenity, you don't have to look so surprised. I'm pretty sure she brought you up as a possible yoga instructor because she knows damn well she and my husband are always flirting all the time. She feels guilty because they're probably sleeping together," Lisa said causally, but I could tell she was irritated.

"Well, I wouldn't assume—"

"Trust me, he's sleeping with her. He sleeps with many of the models he represents. He's been doing it since his thirties. Damn, near seventy years old, and he's still bending ditzy models over the desk."

"Why are you still with him? You clearly don't approve. If it's okay to say, you don't exactly seem like you need anything from him. So, what's the point?" I curiously asked.

"When I first met you, Serenity, I could tell you were one of those open-minded types. If you don't want to be bothered with someone, you don't make excuses; you just leave. You don't attach yourself to too many things or people. But honestly, at my age, seeing that I'm sixty-two, I'm not about to start over. Richard and I have been married for a long time. We met in the modeling industry, which is superficial as hell. We've raised children, have grandchildren, endured money problems, births, deaths, foreclosures, infidelity, life-altering illnesses, and a shitload of other stuff. I couldn't care less about Richard cheating with an impressionable girl. Hell, I used to be that girl in my twenties. But I can't have Richard jeopardizing our legacy. Our net worth is two hundred and fifty million dollars. I don't have time for him to get caught up with some Instagram fitness model who's only using his old ass for money anyway. He's not as sharp as he used to be, and if he's not careful, he could totally mess up what we've built over the last forty years because his dick still works a little bit." Lisa chuckled. "Shit, I'm fucking around myself, but at least I'm smart about it."

"I knew I liked you for a reason."

"Well, even though I couldn't give two shits if you liked me or not, it's nice to know everyone involved in this Fest ain't just here to kiss my ass. I get tired of that shit."

"I can imagine. Well, no ass-kissing is going to come from me, but I really respect your work in the wellness industry. I've followed you and the Fest for quite some time."

"I really appreciate that. So, exactly how do you know Melissa?" Lisa asked.

"Believe it or not, she was dating my ex-husband," I said nonchalantly.

"Wow, no shit. Well, I like your attitude about it. Fuck them."

I couldn't help but laugh. "You're funny, Lisa."

"Listen, if your ex-husband is no longer in your life and he ended up with her, then I question his judgment. You've got spunk. I don't know what the hell Melissa has other than two bowling balls plastered on her chest."

Lisa had me crying from laughing. I couldn't remember the last time I laughed so hard, and she was so serious when she said that.

Lisa laughed. "I hope he's not the reason you've turned to girls."

"No, not at all. Like you said, I'm a little bit freer in my thinking. I've been attracted to both men and women for a long time. I've never labeled myself as anything because I wanted to give myself a chance to just be into whoever I wanted to be into. My girlfriend, Imani, is actually married. We're in a poly relationship."

"Oh, okay, I have plenty of business associates who are polyamorous. That kind of stuff was going on back in the seventies, even when I first got married. We didn't have a name for it other than freaky shit. You young kids are a lot more open these days and don't hide anything, so I get it. Is it only your girlfriend that's coming here, or her husband as well?" Lisa appeared to seem really interested in my lifestyle.

"Nope, just Imani," I said.

"I know you're all doing the threesome thing, but by the way you smiled when you said her name, I could tell there's a lot more going on with you two." Lisa read me without any effort at all.

"Wow, you picked that up rather quickly. I'm quite impressed with your intuitiveness."

"No need to be impressed; I'm just old. I've been around the block a few times myself. When you've lived and seen as much as I have, you can pretty much spot anything. Now go ahead and get to your girlfriend and have a whole bunch a good sex. Lord knows I'm not getting any on this trip. But be sure to be ready in the morning at seven sharp." Lisa smiled.

"Will do." I hurried up to my room.

As I approached my hotel room, I could hear Toni Braxton playing softly. Imani was obsessed with '90s R&B music. She acted as if no other decade of music existed. I thought it was kind of cute.

"Hey, baby!" Imani ran into my arms as soon as I opened the door. It was so good to see her smiling after the night before.

"Hey, babes. Damn, you look great!" I started kissing Imani's neck. She decided to surprise me by wearing a red negligee. I wasn't really the lingerie-wearing kind of girl. My idea of bedroom sexy was a tank top and boy shorts, but Imani could rock anything and look luscious as hell.

"So, you like my outfit? I bought it just for you." She modeled and did a quick spin for me, so I could see all of her.

"It looks amazing, or should I say *you* look amazing. I really couldn't care less about the lingerie. You could've opened the door butt-ass naked, and I would've been fine with that," I said with a seductive grin.

"I know, but I thought I'd try something different on our first night together here in Bali. Are you hungry? I was gonna order room service, but I figured we'd probably be more focused on enjoying each other than trying to eat."

I kissed Imani. "Well, we'll be eating—that's for sure—but not room service."

"I love when you look at me like that," she gushed.

"Oh, like you're the finest thing on this earth?" I asked.

"Exactly. Now, enough talking; I need you now. I've been waiting all day. I've taken a bath and had a nap, so you know I'm ready." Imani eagerly walked me over to the bed.

Imani's aggressive side showed as she began to take the lead and positioned me so I was on my stomach. She laid next to me and slid her hand between my thighs while kissing my back. Imani was such a fucking beast when it came to making love. She just never held back, whether she was in the pleasing role or being pleased. I then aggressively moved Imani to her back and kissed her forehead before slowly making my way down to her neck and then her breasts, which I always enjoyed burying my face in. The sweet smell of almond flower and vanilla, as well as the softness of her skin, kept me hibernating in that space. Imani came alive whenever I kissed her nipples. It was definitely an erogenous zone of hers. When I made my way to the main event, I licked every part of inner thighs, to her lips, and then to her clitoris. I wanted us to preserve our love-making session, so I slowed things down and rubbed my body against hers. Imani began singing in my ear again; this time it was "Sweetest Taboo" by Sade. I could always tell when Imani was in a good mood because she would start humming in my ear. At times, Imani would sing to me in Spanish.

"God, I love you." I didn't realize what I saying until it came out.

Imani paused and looked down at me. "Um, wow. Did you just tell me you loved me?"

"Please know that it just slipped out. I wasn't expecting—"

"So, you didn't mean it?" Imani interrupted my statement as if disappointed.

"Oh, I meant it for sure. I just didn't want to put you in an uncomfortable spot. I don't want you to feel obligated to say it back," I said, though secretly hoping Imani felt the same way.

"Well, you know what this means?"

"Not exactly. What does it mean?"

"It means you're not getting any sleep tonight, Serenity, because I'm about to show you how much I love you too." Imani placed one of my fingers in her mouth and began to suck it slowly while she was looking at me.

"I'm loving this connection we're experiencing right now," I said to her. She looked like the lioness in her was about to appear.

"Oh, me too. I am extremely attracted to you, Serenity, in so many ways. You cater to every part of me. You understand me and just see me. You touch me in a way I rarely get touched. You know exactly what to say and how to say it. You including me on this trip was the sweetest thing because you definitely didn't have to. You could've had a whole other woman, or man, or both in this room tonight."

We couldn't help but laugh.

"Believe me, I didn't want anyone else here but you," I said softly while kissing Imani's lips in between my words.

Imani laid on her back and sat me on top of her, giving me the cue that she wanted me to ride her. Imani held my hips as I slowly bounced up and down on top of her. She sat up and kissed my nipples while still grabbing onto my hips. We began to firmly rub against one another. The moans, the breathing, and the scents from our bodies filled the air. We were truly experiencing ecstasy. We talked dirty to each other, smiled, were playful, and enjoyed every inch of the other's bodies. We explored our curiosity all through the night. Even when we dozed off, we would wake each other up to some oral sex, and it felt even better than the time before.

"Babe, you weren't playing. You are wearing me out! Don't get me wrong. I love it, but I have to be up and out in a few hours," I said.

"I know, I just can't get enough of you." She kissed me. "Okay, can I just taste you one more time? I promise, this will be the last time," Imani begged.

"Dammit, now, how am I supposed to turn that down?"

"Exactly, you shouldn't," Imani demanded, and I politely opened my legs for her to enjoy. If saying I loved her made her act like this, I was going to tell her how much I loved her throughout this entire trip.

As much as I was enjoying this rendezvous, I knew I needed to get some rest or I would be no good for the first day of the Fest.

*****

"What an amazing session that was!"

"Exactly, I've gone to the Vitality Fest every single year, and I've never had such an incredible experience on the mat."

"Where did they find her? They need to bring her back every single year!"

I overheard so many compliments about my naked yoga session, and it was extremely humbling. I couldn't believe the whispers of the attendees singing my praises. I truly enjoyed being a yoga instructor for the past fifteen years, and it was a passion of mine for so long, but to be given such a huge platform to share my gift was beyond my wildest dreams.

"Excuse me, Serenity?" A young woman, who looked to be no more than twenty-five years old, approached me. She seemed a bit nervous, like she was meeting a long-time celebrity idol of hers.

"Yes."

"I just wanted to tell you this session was more than I could've ever imagined it would be. I've been dealing with so much in my life since I was a teenager. I battled childhood obesity and have struggled with it my entire life. I was in a serious car accident when I was twenty-one, and it left some pretty severe scars. I would've never thought with my weight I would be able to do yoga, let alone naked yoga, because I've always been so self-conscious of my body. But I'm here and am so grateful." The young woman's body shook, and her eyes filled with tears.

"Oh my goodness! Thanks so much for sharing. What's your name?" I asked.

"It's Samantha, but everyone calls me Sam."

"Well, Sam it is truly an honor to meet you and share my gift with you on the mat today. Hearing your story and knowing I was able to connect with you truly warms my heart," I said with gratitude.

"The looks I would get from the women were disgusting, as if someone my size had no right to attend such a class. I was always forgotten and even at times asked to place my mat in the back so others could see. And I know this might be T-M-I, but I've even avoided intimacy with men because of my scars.

"One of my best friends noticed how down I'd been feeling, so he insisted I go to this Vitality Fest. He said there was going to be a naked yoga session, and I immediately laughed at him because I just knew he wasn't insinuating I should attend, but he was so serious. I told him there was no way I would have the money to go to Bali, but when he told my parents about it, they insisted I go and even paid for my trip. Part of the reason is they're desperate for me to meet a man, get married, and have children, and for some reason, they feel my best friend is that person.

"But anyway, I'm so glad to be here because I've never seen so much diversity in yoga at one time! There were people of all shapes and sizes, men, women, young, old, all ethnicities, all nationalities, and imperfect but perfect bodies. I felt accepted, embraced, and loved, and the way you facilitated this session made me forget I was even naked. I loved every minute of it, and I really needed this. So thank you so much." Sam began crying even more, and I instinctively reached for a hug.

"Again, I am extremely honored and humbled by your spirit. Thank you for sharing this space with me. This has been a huge blessing to me as well. Are you going to be here for the entire Fest?"

"I sure am," Sam said while wiping her eyes.

"I would love for us to connect over lunch tomorrow after the community gathering."

"Oh my God, are you serious? I would love to!" Sam was so excited she could barely contain herself, and it made me feel amazing having contributed something of substance to her life.

"Great, and please bring your friend. It seems like he's played a very integral part in you being here. I would love to meet the person who is responsible for your presence." I smiled.

"I can't believe this is happening! Of course, I will definitely bring him. His name is Brian, by the way."

"Great, well, bring Brian, and I look forward to sharing a meal with the both of you."

"Thank you so much! This has made my day. Do you mind taking a selfie with me?"

"Sure, if you tag me in the pic." I winked.

"I sure will!"

Sam and I took a few selfies together and hugged again. Having that encounter with her really put me in such a magical space. I spoke with all of the guests, smiled, and took pictures, but Sam really touched my heart with her story. Her energy made me feel at peace, and it reminded me, even though I'd lost the most precious person to me, I am constantly blessed to meet many amazing souls who reminded me I was on a beautiful and unique journey.

I didn't take it lightly either because with the way I felt after Mama died, I couldn't fathom getting out of bed at times. Now, I was soaring. I felt like I was coming in contact with so many great people and being presented with these opportunities because I was allowing myself to heal and to grow. I'd had some really tough times since Mama died and still had moments from time to time, but it was so nice to know I wasn't alone. I seriously thought she placed these people in my life, because every time I felt this sense of peace around someone, it was because they said something that reminded me of her, or they didn't mind hearing stories about her. It was crazy, but I liked it. As soon as she died, I felt like she left me with nothing. More and more, however, I was seeing all the people she surrounded me with. It was amazing how much I was seeing that now. I wished she was physically here with me. I missed the hell out of my mom.

Everyone had disappeared to take their breaks and get ready for their next activity, and I felt the warmth of the tears streaming down my face. I was by myself, but I wasn't alone. Mama was with me, and I felt the strength of her embrace. *Mama, thank you for being here with me right now and for sending so many people and opportunities my way,* I thought. *You knew exactly what I needed. Thank you, Mama.*

CHAPTER

7

"Babe, can you believe it's already our last night in Bali? Damn, I feel like we're really just getting started," Imani said while getting dressed to go to dinner.

"Ha! Maybe you're just getting started, but I'm beat." I yawned.

"Aw, baby. You *have* been working your ass off on this trip. I have really enjoyed seeing you in your element. Obviously, I've seen you at work, but it's been so different seeing you in a leadership role. I loved watching you on stage as one of the panelists for the health and wellness breakout session. You wore those ripped jeans I got for you. You looked so hot!" Imani slapped my ass.

I laughed. "Yeah, I think some other people noticed my hot ass in those jeans as well."

"Oh, trust me, I peeped that. It was both men and women, but I didn't give a damn because I knew you and I were going back to the room together." She grabbed my hips and pulled me close to her.

"I love that about you. I like that you don't get jealous about that stuff because it's so unnecessary." I kissed Imani.

"Like how this shirt and bra you're wearing right now is so unnecessary?" Imani was clearly feeling freaky.

"You know how we can get. I can definitely cancel our dinner plans with the team tonight. Don't play with me," I said while sucking on Imani's bottom lip.

"You know I am never one to turn you down. But seriously, I know you're still technically on the clock, and I don't want you to miss out because you're fucking around with me."

"Fucking around is always a good thing. Maybe just a quickie?"

"As tempting as that sounds, let's just go to dinner with your team. Maybe we can leave early so we can really take our time tonight?"

"Okay, you sold me on taking our time because I want to get all up in that and don't want any interruptions, you hear me?"

"I love when you're demanding about sex," Imani said seductively.

"And you like it because you know even though I'm demanding, I always make sure to please you in every way."

Imani and I began kissing again. We almost lost track of time until Imani's phone rang.

"Oh." Her eyes widened. "It's Alex."

Even though our relationship was very open, there was something about Alex calling during the middle of us being intimate that seemed odd. I still felt like I was doing something wrong because I knew how deep my connection with Imani was.

"Hey, babe. How are you?" Imani answered. "Serenity is here. Wanna say hi right quick?" Imani put us on speakerphone.

"Hey, Serenity. How's everything going? Are you taking care of business out there?" Alex asked.

"I sure am. Things have been great! You've got to come out here sometime. As a matter of fact, we all just need to hang out here." I didn't want Alex to feel excluded from anything.

"Bet. That sounds good, as soon as I can break away from work. I've had a shitload on my plate lately, so a real vacation would do me some good. I'm glad Imani had a chance to unwind. She really deserves it. Thanks, Serenity, for doing that for her."

"Oh my God, anytime. We've had a blast."

"I kind of figured you would. I need you all to come back, though, for real." Alex laughed a bit, and we could tell what he was insinuating.

"Okay, baby, we're going to head out to dinner. I'm looking forward to seeing you when we get back." Imani took Alex off speakerphone as she continued to wrap up her conversation.

"Okay, I love you too." Imani's mood seemed to change all of a sudden after she hung up the phone.

"Babe, is everything okay?" I asked while touching the small of Imani's back.

"I'm not sure how to answer that yet. Something just feels different." Imani appeared disturbed.

"What's going on? You're starting to worry me."

"Well, it's nothing life threatening or anything. I could just tell Alex didn't really want to discuss this openly with you right now, but I'm going to go ahead and say it anyway. He's asking that we possibly take a break from our relationship with you for a while. He said something about wanting to have more alone time with me." Imani sounded sad.

"Imani, that's not exactly the weirdest thing he could've said. I mean, I care about both of you, but you all did have a marriage before meeting me. It's really not that odd he may feel like he just needs a few days of uninterrupted time with you. We have been together a whole week. He probably just misses you," I said.

"I don't know, Serenity. It just seemed like he wants to take a break indefinitely. It was the way he sounded on the phone."

"Babe, honestly, don't worry so much. You know I ain't going anywhere. This relationship has gifted me with way more than I could've asked for. I honestly thought at the beginning you all just wanted to add me in to spice up your marriage or something, even though you all seemed pretty spicy to me from the beginning. But the both of you have treated me very well, and I definitely can't complain."

"Babe, are you forgetting the conversation we had earlier about how you and I feel about each other, though? Our connection? And now he wants me to take a break from that. Oh my God, fuck no!" Imani became upset.

"Babe, I really think you're stressing yourself out for no reason. He's probably just talking about a few days. That won't be so bad. Look, Alex is really a good guy. He's in love with you. I can't lie, I've enjoyed having you all to myself this week, so I get it from his standpoint. It'll be okay. Come here." I grabbed Imani close to me and kissed her slowly.

Clearly, she was really into me, and I loved that. I loved being desired by her, but I also liked our arrangement. I thought, to some degree, I was starting to become her escape from being a wife and even a mom. I didn't take offense to it, but I didn't want her to stress out either. I wasn't planning on going anywhere, and maybe she was concerned about that. I knew her, and Alex seemed to be a little at odds before she left for Bali, so that could've still been on her mind.

"Serenity, you are so fucking sexy, and you know exactly what to say." Imani began kissing my neck, which she knew turned me on.

"There you go again, trying to make me skip this dinner." I felt myself succumbing to Imani's advances.

"See, I need this. I don't want a break from you." Imani kept kissing me.

"Okay, let's get it in quick before we head to dinner."

I unhooked Imani's bra and got started.

*****

I really enjoyed my time in Bali. Imani slept on my arm during the flight back home. I kissed her forehead as she rested on me. I really loved this woman. Spending the whole week with her was one of the most beautiful experiences I'd had in a long time. I loved everything about her—watching her sleep, hearing her sing in the shower, admiring how she smiled and laughed with Yaya on FaceTime. She also listened when I talked about my mom, and I even loved the way she interacted with Alex. I loved watching her get up in the morning and sit on the balcony, drinking her coffee while admiring nature. Imani was beautiful.

I looked forward to the day when she would feel she was ready to really break out into the music scene. Imani's voice was so smooth and sultry. I could tell she was in a whole other dimension when she sang. It seemed like nothing could touch her. I loved seeing that side of her. She was so free with music, just like when she made love.

"Babe, what are you thinking about?" Imani had awakened briefly and was whispering to me in a deep register after getting up from her nap. The pilot mentioned we might be moving into a little turbulence soon and advised all of the passengers to fasten our seatbelts.

"You and how amazing you are." I kissed Imani's forehead again.

"Aw, thank you. I wish we could stay another week. I'm not quite ready to get back to my normal routine," Imani said.

"I know you're not, but it's all good. We'll do it again sometime," I said, hopeful.

"Yeah, but I doubt Alex will be okay with just the two of us going by ourselves again, especially after we talk to him about us."

"So, about that…I'm wondering if we should hold off on talking about our deep connection and such."

"Hold on. What are you talking about?" Imani jumped up as if she was ready to have a very full argument about it.

"See, there you go. Just calm down. I'm thinking about what you said he told you on the phone last night, about missing you and wanting it to just be the two of you for a while. If you come walking in the house, talking about how you and I have a deeper connection, it's going to make matters worse," I explained.

"So, you expect me to just let him dictate the parameters of this relationship? Oh, hell no." Imani pursed her lips. The turbulence began to kick in and so did Imani's attitude.

"Girl, if you don't put your lip back in your mouth…" I said playfully. "You're getting all Bankhead on me, and I'm just trying to help you see things from a different perspective. Trust me, I definitely don't want any of this to end, either, but if you start making rash decisions, this could all backfire. Just take it easy. That's all I'm saying." I tried to slip my hand under Imani's skirt.

"Not right now." Imani moved my hand away.

I was surprised. "You must be really upset. You've never turned that down."

"But we're on the plane." Imani tried to find an excuse not to let me pleasure her a bit.

"That's why we have the blanket. Nobody will know." I started kissing Imani.

"For real, Serenity, not right now." Imani turned away from me and stared out the window.

She was really upset. I'd never seen Imani become bothered this way. Maybe she had more insight into this Alex situation than I did, because I couldn't understand why this was getting to her. I felt like there was more going on with Imani than she was saying.

"I'm sorry, Serenity, I just have a lot on my mind. I didn't mean to turn you away like that," Imani apologized. As her demeanor softened, so did the bumpiness of the plane. The pilot turned the seatbelt light off again.

"I hear you. I just want to understand what's going on with you. It seems like there's much more to this than you're telling me. I get it if you don't want to talk about it right now, but I hope we can discuss it sooner rather than later." I was attempting to be understanding but also direct with Imani. I didn't want us to put this conversation off too long.

"I promise we'll talk about it later. Again, I'm sorry. I guess I'm overwhelmed with the fact that I kind of have to resume my normal lifestyle when I get home. I was really enjoying myself in Bali, not having a care in the world."

"You got me, babe, I'm here for you. I know you've been overwhelmed with Yaya and taking care of your home. I thought I was helping you out a bit with coming over and giving you a much-needed break."

"Seriously, you have, but it's more than that. I loved watching you at your yoga retreat. It made me think a lot about singing and how I really want to pursue that, but time hasn't exactly been available to me these days. Now Alex wants me to take a break from you. That's such a huge slap in the face. At this point, he can just take everything I have." Imani's voice was elevated, and her eyes swelled with tears.

"Okay, calm down. I told you I wasn't going anywhere." I held Imani close. I could tell she really needed comfort. I always thought she and Alex had this family thing down, but maybe Imani was suffering in silence a little bit. "Do you feel like you've been losing yourself?" I asked.

"Yeah, I have been feeling that way. It's crazy; how is it that us women always fall into this trap of giving men everything they want, and we don't get what we want? I know we have a nice life, and I wouldn't trade Yaya for the world, but I've lost myself a lot. Being with you makes me feel so alive. I'm envious of you and how you choose to live your life at times. I wish I could just come and go as I please."

"I've had a lot of lonely days and nights prior to meeting you and Alex. It hasn't always been easy."

"I know. I guess I'm just venting."

I patted her leg. "And you can vent all you want. I'm here to listen."

"I know you are. I'm not sure why I've been feeling like this all of a sudden. Maybe I'm being ungrateful."

"Imani, look at me," I said sternly. "You're not being ungrateful; you're just human. I've seen you and Alex together, as an outsider as well as someone on the inside, and you in no way, shape, or form exhibit any kind of ungratefulness. I think you've enjoyed this vacation and reality is just hitting. Seriously, just because you're not working outside your home doesn't mean you aren't still working. You take care of your family and you've put your dreams on hold for a bit to be available to Alex and Yaya. It's going to take its toll on you from time to time. That's perfectly normal.

"I think Alex is comfortable with the position you're in. He knows that home and Yaya are well taken care of but he's not quite privy to your deepest desires. And you have to be the one to tell him that. Believe it or not, men aren't really the ones that get bored in long-term relationships— it's women. Sometimes men can become so complacent with their partners which causes a woman to need more. Honestly, I wouldn't even be here if it wasn't for you giving this relationship the green light. You wanted this, and there's a reason why."

"See, it's things like that: the way you talk to me and understand me. I know Alex loves me, for sure, but I'm missing that level of understanding from him."

"I hate to break it to you, but it's very rare a man will truly understand how a woman thinks and feels because he's a man. Of course, to some degree, I'm going to understand you better because I'm a woman."

"I guess. It just sucks because Alex pulled this stunt last time before we officially started dating."

"What are you talking about?"

She shook her head, looking away from me. "It's nothing," Imani responded, as if she didn't mean to blurt out what she just said.

"No, you were saying something. I would like for you to finish."

She hesitated before answering, "So, before Alex and I officially became a couple, I was seeing someone, a woman. That was the only other woman I had ever been with. I was a bit confused by it too because I had never identified as gay, but I must admit, I was just really attracted to her and was dating her while I dated Alex. He didn't take the relationship seriously because he thought I was just curious about being with a woman."

"Was it serious?" I was anticipating her answer.

"I mean, pretty serious to me." Her voice became distant. "I fell in love with her."

"Okay, so what happened?"

"Well, Alex and I grew more serious too, and he pressured me to choose, and honestly, I wasn't ready to choose because I loved them both."

"So, I'm assuming you dumped this woman and married Alex."

"Pretty much."

"Do you resent Alex for that?"

"I mean, hell yeah! And he's doing it all over again!" Imani became agitated again.

"I'm not sure how to respond to all of this. I feel like I understand why you were so upset when Alex said maybe you both needed a break from me. Babe, I really don't know what to say." I felt myself becoming distant, maybe because the issue with Imani and Alex appeared to be a pattern, and I was starting to feel like collateral damage. And who was to say she wasn't still in love with this woman?

"Are you upset, Serenity?" Imani grabbed my hand as if trying to comfort me.

"Let's just take a break from this conversation right now. I'm a little tired and want to take a nap." I didn't mean to be cold toward her, but if I was honest with myself, this put me in a very sour mood. The flight attendant stopped by our aisle to offer to pick up any garbage, but I just ignored her. I tried to think of anything to get my mind off of the conversation we just had.

*****

It had been about three days since we'd returned home from Bali. I was back to my regular scheduled program and, clearly, so were Imani and Alex. After our conversation on the plane, we didn't speak to each other much, making it a long flight. I tried to fake a few naps to get out of talking to her. I needed some time to process what she'd told me about her previous relationship. I couldn't believe Alex made her choose between her girlfriend and him. I mean, I knew going into this relationship with the both of them it could be short lived, but after Imani decided to come to Bali with me and Alex acted cool about it, I thought I did more than just fill a void in their relationship. Alex was a cool guy, but clearly, it looked like I had served my purpose in their relationship, and now it was a wrap.

Maybe I was being overdramatic. I should've known by Imani's reaction and how upset she was by Alex mentioning he wanted a "break" that something else was going on.

Since being back home, I hadn't talked to Imani except for a few text messages, or Alex at all. I told Imani to just focus on her family right now and we'd connect soon. She sent me a long dissertation about how she felt like I was giving up on us, but like I told her, that was precisely the problem: it wasn't just her and I. It was the three of us.

Maybe Alex noticed the special bond Imani and I had and was trying to shut that down. Right now, I just wanted to enjoy some peace and quiet. I missed them both, but I really didn't want to be involved if it would cause major drama in my life.

My phone was still on silent mode from work, but I saw it light up from a distance on my kitchen counter. If it was Imani, I really didn't want to talk, so I let it go to voicemail. It started ringing again, so I decided to check and see if it was her, but it wasn't. It was Cynthia. I hadn't talked to her since I'd left for my trip.

"Hey, Cynthia." I knew my voice came off as distracted, and I didn't even try to hide it.

"Poodah! What's wrong?"

"Girl, where do I begin?" I sighed.

"Oh my God! Was the trip not good?"

"No! My trip was amazing. I met some wonderful people, networked, booked some other gigs, and Bali was simply gorgeous!"

"Okay, so why do you sound like you just lost your dog or something? I'm confused."

I told Cynthia everything about my relationship with Alex and Imani, the bond Imani and I shared, and our trip to Bali. I felt relieved to get it all off my chest, but I was pretty much out of breath after that synopsis.

"So, I ain't talked to you in, like, a week and all this shit happened? What in the absolute hell?" Cynthia sounded exhausted.

"I already know what you're going to say."

"No, you don't. What do you think I'm going to say?" I imagined Cynthia with her hand on her hip while asking me that question.

"You're gonna say, 'So, here you go again, keeping things from me,' and, 'I told you to watch yourself with those two,'" I said confidently, like I had just guessed the right answer on Jeopardy.

"See, little do you know, Poodah, I wasn't gonna say that at all."

"So, what then, Cynthia?" I asked with attitude.

"Actually, I don't have anything to say. I'm just here to listen. Ha!" Cynthia laughed.

"Since when don't you have anything to say?"

"Since now. Well, actually since you had that panic attack. I have vowed to be more understanding and more of a listener. I hated that you felt you couldn't disclose to me you were having anxiety. The way I flipped out on Imani wasn't cool, so I'm trying to turn over a new leaf. It sounds like the three of you may just need some time. Everything sounds like it happened so fast. Maybe this is the point where you all need to slow down and take it easy for a while and really get to know each other."

"Um, who am I speaking to on the phone and what have you done with my Cynthia?" I was confused.

"It's still me, hun. I'm just in more of a zen-mode right now. It doesn't hurt that I've been getting good dick on the regular myself these days, but that's beside the point. Serenity, I'm really not surprised you hooked up with the two of them. You've been drooling ever since you met them. And don't get me started on you and Imani. Now, I saw that coming a mile away. I may not be down with the thruple life and wanting to be all up in vaginas all day, but I can detect a potential threesome when I see one. Did you forget I used to be a high-class call girl back in the day?" Cynthia said with a bit of sassiness and, possibly, pride for her not just being a hoe but a high-class hoe. "Poodah, it sounds like you may have your work cut out for you with this one. It doesn't seem like you were expecting things to get this complicated, especially this soon."

"It's not really that complicated," I tried to convince myself.

"Well, it kind of is, boo. And you know why? Because who you really want is Imani and you're butthurt that she may choose Alex again."

"Oh, shut up. When did you become Iyanla overnight?"

"Well, that's what good quality dick will do for you. I ain't got a stick up my ass, so I'm calmer and can see clearly what's going on. Well, maybe not exactly that kind of stick up my ass." Cynthia started laughing.

I groaned. "Now you gave me a mental picture."

"Whatever, Poodah, you're over here fucking a married couple while trying to steal away someone's wife." Cynthia was laughing too hard at this point.

"Okay, I see you're really getting a kick out of this."

"I'm just trying to get you to relax. You're usually the one floating on a cloud. You need to just chill. It'll be alright, hun. I'm pretty sure you'll all work this out in no time. So, by the way you're acting, are you in love or something?" Cynthia was really hitting the nail on the head today.

"Yeah, I won't lie. Imani and I said we loved each other while we were in Bali."

"Oh, shit."

"Oh, shit, nothing." I was pouting at that point.

"This is too funny. My Poodah done messed around and fell in love. So, does this mean you're in love with Alex too?"

"Now that's a good goddamn question. I didn't even think about that."

We both broke out into hysterical laughter because saying all of this out loud sounded ridiculous, but I had always been about following my heart and letting the wind take me where it wanted to go. This was even new for me. Part of me was happy I could feel again and experience being in love again.

"Listen, Poodah, live your life. You've been through enough and it's taken some time for you to get to a place like this again. It's okay to be hurt. I was just messing with you. I support whatever you want to do. All of this will work out the way it's supposed to. Give them a couple more days, and if you don't hear from them, maybe invite them over for dinner or something. Just don't make too big of a deal out of it. Just live your life and have some fun. You deserve that."

"Yeah, you're right. I guess that good dick you've been getting has helped you with giving good advice, huh?"

Cynthia exhaled. "Girl, it's been amazing!"

"So, who is the special guy?"

"Believe it or not, it's Dennis."

"Your *boss?*"

"Yep."

"Shut the front door."

"Girl, yes, I'm having a little cream in my coffee these days."

"I ain't tripping 'cause he's white. I'm tripping because he's your boss. You've always had a strict policy on not mixing business with pleasure. Why the change of heart?"

"Honestly, I'm trying something new these days myself. I'm tired of what I've been attracting lately, and Dennis has been trying to get with me for years. I'm tired of these broke niggas. I'm too old and too goddamn rich to be taking care of some man. I know Dennis has got money, seeing that he's my boss.

"He's been amazing, Serenity. We barely see each other at the office because we're both so busy, of course, but he always makes time for me outside of work. We're always doing some fancy shit because, hey, we're rich. He gives the best massages and loves to rub my feet after a long day at work. He's got that old-school soul in him, so he's always playing some blues music and loves singing to me with that Michael McDonald voice of his. I love that he's got grown-ass kids, so I ain't gotta deal with nobody's little monsters. And you know the head is amazing!"

"Well, not trying to sound stereotypical, but I kind of figured it would be. But, um…"

"Yeah, child, he's an anomaly. He's hung, honey."

We couldn't stop laughing. It felt so good to talk with Cynthia. I was glad she wasn't upset with me for not telling her about Alex and Imani sooner.

"Seriously, though, I miss you, Cynthia. I hate that you had to cut your visit a little short when you were here."

"I know. I was bummed about that too."

"It's all good. I'm glad things are working out with you and Dennis, though." I clapped my hands together. "Ooh, let's have some fun and Facebook stalk these people we're fawning over."

She chuckled. "Let me put you on speaker so I can pull up the app on my phone."

I found his profile easily. "Wow, Dennis is friends with Lisa," I said while scrolling curiously through his page.

"Who's Lisa?" I detected a little jealousy in Cynthia's voice.

"Oh, Lisa is just the creator of the Vitality Fest."

"Is she pretty?" Cynthia always cut straight to the point.

"If you're into the blonde, Amazon type."

"I ain't got shit to worry about then. Now, if you said Megan the Stallion, I probably would've been like, *um*, the fuck? Dennis clearly likes his women brown and round."

"Cynthia, you are a whole mess."

"Listen, I'm just telling the truth. I swear, Dennis's granddaddy had to be black because he's definitely got that soul in him."

"Girl, I will throw this phone." Cynthia was a riot. "You know what? I ain't never stalked Alex or Imani's pages."

"What the hell is taking you so long?"

"You know I only get on Facebook once every three months or so anyway."

"Yeah, you're right about that. Wow, are these pics of Imani from college? Didn't she go to Spellman?"

"Yeah, she did." As I was scrolling through the pictures, I could tell they were from the early 2000s by the looks of the camera and the clothes. Imani was definitely much slimmer, and her hair and makeup were reminiscent of the singer, Aaliyah. Imani was gorgeous even in her early twenties, and her smile was so innocent. As I continued to scroll through the pictures, I noticed a woman who Imani took many pictures with. In some of the pictures, they just looked like friends having a good time on campus, while others looked a bit questionable, like they were rather close. I tried to see if the images were tagged so I could see who she was, but I got nothing."

"Hey, Poodah, who's this chick in all the pics with Imani?"

"I peeped that too. None of them were tagged."

"Oh, trust and believe I can find out." Cynthia could easily sniff out the truth via social media, but she couldn't figure out her last boyfriend had a whole baby mama she didn't know about. "Okay, it looks like the woman's name is Iris. She looks to be about five foot three, one hundred and fifty pounds, was married, now divorced with three kids, all under the age of ten." Cynthia was acting as if she was reading the profile of a suspect in a murder case.

"Damn, Cynthia. I've never known you to have this kind of time on your hands."

"What can I say? I'm dating the boss now."

"Seriously, though, I'm getting the feeling this may be the woman that got away." I was becoming more curious by the minute.

"Oh, you're talking about the woman Imani had to let go of because of Alex?"

"Yep. I know Imani and Alex met in college, and Imani said she had only been with one woman her whole life besides me, and, well, she did go to an all-girl school. They just look really close. I can't say Imani has a type because I don't feel like I've even known her long enough to know her type, but this girl is gorgeous."

"It looks like Imani and Iris have been in contact on here rather recently."

"Cynthia, what are you looking at?"

"I'm looking on Iris's page now. She posted a pic of herself in the Bahamas wearing a barely there swimming suit. Look at the comments."

"Damn, you look so good, Iris. You haven't missed a beat since college. I've missed you so much."

My lips pulled down. By the look of that comment, Imani seemed to still be into this woman. She left a comment under the pic just two short days ago.

"What're you gonna do, Poodah?"

"Honestly, what can I do? I don't even know if this is the woman from her past. Even if it is, how am I supposed to bring up the fact that I was stalking her page? I'll just leave it alone," I said, feeling defeated.

"You're a good one, honey, because I would be like, 'Who the fuck is that?'" Cynthia always exuded attitude.

"Seriously, though, I can't control Imani, Alex, Iris, or whoever else. I can only control myself. I don't like how I'm feeling right now, but I refuse to be all up in Imani's face about this. The beauty of our relationship is the trust. I have to trust this will all work itself out."

"I'm so proud of you, Poodah. I want to know who the bitch is, but I'll follow your lead and let it go."

"Yeah, it's really not worth it at this point. I don't even know what's going on between the three of us or if there is even still an *us*. I'll just wait to hear from Imani."

"Girl, I swear you're a good one 'cause I can't with this madness. But anywho, your brother James called me the other day."

"He did? What for?" I asked curiously.

"He made it seem like he was worried about you, but it really seemed like he just wanted to see if I was dating anyone."

"His divorce ain't even been final two days and he's already reaching out to you, huh?"

"Well, actually…"

"Well, actually what?" I was becoming a little bit irritated.

"We hooked up a few times a couple of years ago."

"While he was still married?" I scowled. "When were you going to tell me about that?"

"Never, actually, but since you've kept a couple of secrets from me, I don't feel so bad about telling you now," Cynthia said nonchalantly.

"I'm not sure how to take that. I'm definitely not judging you because that's not my place, but I wish you would've felt like you could tell me."

"You were in a really bad spot when James and I were kicking it. I really didn't want to bombard you with all of that. And honestly, James and I really just hooked up for nostalgia's sake. We hadn't been together since I was in college. He was lonely, I was lonely, and it seemed to make sense at the time."

"Well, I'm glad his wife, or should I say ex-wife, didn't find out. She's batshit crazy."

"Trust me, I know. But I'm done with all that. Dennis and I are doing our thing, and I'm really happy."

"I'm glad to hear that."

"Things will work out, Poodah, don't worry." Cynthia tried to comfort me.

"I'm not worrying. I'm a little sad but okay. I just hope we can work through this because being with Alex and Imani, I've been the happiest I've been in a long time."

I heard my doorbell, so I told Cynthia I'd call her back. When I looked out of the window it was Imani. I invited her in.

"Hey, I'm surprised to see you." I said curiously.

"I really miss you, Serenity." Imani hugged me tight, and I could feel she needed some time with me. We walked into the living room, and I offered her some wine.

"Does Alex know you're here?" Imani sighed.

"You know he doesn't."

"So, what are we going to do?"

"Honestly, I don't know. Can we just enjoy this wine and talk about any and everything besides Alex?"

"If that's what you want…?"

"I feel bad because I know you need answers from me. I just don't have them right now." Imani began poking her lip out.

I lightly grabbed Imani's wine, placed it on the coffee table, and I held her in my arms. As much as I felt like we needed to deal with the elephant in the room, which was Alex, I knew I wasn't going to get answers from Imani tonight. I turned on some jazz music and began giving her a back massage.

"That feels amazing."

"I can tell you need some TLC."

"Oh, I definitely need some TLC."

I grabbed Imani's hair, positioned it to the other side of her neck, and began kissing her. I lifted up her shirt over her head from the back and unhooked her bra.

"Serenity, I promise I didn't come over here just for sex. Don't get me wrong, you know I want you. I just don't want you to think that's what this is all about."

"I know it's not. I can just tell you need some relaxation, and you look and smell so good. It's turning me on. But promise me we'll discuss this Alex situation very soon."

"You got it." I couldn't really tell if Imani was serious or if she was just aroused by me caressing her breasts. Either way, we were going to enjoy each other tonight and deal with our feelings another time.

8

It had been months since I'd seen Dr. Wilson. She was no longer working at the office, but even though her dementia had gotten a little worse, she hadn't completely forgotten who I was or what we'd talked about. Clearly, she wasn't a therapist anymore, but she would always be *my* therapist. I didn't give a damn about dementia. Dr. Wilson's daughter was spending more time at her house to ensure she was okay. Gigi was about five years older than me; about five foot six; with beautiful, flowy red hair; and she was so caring and attentive, much like her mom. I approached Dr. Wilson's door and rang the bell.

"I'm so glad you could stop by, Serenity. Mommy's been asking about you a lot lately." Gig motioned me to come in. "She told me to promise not to tell you this, but she said you were always one of her favorite clients. I guess, professionally, she's not supposed to be biased." Gigi smiled, handing me some tea.

I thought it was the cutest thing that a forty-five-year-old woman still called her mother, "Mommy."

"Well, I'm honored because I love your mom. I really appreciate you reaching out and inviting me over. I've been needing to connect with her.

So much has been going on in my life, but I also know there's plenty she's dealing with as well. I didn't want to be selfish."

"Listen to me: wanting to share what's going on in your life with Mommy is never being selfish. Trust me, she wants to hear it. As a matter of fact, her doctor said that having people around her she enjoyed conversing with could help her stay positive and not get depressed. I know it seems weird to even consider Mommy getting depressed, seeing as she was a therapist, but it can happen." Gigi sounded educated and well-versed on Dr. Wilson's prognosis.

"If you only knew how much it meant to me to know that your mom enjoyed my company that much. I've been kind of struggling a little bit with some things going on in my life, and your mom was that one person who always knows exactly what to say."

"Serenity, is that you?" Dr. Wilson walked into the living room looking a bit thinner, but overall, she still seemed like herself.

I quickly walked over to Dr. Wilson and greeted her with a big hug. I was so happy to see her. Dr. Wilson rubbed my head with one hand while she held me with the other. Her touch was soft, as if she was starting to lose muscle strength. We hugged and took a few deep breaths together, which was how we always began our sessions. I wasn't sure if she'd remember that, but she did.

"It's definitely me, Dr. Wilson. I've missed you so much!" Dr. Wilson continued to hold me, and it was exactly what I needed. Even in her sickness, she managed to know exactly what to do.

"I'm going to run a few errands and give you all time to catch up. Serenity, here's my number if you need me. It was great to see you." Gigi wrapped me in a hug before giving Dr. Wilson and I some much-needed quality time.

"It's so good to see you, Serenity. Remember what I said: I'm not dead yet. I just have a little memory loss, but I will always make time for my favorite client." She smiled at me.

"Dr. Wilson, I don't think you were supposed to tell me that," I whispered as if someone was listening.

"Girl, nobody's here, and I'm no longer a therapist, remember?" We both laughed

She and I sat down on the couch together, and she held my hand tight.

"I've missed you so much," I said. "So much has been going on." I dropped my shoulders.

"Feel free to talk to me about it. I seriously have nothing but time these days," she said eagerly.

"Are you sure it's not too much?

"What did I say?" Dr. Wilson said in a stern voice.

I chuckled. "I know, you're not dead yet."

"I actually want to know what's been going on in your life. How are your friends doing? That young married couple?"

"Oh, I'll get to that in a minute because that's a long story. The good news is I went to the Vitality Fest in Bali a couple of months ago. They loved my work, and I was able to make some great connections."

"That's great, dear! Can you refresh my memory regarding what that was about?"

I filled Dr. Wilson in on the details.

"Oh, the drama." She laughed.

I playfully swatted a hand at her. "Don't make fun of me."

"I'm not, sweetie. I'm just glad to see you and hear about what's been going on."

"Well, I'm glad you're happy because I've been on a whirlwind the past few months. So much has been going on with me. Alex and Imani…" I proceeded to tell Dr. Wilson about my poly-relationship and what transpired to this point.

"So, since you've been back from Bali, have you spent any time with them?"

"Only Imani and that was short-lived. Like I said, Alex wanted to take a break, and Imani was frustrated. Imani and I have basically been sneaking around which is so not my thing. I like openness."

"So why are you allowing it?" Dr. Wilson put me on the spot.

"You and I both know I can't control them."

"I'm not talking about them. I'm talking about you. You just said this isn't what you want, so why are you allowing this for yourself?"

"You know, for someone who's losing their memory, you sure are pretty sharp," I said.

"I know! Don't you love it!" Dr. Wilson was so geeked. It was actually really cute.

"But seriously, I'm really feeling Imani, and I want to be with her. I mean, I like Alex too, but quite honestly, I'm not losing any sleep if he doesn't want a relationship at this point. It's Imani who I want to be with."

"Well, it sounds to me like they're a package deal. If you two are having to sneak, it takes away from the arrangement you once shared. Now, boundaries can change, of course, but a conversation should be had so you can really experience the true honesty and intimacy you desire. I don't want you to shortchange yourself." Dr. Wilson had always been blunt. I really appreciated that about her, and I was glad she was still able to give it to me straight.

"I'm just disappointed because, for a minute, things seemed to be going so well."

"Of course, they did because you were experiencing the newness of the relationship. You know how this goes, Serenity," Dr. Wilson said as if I should know better.

"Man, you're coming at me kind of hard today, aren't you?"

"No, I'm not. It's just tough for you to hear because you're fully invested in this relationship, that's all."

"You make it sound so easy, like I'll get over it soon."

"Serenity, that's not what I'm saying at all. I know sometimes it's hard for us to truly face certain things head-on because we're emotionally invested and worried about the outcome. I want you to be honest with where you're at right now. Don't lie to yourself. Yes, you value honesty and openness, but right now, you're willing to forfeit some of that honesty to still engage with Imani."

"I wish I knew what to do." I placed my head in my hands.

"Everything you need to know is within you. You have to make the decision regarding which route you want to take and be willing to face whatever those consequences are. There's never a cut and dry answer when it comes to matters of the heart. I mean, do you even want the both of them, or just Imani?"

"Well, I really like Alex. To say he's alluring is an understatement. He's intelligent and driven but also pretty laidback, which I like. I can definitely talk to him, and of course, the sex is amazing with or without Imani. The only thing is…I don't feel that connection with him. I could tell from the beginning how much he adored Imani by the way he looked at her. It doesn't bother me that he doesn't look at me that way. I do feel like Alex enjoys me for a little extra fun or maybe to watch Yaya if he wants to take Imani out on a date, but that's about it. Now, he's pretty much swooped Imani away from me because he's been wanting her all to himself, and I'm, like, damn, I thought it was the three of us."

"But didn't you say you and Imani were getting closer and the two of you were wondering how you would tell Alex? Are you upset he beat you to the punch?"

"I guess. I never really looked at it that way. I mean, seriously, Dr. Wilson, I know Imani is committed to Alex. She's not looking to leave him. I have absolutely no problem with sharing, which is why I'm so frustrated because I thought Alex didn't have a problem with it either." I was trying to figure out how to solve this issue.

"I'll be the first to say I'm not well versed in the poly lifestyle, but maybe you were more ready for this kind of relationship than they were. Think about how quickly you all formed this relationship with no real conversation regarding how it would work or its boundaries. You all seemed to just dive in head-first, which is fine, but this is all still so new to each of you.

"It seems like Alex is calling all the shots here, and I know this doesn't pair well with your free-spirited nature."

She had a point. I hadn't even challenged Alex or Imani about the trajectory of our relationship because I didn't want to upset or lose Imani. It had been almost two months since we'd returned from Bali. I'd barely seen Imani and I hadn't seen Alex at all. The few times I snuck in and had sex with Imani just made me yearn for her more. How did I grow complacent with this arrangement? Like Dr. Wilson said, I was making excuses for this situation because of what I wanted so badly.

"Doc, are you sure you have dementia? You seem on point to me."

"Well, Gigi has really done her research on how to delay the progression of its symptoms, so to speak. Leaving work played a huge role in that because it simplified my life tremendously. Meeting with so many clients regularly and trying to keep up with their diagnoses and what we've talked about in our sessions could've sent me into a tailspin. Also, I've been making physical activity more of a priority these days. The doctors also stated they haven't detected any signs of stroke, bleeding, or tumors in my brain scans, and even though my neuropsychological tests indicate some minor issues with cognitive functioning, my memory is still pretty good. I'm blessed. I just try not to worry about the future. Since I've left work, Gigi and I have been on a vacation together ourselves. That's one thing I never made a priority because I loved my work so much. I rarely took days off. I'm actually enjoying this time. I'm seeing the beauty in other parts of my life right now."

"I love your perspective on all of this."

"There are so many ways to deal with adversities and challenges, Serenity. I'd rather be at peace about it all. There's been a lot of good that's come from this prognosis, and then there's a lot I'm personally struggling with as well. The unknown is scary, but I have so much life left in me. I live for moments like the one we're having right now. You and a few of my other clients that have come to see me have really brought me joy."

"So why walk away from your career now if you're still able to manage?"

"Actually, my body is deteriorating. Everyone's body is deteriorating. It's a part of life. I can honestly say finding out I had dementia revealed to me I don't want to work until the very end. As much as I enjoy it, I really want to not be tied to my work. I'm still whole even without being a practicing therapist. Even in my older age, I'm still whole. Sometimes stripping away all of the things that define us and just *being* is the most beautiful thing we could ever experience."

My eyes welled with awe. "Man, I have missed you *so* much "

"Aww, I've missed you too, sweetie. I can tell Imani is a very special person to you because something about her connects you to your mother, and anything that gives you that feeling of her presence is hard to ignore. You said it yourself, when you first met Alex and Imani, Imani was the one who wanted to know more about your mom. She would listen to you talk about her no matter how long, and she genuinely seemed engaged when you shared memories and stories of her. At that time, that's what you needed. It's okay to be totally enamored by her because of that, which is all the more reason to have a real conversation with the two of them to see where you all stand. You owe that to yourself, but don't focus on the outcome and what they choose to do because you can only control yourself. Don't give in because it feels like the easiest thing to do."

"I do feel at times what I'm allowing right now makes me feel a bit of anxiety." I could feel the tears coming again.

"And this is because you're not living your truth. You are the kind of person who craves authenticity, but you're silencing yourself in fear of experiencing anxiety. In turn, you're actually feeling anxious because you are not expressing yourself."

"I know, Dr. Wilson, but I've been scared. I felt really lonely after Mama died and then Dave and I divorced. It's like I wanted company but didn't want to be bothered, and I fear that if I let Imani go, I'll be back at square one—feeling isolated."

"This is your truth coming out right now. This is what you haven't admitted to yourself. This is the inner work that comes with loss. Hell, this is the inner work we all need to do on a daily basis to stay sane and in the moment. The connection you shared with your mom was like nothing you've ever experienced in life. You're afraid it's not out there, so you're willing to put up with what's going on with you, Imani, and Alex out of fear. If anything, what you experienced with Alex and Imani early on lets you know what could be. You have to be willing to try."

"I did try, when I opened my heart up to them." I felt myself getting upset and crying more.

"Of course you did, but you can't stop opening your heart. You're still going to be faced with challenges from time to time, even in a relationship you thought was ideal. If you really want to see where this can go and experience true authenticity and connection, you have to share how you're really feeling with them."

"Dr. Wilson, I wish I could just take you everywhere I go. I've been needing this advice."

"For someone who's losing her memory, I feel like I'm the one constantly reminding you of what we talked about." She chuckled.

"I know. Everything I need is inside of me," I repeated.

"Exactly. You don't necessarily need me, but I'm a reminder for you. I'm not sure what the future holds for you, Serenity, but for some reason, I think it's going to be great. I can't promise this road is going to be easy. You're still going through the grieving process, but since the first time I met you, I've witnessed so much growth in you. You're no longer in despair; you've been able to move on from your divorce, have core friends you can rely on, thrive at work and enjoy it, and even though you're having some issues with Alex and Imani, don't forget there have been some absolutely amazing times shared with them. Forgive me for being crass, but some good sex has been had as well." Dr. Wilson broke out into an infectious laugh that cheered me up.

I was so worried after Dr. Wilson told me of her diagnosis of dementia. I never would've imagined we would have an opportunity to sit down and talk like that again. Dr. Wilson hadn't only been my therapist, but she was a mother figure and friend too. I could tell her anything. I was glad she explained to me more about dementia because I honestly didn't know much, and I thought it was a death sentence. I couldn't bear the thought of losing Dr. Wilson anytime soon. It seemed like she had an idea of how to delay some of the symptoms such a memory loss, and Gigi was a champ. I was so glad she had her daughter to look after her.

"Crass is good." I grinned. "And let me tell you, the sex has been through the roof!"

"Now, cheers to that!"

Dr. Wilson and I tapped our mugs together filled with warm chamomile tea. We laughed even more.

"Of course, there are so many other great qualities about our relationship, but I must admit, there has never been an issue when it comes to sex with the both of them, or even with just one of them. We complement each other very well sexually," I said proudly.

"Well, physical expression can definitely play a huge role, for sure. I'm glad you're experiencing that, though. You're still young, healthy, and, of course, gorgeous. This is the time to be having some great sex. You're in your prime.

"You know, I was never married, but I had a few great committed relationships and a lot of good sex myself. I would encourage all people to have good sex in their lives—protected, of course."

"Most definitely protected."

We enjoyed a good laugh again, along with some good tea. Dr. Wilson and I talked for a few more hours about any and everything. I felt so relaxed and at ease with my situation. Talking with her definitely gave me the confidence to work things out with Alex and Imani.

*****

"Baby sis, where the hell you been? I ain't heard from you in over a month!"

My brother James was probably the only person who would FaceTime with me no warning. James never gave a damn about anything. I was just getting home from doing some much-needed grocery shopping. I hadn't really been cooking lately; mostly just going out to eat because living alone, sometimes cooking full meals just felt like a waste of time.

James and I grew up really close, as he was barely two years older than me. Ellis was seven years older, so he was out of the house by the time I got my first training bra. James and I were more like twins. We did everything together, and Mama even dressed us alike, in striped t- shirts and flooding corduroy pants most of the time. If it wasn't for my ponytails, I was pretty sure I would've been mistaken for a boy. James and I wrestled, fought, climbed trees, and slept in the same bed together for years before Mama decided I needed my own space because I was becoming a woman. James hated when his friends would try to talk to me. He fought every single boy who even looked my way.

James was tough, and I looked up to him so much. Growing up in Baltimore, he protected me from a lot of stuff. He said I was too clumsy to be out in the streets. He would say, "I know you're a tomboy and all, but you're still pretty and kind of naïve, so I gotta protect you at all costs." James and I looked out for one another. He used to pay me money not to tell Mama he was sneaking girls into the house when she was at work, and he would pay me extra for not mixing up their names in front of them.

Ellis, my other brother, went into the Navy at seventeen and traveled the world. I barely saw Ellis until he returned home at the old age of twenty-five. He was clean shaven like a Muslim, physically fit, and already had a wife and two kids when he moved back to Baltimore. Everyone on Daddy's side of the family said Ellis was a sellout because he married a white woman, but they always forgot Mama was half white and black herself, so in a sense, they were dismissing us as well.

James, on the other hand, was a street dude. He started selling drugs at twelve, had his first child at sixteen, and dropped out of high school shortly after that. James wanted no part of school. He finally got out of the drug game when he turned twenty-two after being shot and almost losing his life. James took his drug money and started investing in real estate and became very wealthy. He finally settled down with Blanca, who was a fast-talking, voluptuous, and highly intelligent Cuban he met at a New Year's

Eve party in New York when he came to visit me. They were off and on for years before they started having kids. Blanca was feisty and could run circles around anyone from an executive on Wall Street to a politician. She loved James's street edge and couldn't get enough of him, but she was crazy. She slashed his tires once when she thought he was cheating, she followed him on a business trip, and hid out in a room on the same floor as his suite. She admitted to hiring a private investigator to see if James was still sleeping with his first child's mother. The chick was certified nuts, but James said she had that "superhead" gift which was too much information for me, but again, we were always so close.

"Um, minding my damn business. Where've you been?" I asked with attitude.

"Since you wanna talk shit, I've been minding my damn business too. I'm just trying to make sure you've been alright." James gave me that same attitude back.

"Damn, big bro, I missed you. Thanks for checking in on me."

"You know I'm always gon' look out for baby girl. Yo, so what's been good?" James's Baltimore dialect was still so strong. Mine had pretty much dissipated over the years. These days, I probably sounded like any other chick in Scottsdale.

"I've just been working, doin' my thang." Whenever I would talk to family or friends back home, the slang would pop out every once in a while.

"Yeah, I heard about your trip to Bali. You could've called a nigga or something. I could've come through."

"First of all, why you talkin' like Bali is up the street? Secondly, I'm pretty sure you found out from Cynthia."

"There you go. Okay, so what? Me and Cynthia kicked it a bit. It ain't no thang. We been had that friends-with-benefits thang going for a while. Cynthia's my girl—always will be. She might be all corporate and what not, but she's cool as hell. She got her a white man, but I done already told her if he can't lay that pipe, she knows who to call." James laughed mischievously.

"Ugh, I ain't trying to talk about this with you."

"C'mon, sis, and quit acting like we don't talk about everything. We always have."

"Well, technically we don't because you didn't fill me in on the fact that you were still hooking up with Cynthia."

"Get off that. You want me to call you every time I'm fucking somebody? C'mon. Anyway, Cynthia been keeping me in the loop because you ain't been calling me to let me know how you doing. I've been wanting to come out there and visit you like old times and shit."

"James, you could've picked up the phone and called me."

"Nigga, that's why I'm calling you now!" I could tell when James started getting worked up for no reason, so I thought I'd change the pace of this conversation.

"So, how's business going?"

"Man, it's been beautiful. Another reason I wanted to hook up with you is because I wanna scope out some properties out your way. There's some new developments I wanna check out, so I figured I'd come see you too."

"Aww, how sweet!"

"Serenity, don't start all that sappy shit." I could tell James was serious when he called me by my real name just like Cynthia.

"Okay, I'll quit messing with you. Anyway, let's get together because I miss my niece and nephew. I know they're getting so big."

"Yeah, Taj and Terrell are eight and ten. But Deja is twenty-six now."

"Damn, Deja is a full-grown woman. It feels like yesterday when you told me Vanessa was pregnant with her."

"I know, right? I was scared as fuck. Being only sixteen and hustlin' was no way to bring a seed into this world, but Vanessa was not tryna get no abortion, no matter how much I pressured her. Looking back on it now, though, I'm so glad she didn't listen to me."

"Yeah, me too. Look at Deja now; she's so smart, graduated from college, getting her master's in business administration, and even running her own business in wardrobe styling. I'm so proud of her."

"Hell, me too! The way my life was set up, Deja didn't look like she had a fighting chance. Thankfully, Vanessa kept Deja away from the streets and made sure she was focused on school."

"Please try to see if Deja can come out as well when you visit. I really need to see her."

"I will. So, what's good with you, for real? Cynthia told me you was having some anxiety or some shit. What's up with that? Why you didn't tell me?"

"I really didn't want you or Ellis to worry."

"Oh shit, you didn't even tell Ellis? You know he gon' trip. You know he's always been like your daddy since the motherfucker that was supposed to be our father was just a true fuck-up and abuser."

"I really don't want to talk about him. For the longest, I couldn't even sit on Mama's couch without thinking about how he beat the fuck outta her."

"Is that what you've been having anxiety about?"

"No, it just took me a long time to really come to terms with Mama's death."

"Now, that's what I don't wanna talk about. Mama was my everything. Shit's still hard. Some of my favorite memories was when me, the kids, and Mama would visit you in Arizona and just kick it like old times, and she never had to worry about anything because we took care of it all."

"Yeah. God, I miss her."

"Fuck yeah. You remember when we convinced Mama to sit out on your balcony and just roll a blunt with us? She never wanted us to know she smoked weed when we were kids, but then when we were at your house that time smoking, and she said pass that, we both fell out laughing. She was a pro at it too, and that was the first time we all smoked together."

"Oh my God, I remember that like it was yesterday." It grew silent on the phone. A tear fell from my eye, and I knew James was having a moment too, but he hated when I called him out on being emotional. I acted as if I didn't hear a slight sniffle on the other end of the line. I wiped my eyes and proceeded to change the subject.

"Oh, I meant to ask you something."

"Yeah, what's up?"

"By any chance, do you know a woman named Iris Senegal? I thought I saw you two were friends on Facebook."

"Yeah, I know Iris. She dated a partner of mine a while back, but she was married for a minute."

"Was?" I asked curiously.

"Yeah, they got a divorce not too long ago. My partner is still cool with her. That's how I know her. What's up with the questions? You got beef with her or something?" James always had that street mentality and figured someone wanted to fight me.

"No, it ain't no big deal. I just happened to be scrolling through Facebook and saw that you knew her."

"Cut the bullshit, what's up? You don't just be asking about shit like that. Plus, you ain't never even on Facebook."

"Okay, so it's a pretty long story…" I proceeded to give James the run down.

"Man, you know y'all females are always on some detective type of shit. We gon' get to the part where you fucking women now? How my man's Alex got the sweetest set-up with two women, but he's asking you to leave? Anyway, when I talked to my partner who used to mess around with Iris, he did say she was into women and they had threesomes all the time. Word on the curb is that she divorced her husband to be with a woman."

I was sick to my stomach. Was Imani still interested in Iris, and was there maybe something going on with them now? I hated feeling jealous. I could be blowing all of it out of proportion, but for some reason, I was getting the sense there was more going on with this Iris. I wondered how I would bring it up to Imani.

"Actually, all this stalking shit is not my usual style. I just really haven't been myself lately, and I was trying to figure out what was going on."

"Damn, did you ask her?"

"I haven't talked to her in a while. We've met up a few times without her husband knowing."

"I'm still trying to figure out why the nigga don't want two women, though. Did he ask for this threesome?"

"Actually, they both wanted it."

"Shit. If my lady tells me she wanna add a chick in our shit, I ain't gonna block that. Goddamn!"

"Well, it doesn't matter anyway because it's not gon' work."

"Look, I don't know anything about these people, and you're all the way in Arizona, so I can't see what's going on. If you're feeling Imani like that, which it seems like you are, you gotta go get yours. Let Alex fuck up. Imma be out there beating his ass!"

"James, it's not even like that. He's a good guy. He probably just feels his wife slipping away."

"Well, then he needs to give her what she wants. Shit, you can't let your wife be wanting some pussy over some dick. If that's happening, then as a man, you ain't doing your job. I swear I can't get with these new age niggas."

James's reasoning was still a little prehistoric and chauvinistic, in my opinion. I didn't like the idea that men have to be doing this and that to keep their women happy and vice versa. I felt that people needed to be in tune with themselves, which in turn would naturally make each other happy. The three of us really had something going for a minute, but it felt like Alex wasn't deeply invested in me, which I got because I was the third person in the situation. It seemed like Alex didn't want to get that deep, but he probably just enjoyed the sex.

"I'm all good, big bro. I'll figure it out. I promise, I'm good. I love you for always looking out for me."

"You know that's always gon' happen. Hit a nigga up so I can come through. I'm trying to make a few deals out there, the sooner the better."

"Most definitely. And kiss my niece and nephew for me. I miss them so much. I'm going to call Deja too."

"Yeah, she would like that."

"Okay, I sure will. And big bro?"

"What's up?"

"I love you and miss you so much."

"I love you too, man. You've always been my world. Now let me get outta here so I can take care of some business. If a nigga ain't grindin', a nigga ain't eating, and I don't play that shit."

James had worked since he was twelve, even if it was selling drugs. He refused to let a woman take care of him, even if it was Mama. He never even accepted money from me. He didn't believe in that. For the life of me, I never understood how my brothers became self- sufficient because Daddy could barely keep a job. But then again, maybe that was why; we wanted to be nothing like him.

"I know how you are. Okay, babes, I'll hit you up soon. I love you."

"I love you too, baby sis."

After hanging up with James, so many memories began flooding back from my childhood. I could hear music from Soul Train playing in my head. I could see us cleaning up the house on a Saturday morning and smelling the bacon Mama was frying in the kitchen. Most of the time, Daddy wasn't there because he would be out running the streets the night before. He wouldn't stumble into the house until the early afternoon sometimes.

Ellis made a comment once when he was having an argument with Mama about Daddy beating her. He screamed, "How you gon' let that nigga have a baby on you, Mama?" I never questioned either of them because I didn't want to be caught eavesdropping and Mama didn't play that. She never talked about it, so I never knew for sure if we had another sibling somewhere out there. I never really cared what he did. As far as I was concerned, it was just me, Mama, James, and Ellis.

Me and Mama were so in tune with each other. It was crazy how I could feel Mama's energy all the time, even as a little girl. I could be at school and all of a sudden, I would get a headache, or my stomach would hurt, and when I would come home, I would find out Daddy hurt Mama, or Mama had a rough day at work. We were so connected, and she loved that about me. She said even though I could play rough with James, I was also such a sweet spirit. She said I never questioned her about stuff and was always a good kid. I never gave her any problems, not even in the womb.

I oftentimes wondered why Mama would let Daddy beat her like that, but later on, I found out her mom was in an abusive relationship too. We never knew her because she died before me and my brothers were even born. That cycle didn't continue with me. I was never even attracted to men who were controlling and abusive, so I didn't surround myself with that. I guessed my name being Serenity played a role in that.

There were days when I just couldn't believe Mama was still gone. Whenever I had to teach evening classes, I reflected a lot during the day. I also had developed this unspoken ritual of getting up in the morning, making some tea, and sitting on my Mama's old couch. I used to cry every single time and didn't understand why I was putting myself through that, but it was the one thing that made me feel the closest to her. I can still envision her red, curly hair, hazel eyes, and gorgeous smile. Even with a scar above her right eyebrow and tiny one above the left side of her lip from the abuse she endured, her beauty remained.

After meeting with Dr. Wilson, I took a big step and decided to get the couch reupholstered. I felt it was time to change the narrative in my mind, and I felt the couch, being in the condition it was in, had brought an energy around me I didn't need. Mama was gone, physically, but not from my heart. It was okay to keep the couch, but I needed a new perspective. I didn't want to grieve like I had been. Mama would've wanted that for me. Once I reupholstered the couch, I decided to do some remodeling around the house. I hired some carpenters and had my home repainted, remodeled my kitchen, got some new light fixtures, and new flooring. I swapped out some home decor and renewed my space. I still kept my plants, but I added pops of color everywhere. It was time; Mama was gone. Dave and I no longer shared the house together, and it was time.

I gathered my things for my evening class, and as I was checking my email before heading out, I noticed an old DJ friend of mine from college was going to be in Phoenix that night, doing a set at one of the clubs. I couldn't believe it. DJ Tam's skills were amazing. I had been following her recently on social media. She would post videos of herself all around the country spinning hip hop, house, funk, R&B, and even freestyle. At the spur of the moment, I decided it was time to get out, and I wasn't going to ask anyone to go with me. I was going to get my dancing shoes and shake my ass to her beats. I couldn't wait.

9

I had a really good feeling about Tam's gig for some reason. I was blasting music while eating chips and hummus and drinking some really good wine. I still hadn't gotten a chance to talk with Alex and Imani, nor did I ask Imani about Iris. I definitely wasn't interested in sneaking around anymore, so I took a step back for a couple of weeks to get my mind right. I decided I would call them tomorrow because tonight was all about me.

When I walked past my full-length mirror and took a long look at myself, I thought I looked hot. I was wearing my backless, flared mini dress with spaghetti straps. My skin looked so smooth, the curls in my hair were popping, and my body was lean. Yoga was really doing some good. I sprayed on a little perfume, touched up my lipstick, and slipped into my mama's black Donna Karan heels. I was definitely ready for a night on the town. I locked the door behind me, hopped in the drop-top because it was humid as hell, and I took off for Phoenix. I was hoping the humidity wouldn't totally knock out my curls before arriving at the club. I continued to blast music in my car like I was back in Baltimore. I could only imagine what some of my white neighbors were thinking, but I didn't care. I wanted to let loose and be free; I didn't want to worry about a thing.

When I finally pulled up to the club, there was a long line outside, but thankfully, I knew the bouncers due to Dave's connections. I could hear DJ Tam spinning, and from watching her on social media, I was able to detect her distinct style. Being from Baltimore and going to school in New York, I was used to clubs that play the best hip hop music, which was why I rarely bothered going out much for the nightlife scene in Phoenix. They definitely came nowhere near the party scene in New York. When I saw DJ Tam was coming through, I knew it was going to be hot.

It looked like everyone in the city of Phoenix was in the building. I even saw a few reality television stars. VIP was packed with girls, and both levels were crammed to capacity. I briefly ran into Melissa, who wanted to talk to me about why she couldn't go to the fest in Bali at the last minute. I had to politely explain to her I wasn't interested in talking shop tonight. I was letting my hair down and that was all I was concerned about. A few other yoga instructors from the studio were wandering around. I saw plenty of Dave's friends but no Dave. I even spotted a few of the workers from the local Target. The music was blazing, and I took a quick shot of tequila to get my evening going right. There were so many people I knew who wanted to do the small talk thing, but I just wasn't interested. All I wanted to do was dance.

I was finally able to get through the crowd and greet DJ Tam. She screamed so loud and hugged me.

"Honey! I didn't know you lived here!" DJ Tam was yelling over the speakers.

"Yep, been here for a little over ten years now. You are killing it tonight. I've been following you on Instagram. You're definitely doing your thing. I'm so happy for you!" I was genuinely excited.

"Oh my God, thank you! I'm doing what I love. You know this has been a dream of mine since NYU, and now I'm here."

"I know, right? You always got the parties cracking there. Well, I ain't gon' keep you and flood you with requests. I just wanted to say hey, and I'm so glad you're here in Phoenix livening this place up."

"Ha! Bet! And I got a song just for you. Don't you worry at all. And damn, Serenity, you look so fucking good, but you always have." DJ Tam winked at me.

As I walked away, I could feel her still looking at me, and when I turned around, sure enough, she was. DJ Tam and I flirted from time to time in school, but we were never a thing. We never even kissed, but we were always cool. I must admit, I swayed my body a little more seductively because I knew she was looking, but it was all in fun until some drunk dude tried to push up on me, but I weaseled myself away from him. I went to the bathroom to check my hair and makeup, and everything was still intact. As soon as I stepped back onto the dance floor, I could hear the bass of Chaka Khan's, "I Know You, I Live You" come on. I couldn't believe DJ Tam was playing this. That was another one of Mama's favorites, and I used to play it in my dorm room all the time when DJ Tam and I lived on the same floor. I would lose my mind and go into a trance whenever I would play this song. When DJ Tam started spinning around campus, she would always play this song for me knowing I would get the party started with my dancing, and it was no different tonight.

I tuned everything and everyone else out and lost myself in the strong bass lines, the low- pitched instruments, and heavy syncopated beat. The sound of the drums, electric guitar, and horns in Chaka's song always drove me crazy. My body moved effortlessly, and I could feel myself captivating the attention of both men and women. No amount of alcohol could make me move like this. My hips continued to sway without my permission as I raised my arms up high. Before I knew it, I felt someone's arms wrap around my waist and felt a gentle grind on my ass. Then I smelled that perfume. I knew that scent. I knew that touch. I turned around, and it was Imani.

We didn't say a word to each other; we didn't have to. We continued to dance as if no one else was in the room. We stared intensely into each other's eyes. I could feel the heat of passion all around us. She turned my body around quickly, so my back was to her and she could continue to grind on me. Imani danced on me as if her life depended on it. At one point, she even moved my hair over to the side and gently kissed my neck while still holding my waist. I could see men out the corner of my eyes looking as if they were getting off on this free show we were giving them. I even saw a few phones out and people recording. I hated that they felt they could record us without our permission, but nothing phased me at that moment. I just didn't want the moment to end.

"Imani, what are you doing here?" I asked. I felt she had no right to be here even though I was more than excited that she was.

"Does it matter?"

"Yeah, it kind of sort of does. I've barely talked to you in the last month, except for the couple of times we had to basically sneak around to see each other and now you're all on top of me like this." I wanted answers from Imani. I was definitely enjoying the moment we were having but not enough to forget we really needed to talk.

"Babe, why can't you just get lost in the music with me for a little while longer? We've got plenty of time to talk, but right now, seeing you in this dress is doing something to me. I want you, and I need you even more." Imani kissed me softly on my lips but was also insinuating she wanted to take me home right now.

"What about Alex?" I asked, trying to see if the pin would drop, so to speak.

"Babe, look around. Do you see him here? Now, what we need to do is stop talking and get the fuck outta here and head back to your place."

Who the hell did Imani think she was being so demanding and not giving me any answers? But dammit, I was turned on. I threw caution to the wind, and we left almost immediately. Imani mentioned she took an Uber to the club because she didn't know how much she would be drinking. We hopped in my car, and she barely said two words about Alex; she just kept touching my thighs while I was driving.

"Don't make me pull this car over. My panties are soaked right now because you're over there being all seductive and shit."

"And you know you like it, so quit tripping."

Imani was teasing me, but I was loving it. "What the hell has gotten into you, girl? You think you can just not talk to me for the past couple of weeks, see me in a club, drag me outta there with no explanation, and take me home to have your way with me?"

"Isn't that what I'm doing right now?" Imani chuckled and grabbed my hand and sucked one of my fingers while smiling at me.

This was really hard. As much as I wanted Imani, I really wanted us to be truthful with one another and with Alex. I thought the whole point of the poly-relationship we had going was to be able to freely express ourselves to the fullest, without dodging each other's questions and sneaking around. If I didn't know any better, I would've thought Imani was getting off on keeping shit from Alex.

"Imani, listen, I just want us to—"

Imani cut me off at the light and kissed me passionately, putting her hands under my dress. This chick was relentless, and quite honestly, the shit was working. We couldn't get back to the house fast enough. I pulled up to my driveway, and we sprinted toward the door as if we were both competing in a relay race. Before I knew it, the door closed, and our clothes started flying. We were aching for each other. I knew in the back of my mind something wasn't right, but I was magnetized by the intense passion.

"We really need to talk," I said while Imani was kissing my neck.

"Honestly, Serenity, I'm not trying to talk right now. You know this is what you want, so please stop stalling and let me please you the way you'd like to be pleased."

I couldn't think clearly when Imani looked at me like that, standing naked in front of me. Why was I allowing her to do this to me? I believed our threesome could work with communication and some rearranging of boundaries, but Imani was determined to get what she wanted, and dammit, I was going to let her; she had me hooked.

The evening was filled with laughter, kisses, and some intense lovemaking. I didn't want it to end, but Imani had to head back home. Even though she lived only a couple of blocks away, I offered to drive her back. I didn't want her walking alone in the dark, but she insisted I didn't because she didn't want Alex to know we saw each other at the club and had a quick midnight rendezvous. And just like that, she was gone, again.

This sucked. I was at her mercy. What started out as a fun-filled evening ended on a pretty muddled note. I felt more confused than before. There was so much that needed to be worked out. I felt like I was getting too old for this shit. I wasn't trying to play these games. Although I was attracted to both Imani and Alex, of course I was a lot more attracted to Imani, so I needed to know where all of us stood. I was going to call Imani and Alex sooner rather than later, and I was not going to allow her to change my mind with her pussy.

*****

Hey, Alex! It's been a minute. We haven't spoken in a while. I just wanted to catch up with you. Maybe you, Imani, and I could get together for dinner when your schedule allows.

I was nervous about sending Alex that text. We hadn't spoken in a while, but I needed to get to the bottom of what was going on in our relationship, and I wasn't getting anywhere with Imani. I waited for those three little dots to appear on my iPhone to indicate someone was responding back. Nothing was coming through. I was getting ready to teach another class anyway so maybe once the class was about to begin, he would respond. Ten minutes later and still nothing. I checked my phone again after my hour class was over and still nothing. He was at work, and I was pretty sure he wasn't checking his phone throughout the entire day. Maybe he was just ignoring me, though.

Hey, Serenity. Wow, it has been a while. I'm sorry I haven't reached out to you sooner. To be honest, when you and Imani returned from Bali, I felt like I needed a little more quality time with my wife. I didn't mean to just cut you off without really speaking. I would actually love to get together for dinner. We have a regular babysitter now for Yaya, so would you be open to meeting tomorrow evening?

Thank God he answered my text. I was on edge about all of this. Imani was probably going to kill me when she found out I was scheduling this dinner, considering she didn't want to have a real conversation about our relationship. I didn't care, though. My feelings were at stake, and I didn't feel like she should be the only one steering the ship.

I would love that. I look forward to seeing you both tomorrow evening.

I responded as if I hadn't seen Imani since Bali. I hated lying to Alex— I hated lying period— because I really liked him and could still see us all being involved. The question still remained: why didn't Imani want to work all of this out? I guessed I'd find out at dinner.

I packed my bags and began to head out for the evening. Class had been mediocre. I gave about fifty percent effort with my poses and allowed my students to do the same. I wasn't leading them like I should. My head wasn't in the game; I was too consumed with thoughts of Imani. Last night was amazing yet so disappointing. Running into Imani at the club was something I didn't expect, and I didn't expect us to connect like we did on the dance floor. Whenever we made love, it was exhilarating. The way we could please one another was magical. The times Alex and I made love were great too, but I didn't get the same feeling I got with Imani.

I got angry with myself because I'd allowed fear to guide me instead of confronting Imani and demanding answers. It seemed like there was more going on with her, which saddened me because I thought we were truly linked. I still got a feeling there was more I should know about Iris. I knew it was just a Facebook comment on a picture, but for some reason, I thought there was more to that story. I didn't want to become a jealous girlfriend, but I also wanted to know if Imani was just going through some phase with me, or if she really wanted this.

I hopped in my car and let the evening breeze flow through my hair. It was a hot wind, but after living here for over ten years, I had gotten used to it. I turned the music up and started singing along to Jill Scott's, "Golden." At times, I felt I was far away from living my life like it was golden, but other days, I felt closer to that thought.

I began to think about Mama. I decided to take a detour home from work and drive down different streets and places I would take her when she visited me. For some reason, that always made me feel close to her. Sometimes I would even talk out loud to myself, as if she were sitting right next to me. I knew it sounded crazy, but it was just my thing. With all this stuff going on with Alex and Imani, I would've loved to be able to chat with her and ask her for advice. Her words always encouraged me and made me feel like I could do anything. I didn't fear anything until she died. Things that worried me now never used to worry me before. All this second guessing and uncertainty never existed with me before. It seemed like as soon as Mama died, I lost that part of myself. I felt like I was getting it back some days, but other times, I felt like I failed miserably.

*****

I was nervous to meet up with Alex and Imani. I was about thirty minutes early for dinner, so I just sat in my car. I tried to think about anything and everything to get my mind off of the worst-case scenario happening. What if Alex said he didn't want a relationship with me anymore and, in turn, forced Imani to not have any communication with me too? What if Imani got upset with Alex and left him then assumed I was ready for another marriage? I needed to relax.

My phone had vibrated with a message from Lisa. *I have a HUGE opportunity for you. Please contact me ASAP!!!*

I wondered what kind of opportunity could be so urgent that I had to contact her immediately. With the extra time I had, I decided to give Lisa a call.

"Hey, Serenity! Thanks so much for calling me so promptly! I promise, you won't regret stopping whatever you were doing to contact me."

I could feel the excitement radiating from Lisa's voice through the phone.

"I can only imagine what opportunity has you so enthusiastic."

"First, you were a major hit in Bali. We've already talked about that. One of our major sponsors of the Vitality Fest is opening five major yoga studios over in the East Coast called Yoga Theory. The owner, Kevin, is a major power player in the wellness industry. He's looking for a Director of Operations who's willing to oversee all five studios. This business is all about who you know, so he told me specifically he was not going through a string of interviews. He wanted someone who was handpicked, so of course, he came to me for leads. I said, hands down, it should be you."

My jaw dropped before I stuttered, "O-Oh, wow."

"Serenity, are you serious right now? *Wow* is all you have to say?"

"I'm so sorry, it just kind of caught me off guard because…well, it's corporate. I find my own students, create my own schedule, and I'm not bound by the politics of a job. I only rent space at the studio, but I don't work for them."

"I totally hear what you're saying, but this could be a major business move for you. You could learn the ins and outs of running numerous studios, all while making a shitload of money because the suggested salary is extremely nice."

"I'm not exactly driven by money, though, Lisa. I mean, I know we all need it, but I would be perfectly fine living in a studio apartment if I had to. Honestly, these days I've been considering downsizing significantly anyway."

"Okay, so what are you driven by?"

"Autonomy. I like being free. I'm not interested in wearing suits to work, and I'm definitely not interested in giving up my yoga classes. I'm sorry if I've ever given off the vibe that being a director of numerous yoga studios was my goal."

"Serenity, when the team met in Bali, you jumped right in and handled the business aspect of that fest like a pro. I honestly wondered why you were content with just teaching classes."

"Well, my ex-husband is a serial entrepreneur, and you can't be married to a person like that for five years and not learn a thing or two. I'm pretty sure this job will require me to move, and I'm definitely not interested in returning to the cold weather. I'm so sorry to disappoint you. I don't want to seem like I'm ungrateful. I really appreciate you thinking so highly of me and my work."

"Just sleep on it before you totally close the door on this opportunity. There's so much to gain from this besides money. Trust me on this. Call him in a couple of days," Lisa insisted.

"Lisa, I really appreciate—"

"Serenity, trust me, I think you'll regret this if you don't at least think about it."

"Okay," I said, though with hesitation. "I'll do that." I told Lisa what she wanted to hear, but I knew I wasn't interested. I was going to call Kevin tomorrow and let him know my decision. It made no sense to entertain the opportunity knowing my heart wasn't into it.

"Okay, great! Listen, I have to go into a meeting in the next five minutes. I didn't expect you to call me so soon. Feel free to connect with me once you've talked with Kevin."

"I will, and Lisa, again, I really appreciate you believing in me," I said.

"It's my pleasure. I just see so many great things happening for you, Serenity. I feel you have so much more to offer. But I gotta go. We'll chat soon."

I was surprised Lisa thought I would want a job like that after meeting me and getting to know me. I did enjoy business, but I wasn't interested in that whole corporate vibe. I knew I didn't make tons of money as a yoga instructor, but I thought I did pretty well for myself bringing in about sixty-five thousand a year. That director of operations position sounded like I would probably make three times as much, but at what cost? I could see how Cynthia worked, and I knew she loved it, but that wasn't my goal.

I loved meeting new people and loved connecting with them in a way that was authentic. The experience I had in Bali was amazing. If I could do more yoga retreats and speak to people across the world about wellness and mindset, I would love that. I would do that for free. Financially, I was in a good spot. While I was married to Dave, I was able to tuck away a lot of money that was doing very well in the stock market. Dave left me the house and it was paid off, so I could sell it, downsize, and invest the money. I was free to do what I wanted.

I'd call Kevin and tell him thanks but no thanks. I doubted his feelings would be hurt. Once I turned down the offer, I was sure he'd find someone within a few days. Opportunities like that didn't remain vacant for long. There were plenty of people who craved that kind of work life; it just wasn't me.

My phone began to vibrate again. I knew it couldn't be Lisa again, and if it was, what could she possibly have to say?

Hey, babe, please don't tell Alex about the few times we've seen each other. I don't want to get into all of that right now.

Imani's only concern seemed to be blowing our cover.

I just really wanted to spend some quality time with the both of you. I'm not here to turn your life upside down.

I responded back, but I wasn't happy. I should've not responded and made her sweat throughout the entire dinner, but that wasn't my style.

Okay, thanks, babe. See you soon. We're about five minutes away.

I didn't bother responding back to Imani's last text. I went inside the restaurant and secured our table. The few minutes I had left before they arrived gave me time to get my mind right. Who knew how this evening was going to play out?

"Oh, there she is." I heard Alex's voice.

When I looked up, it was the two of them walking over to our table. Imani definitely looked nervous, and Alex's demeanor seemed like he was approaching me for a first date as if we'd never seen each other in person.

"Hey, you guys." I smiled and hugged Alex first and then Imani as I was trying to come off as if I hadn't seen them both since Bali.

"It's good to see you, Serenity. You look beautiful," Alex said but almost a little formally. "It is great to see you," Imani also greeted me but with a fake-ass hug.

I couldn't but help admire how great the two of them looked together, but also, I immediately felt this might be our last time together. Something felt off. Maybe this was just a threesome that wasn't supposed to last this long. Maybe I was yearning for something more than what it was.

"I really appreciate you two agreeing to meet up with me. I miss you. It's been a while." I tried to sound convincing.

"It has been a while, and I can speak for Alex as well as myself. We miss you too."

Imani had on a fake smile. She wasn't too convincing. I was surprised Alex hadn't picked up on the energy between Imani and I yet.

"So, Serenity, what have you been up to since Bali? I can imagine you've made many connections since then." Imani looked at me as if she were trying to divert the attention away from her.

"Um, actually, yes. I made a lot of great connections. As a matter of fact, right before I walked in the restaurant, Lisa and I were talking about an opportunity she wants me to consider. The only thing is, it's a corporate job, and it would require me to relocate."

"Oh, where to?" Alex asked.

"The East Coast." I said while looking at the menu. I didn't want to look at Imani's face.

"Well, you despise the cold, so I can't see you taking that opportunity," Imani said.

"Well, I'm not a fan of the cold, but I'm also not really interested because corporate is just not my thing. I have a fantastic business here as a yoga instructor. I wouldn't dare give that up."

"So, what is the position?" Alex inquired.

"Director of Operations over five new yoga studios in Washington DC, New York, New Jersey, Maryland, and Virginia," I said nonchalantly.

"Wow, Serenity, that's huge!" Alex was really excited.

"It's not that huge. That's not my calling."

"But don't you want more?" Alex was starting to get on my damn nerves.

"I'm not exactly sure what you mean by more because if it's money, I have that. If it's a fake lifestyle that makes it appear like I'm doing big things, I don't need it. I am very content with where I am in life. I like connecting with people, and I get that when I teach yoga." I was trying not to look completely disturbed by Alex's comment.

"I wasn't trying to insinuate your current business wasn't enough. It just seems like a great opportunity." Alex sounded remorseful.

"I'm sorry if it seemed like I was going off. I just know we all have different goals in life, and I refuse to hide how I really feel about things."

I was directing that statement toward Imani because she wanted to keep what was really going on between her and I from Alex. By the look on her face, I could tell she felt every bit of my statement.

"It's all good. I understand your passion for what you do, and I respect it," Alex said.

"So, have you all finally decided what you want to eat?" Imani asked looking down as if she was trying to avoid eye contact with me.

"Babe, I see what you're doing. You're trying to get us to order and not allow this conversation to get too heated," Alex said and kissed Imani.

She was clearly uncomfortable kissing him in front of me.

"I'm just going to get an appetizer for now. I'm not really that hungry all of a sudden," I said while trying to remain cool.

"You sure? I heard the vegan tacos here are amazing," Alex offered.

This wasn't a good idea. I couldn't deal with how fake this all felt. "Maybe later," I said while continuing to look at the menu to avoid any eye contact.

"Serenity, I know I've said this before, but thanks again for getting an extra ticket for Imani to the Vitality Fest. She came back really relaxed and refreshed. She's been holding it down at home and taking care of Yaya like she's Superwoman. I know she needed that alone time to be on her own and think about herself. Imani said you were able to get her a fantastic suite at the hotel even though it was practically booked by the time you invited her to go."

So Alex thought all this time Imani and I didn't even share a room. I thought he knew we were fucking on this trip, but apparently, he thought Imani and I were just friends. He really didn't have a clue how we felt about each other. I could tell by the look on Imani's face she knew she had dug herself into a hole. Why did she feel like she had to lie about us sleeping in the same hotel room? That made no sense to me.

"I just knew Serenity was going to be busy on the trip, and I didn't know what she had going on or if she wanted to entertain someone else while traveling. I definitely didn't want to get in the way of that," Imani said. She was trying to continue convincing Alex that there were no real feelings involved in all of this.

"Like I said, I appreciate it, Serenity. We know you have your own life, but you decided to include Imani, which meant a lot to me. I wasn't trying to shut you out after you all came back from Bali, but Imani and I really needed some time to ourselves." I could tell Alex was not privy at all to the current situation.

"Honestly, it was my pleasure. You're both amazing. I appreciate we're able to have a relationship like this." I bit my tongue and didn't say what I wanted to.

"No doubt. I really like how we can enjoy a good meal together, hang out, have good sex, and I don't feel like you're trying to destroy our marriage. You complement us."

I couldn't believe my ears. Alex was obviously in the dark about Imani. The more I thought about all of it, I realized Imani was more attracted to women. I saw how she lit up every single time we talked to women when we were in Bali. The way she made love to me was intense. She was hiding behind her marriage and co-signing threesomes as if it were just something they did from time to time, but she really loved women. I was positive Iris was still floating around somewhere in the picture.

"That reminds me, Alex, I said to Imani that the three of us will have to return to Bali sometime together." I waited to see how Alex would respond.

"I would love that. I kind of figured it was a beautiful place because when Imani came back home, she talked about it so much. I haven't seen her that excited in a long time. She was definitely in a good mood when she returned." Alex smiled.

I was sure she was after the time we spent together in our suite, but Imani wasn't going to include that part.

"So, Imani, did you tell Alex all of the things we did on the trip?" I felt myself getting heated at this point.

"I sure did, like when we got an opportunity to go sightseeing and when I saw your yoga classes."

Imani was a trip. She knew we spent way more time together than she led on.

"Listen, we're all grown around here. I can't lie, Serenity. I asked Imani one night if she could record you all having sex while you were in Bali. I was missing you both, and I wanted to see because I kind of figured you two would hook up." Alex had a goofy grin on his face.

"Wow, I would've loved to do that for you, Alex. Imani, why didn't you mention this to me?" I asked curiously.

"It was such a busy day that day, and when we got together that night, it totally slipped my mind." I could tell Imani was lying her ass off.

"Yeah, I was pretty bummed out about that. Imani told me you all really didn't have much time together anyway because you were so busy working."

"It was a busy trip, but if I would've known that, I would've made sure you were well entertained." I winked at Alex even though I was mad as hell.

I continued the conversation while we ate dinner. Imani was clearly living a lie. I guessed I really was a toy, picked up from time to time according to Alex, but I thought Imani and I had so much more. I didn't get why she didn't feel like she could be honest. Maybe she thought if she told Alex how she really felt, he would get upset. Even I didn't want to discuss it with Alex before the trip in fear of him not wanting Imani to go. Maybe we were both guilty to some degree. Maybe Imani felt she had more to lose. In some ways, she did.

I was still angry with her, though. I wish she would've just filled me in rather than kept me in the dark. What if I would've slipped up and said something at dinner that would've blown this whole situation up? Apparently, Imani knew me better than that. She knew I wouldn't put her out there like that because I cared about her too much.

"It's all good, Serenity. There will be other times," Imani said seductively.

This wasn't what I wanted so it was time for me to say something. "So, I was thinking, since we've gotten pretty acquainted with each other, I want a little more clarity on the boundaries of our relationship. It seems like we're all pretty open, and I've spent time with the both of you as well as individually. I just want to know if there were any specific rules to this?" I was nervous, but I demanded answers. I didn't want to keep lying.

"What do you mean?" Alex was perplexed.

"I want to know how you both feel about me. Is this strictly a sex thing, or are we in a real relationship? Also, do we need to inform each other if we're meeting up with one another privately? I guess I just want more clarity on our situation-ship."

I was determined to speak my mind and create some boundaries. When I looked at Imani, I could tell she was irritated by me putting them both in the hot seat.

"I was under the impression you were kind of like our third. Not necessarily a part of the relationship Imani and I share but definitely someone we can chill with from time to time and, of course, someone we have sex with on occasion. I'm personally not comfortable with myself or Imani meeting up with you, or having sex with you, without each of us knowing. I feel like that's deceitful and unfair, and I'm not comfortable with that. What do you think, Imani?" Alex looked to Imani for a response.

"I'm in agreement with you, Alex." Imani's response was short, and she barely looked at me as she spoke. As far as I was concerned, this dinner was over. Imani was not ready for the open and honest relationship I wanted. I felt like I received more transparency from Alex than I did from Imani.

"If it's okay to say, I really like the both of you and appreciate your honesty, Alex. I'll be frank, I'm not exactly interested in being just someone's third. Alex, I think you are incredibly sexy, driven, and an amazing father and husband to Imani. When I first met the both of you, I could tell how much you adored Imani, and I thought that was really special. Imani, you and I connect on a level I've never experienced with another woman before. I feel like we have a lot in common, like the hobbies we enjoy, the same taste in music, and you're always in the present moment with me when I talk about my mom, which I think is so magnetizing. I would love to continue this with the both of you, but if I can be completely transparent, I have found myself even more attracted to Imani than I thought I would be. Alex, I am not here to disrupt what you and Imani share. I heard you loud and clear about what this is for you, and I respect that. With that being said, I would love to still be friends with the both of you, but I won't be able to continue what we've had going on." I was nervous, but I felt it was important for me to be direct.

"I understand, Serenity, and I really appreciate how honest you've been with us. I feel like from the beginning you were clear about where you were in life. Thank you for respecting the boundaries I have for my marriage with Imani and not trying to disrupt what we have." Alex appeared very calm and confident about his marriage with Imani. Imani, on the other hand, looked extremely disappointed.

"I…wasn't expecting this today. I've actually really enjoyed having you in our lives, but I respect your decision," Imani said solemnly.

I was so disappointed with Imani. I bared my soul and felt like what I said gave her permission to be forthcoming as well, but she wasn't ready, it seemed.

Dinner was awkward after that, at least for Imani and me, but Alex acted normal. He didn't suspect a single thing, and I was fine with keeping it that way so I could move on. As we concluded dinner, I was eager to just leave. I knew there was a possibility this would not go the way I wanted. I wasn't expecting Imani to admit to what had been going on between her and I behind Alex's back, but I still felt like she wasn't being truly authentic, which was what I valued most about her. It wasn't my place to decide when and how she was ready to be truthful. That was her journey.

"I'm glad we had a chance to have a dinner and talk. I appreciate what we've shared." I tried to remain as cool and relaxed about this as I could.

"Well, this doesn't have to mean goodbye. I get that the parameters of our relationship have changed, but I hope we can stay in touch with you," Imani said optimistically.

"I think time will tell on that one." I gave a half smile. I looked at the clock and decided to position myself to leave.

"Well, it's getting kind of late, you guys, and I think I'm about to head home."

"Be safe driving home, Serenity, and I guess we'll see you when we see you." I could tell Alex was trying to be kind but really didn't know what to say.

"Have a good night." I gave Alex and Imani a hug and proceeded to my car.

I was hurt. I tried not to be; I should've known what I was getting myself into, but this shit still hurt. I wasn't afraid to admit that to myself. As I continued to walk to my car, I heard Imani yell for me to wait.

"What is it, Imani?" I was really annoyed and couldn't understand what else she could say.

"I just wanted to say I'm sorry. I'm so in love with you, Serenity. I haven't felt this way about anyone in a long time, including Alex. I couldn't crush him like that in there. He's pretty open to having a threesome but having some serious feelings for another woman is just not going to work for him." I noticed Alex walking out the door, heading toward their car.

"He's waiting for you at the car. I'd rather not get into anything heavy right now. I get where you are in your life. It doesn't match up to where I am, so I knew I needed to be honest with myself and to the both of you and let this go."

"So, what did you expect me to do, admit my true feelings for you and leave Alex?"

"I honestly don't care what the hell you do. I can tell you're not in the space right now to make any major decisions, and all I can do is respect that. Quite honestly, I would've been fine with it still being the three of us, but yes, I'm more attracted to you. I don't have a problem admitting that. If Alex isn't willing to allow you to explore something more with me, then I can't do this."

"Wait a minute. He doesn't *allow* me to have anything!" Imani became upset and defensive.

"Imani, stop lying to yourself, please? Deep down inside, all of this is upsetting you because you feel he calls the shots, and you're not ready to admit that. I get it. He takes care of you and Yaya, and right now, you're pretty dependent upon him. I won't come in between that."

"Babe, please don't leave like this," Imani pleaded.

"Can I ask you a question?"

"Anything. What is it?" Imani said desperately.

"Who's Iris Senegal?"

"What?"

"Who is Iris Senegal?" I slowed down my question. I could tell Imani wanted to act like she didn't know what I was talking about.

"Okay, that's a random question. I have a friend from college by that name, but how do you know her?"

"I just want to know if Iris was the woman you had that relationship with, the one Alex made you leave for him?'

"Serenity, listen, I don't know what you're getting at."

"I know you've gotten away with lying to Alex about us, but please don't lie to me. Is Iris the one that got away?" Imani's eyes began to fill with tears, and I had my answer.

Imani was stuck, really stuck. She loved Alex, but this would've been the second time she gave up what she really wanted for him. Both times, it was a woman she really wanted to be with.

"Imani, this is not what I want. I want freedom. I want to live my life according to who I am. I don't want to hide, and I damn sure don't want to lie to myself or to anyone else about how I feel. I love you, but we can't do this. If you keep talking to me too long, Alex will suspect something. If you have tears in your eyes, he's really going to know something is going on. I wish you the best. Please, all I ask is that you find a way to be true to yourself. That's what I want for you. I love you, and don't ever forget that." I blew Imani a quick kiss. I didn't want Alex to start getting suspicious.

I got in my car, and even though I knew I made the right decision, I couldn't help but feel bad for leaving Imani that way. I knew deep down it wasn't going to work. It was time for me to move on.

I attempted to enjoy some time on my back patio. I wanted to take a quick swim in my pool, but all I kept thinking about was the last dinner I had with Alex and Imani. What sucked about ending our relationship was that it felt like a huge loss. It wasn't the same as losing Mama, but it still fucking hurt. I knew Alex, Imani, and I hadn't been together long, but it felt like we'd done so much in that time, especially Imani and me. The thought of her smile, like when she was excited to see me, the way her body moved when she walked, the caring and nurturing side I saw when she played with Yaya, her voice when she sang, and the look in her eyes when I pleasured her. I really missed her. I wanted to call her, but I couldn't. I didn't want to get sucked back in, and I didn't want to disrespect Alex either. I may not have agreed with his idea of a poly- relationship, but I still had to respect it. The reality was I fell hard for Imani. Deep down inside, when I thought back to when I first met them, I was really drawn to her.

I had never officially dated a woman, but I had sex with a couple of them. I was never interested in a relationship though. I was not opposed to the idea, but I'd never met anyone who really grabbed my attention like Imani. When I saw her, I knew I wanted to know more about her. As I got to know her, I wanted to be intimate with her. For some reason, I always thought if Mama met Imani, she would've loved her.

There were many times I thought about Mama and wondered if she were actually gay herself. I remembered her friend Amanda, who used to come to the house all the time and help out, especially when Mama and Daddy had a bad night. When Daddy would rough Mama up, Amanda was always around to wipe her tears. They hugged a lot. Sometimes they even held each other while they were watching a show on TV. As a little girl, I assumed they were just best friends, but they would only act like that around me, usually when my brothers were outside playing and I was in the house. Maybe they thought I was too young to know what was going on and that my brothers would catch on if they did that in front of them. Many times, when Daddy would leave and not come back for weeks, Amanda would come over and spend the night with us.

One night, Amanda was at the house when Daddy came home, and Mama was out grocery shopping. My brothers were out running the streets and Daddy and Amanda got into a really big argument. I don't remember what it was about. They started yelling, and before I knew it, Daddy had slapped Amanda, and she fell to the floor. They started wrestling, and I remember Daddy punching Amanda, and I started screaming, "Daddy, stop!" They kept grappling, and that was when Mama walked in with groceries and dropped her bags. The three of them fought, and Mama tried so hard to help Amanda. I just remembered Amanda saying, "Get the kids and come live with me." Mama kept telling her she couldn't. Amanda stormed out and that was the last time we saw her. Daddy screamed, "Why is that bitch always here? Y'all fucking or something?" Mama sobbed while my dad demanded answers. Mama never answered him.

We stayed, and Mama continued to get abused. When we finally got away from him, I never saw another man in Mama's life. When I was a teenager, I asked Mama whatever happened to that woman named Amanda. She said she was surprised I remembered her because I was so young, but she answered. She lost contact with her, and she moved to another state. When Mama passed, I was going through her phone to inform her old co-workers, friends, and the few family members in Baltimore that Mama had died. I saw a contact that said Amanda, and when I reached out to her, I told her she might not remember me, but that I was Judy's daughter. She responded with so much excitement, stating she remembered me. As soon as she asked how Mama was doing, I broke the news to her. Amanda sobbed uncontrollably, and I just knew there was more to their friendship. I never questioned Amanda about their relationship. I figured if she wanted me to know, she would've told me. I still had Amanda's number, but after Mama died, I was so focused on my own grief and never really thought to call Amanda back. Maybe someday I would.

Who I needed to call was Kevin in New York. I told Lisa I would think about the opportunity, but I still wasn't interested in the corporate scene, so I knew this phone call would take no more than a second. I walked back into my air-conditioned home. The sun was blazing.

"Hello?" A deep voiced man answered the phone.

"Hi, can I speak to Kevin Lattimore?"

"You're speaking to him."

"Oh, great. My name is Serenity Hayes, and I received your information from Lisa Fletcher."

"Oh, yes, hi, Serenity! I was hoping I'd hear from you soon. I'm pretty sure Lisa told you about the position. Did you have any questions I could answer for you? Lisa spoke highly of you."

"No questions. I just wanted to let you know that I appreciate you even considering me, but I am currently not looking for a new job. But thank you for even being willing to talk with me."

"I'm really glad you said that because I don't want you for the position."

"Um…okay?" I was kind of confused.

"Let me explain. Lisa knew I was looking for a director of operations for my new studios, but when I had an opportunity to view your business website and saw what you've been up to, I was hoping you would be more open to doing something else within my company. I think it would be an even better fit for you."

"Really? What is it?" I was intrigued to hear what Kevin would say.

"So, Lisa might have explained to you that I'm opening five studios in the East Coast area, but my headquarters will be in New York, and my largest studio will be here too. I want a dynamic, lead yoga instructor here in my New York location with me. I would also like for that person to be a part of our marketing and publicity for its opening in October. Basically, that person will be the instructor on camera for all of the videos and press releases, talking about the studio to the public, but you'll also get a chance to still teach.

"I read your bio on your website, and I could tell how much teaching meant to you, and I honestly couldn't see you in the director role. I know you have a life there in Arizona with clients, so I understand this would be a major move for you. You have amazing credentials, and to have someone like you leading my New York location would be phenomenal. If Lisa is vouching for you, that speaks volumes. She's been in the health and wellness industry for a long time and knows her stuff. She didn't know I was looking for an instructor of this magnitude at my New York location, which is probably why she recommended you for Director of Operations. She said you were very business savvy and felt like you had so much to offer. I know that was a lot, but what are your thoughts?"

I didn't know what to think. This was something I could get into, but I still wouldn't be my own boss. As much as I loved and missed New York, was I ready to pick up the life I'd made here for the past ten plus years and move cross country? I knew Cynthia would be ecstatic if I moved back to New York. While I knew Imani and I just weren't an option right now, a small part of me was kind of holding out hope.

"It sounds like something I might be interested in, but I really need to think about this. I've been my own boss for so long."

"Trust me, being an entrepreneur myself, I can definitely understand that. The position would come with lots of flexibility and amazing benefits, but the difference is you'd be exposed to so many more opportunities to share your love of yoga with a wider audience. You would automatically be considered to lead plenty of yoga retreats and gain sponsorships for various events."

"Now I'm excited. I know this sounds crazy, but while I went to NYU and I love New York, I'm not a fan of that cold." I chuckled.

"Tell me about it. I'm actually from Texas. I moved here about seven years ago, and I still haven't gotten used to it, but my business has grown so much since I've been here. It was a great move for me. Before you make your decision, how about this? Come visit. See the studio here. There's still construction going on, but I just have a feeling you'll love it. We'll schedule an interview before the month is out."

"Well, during the week, I'll be swamped with classes."

"Okay, I'm willing to meet on a Saturday. It's not something I typically do for interviews, but I'm really interested in what you could offer my business. You have so much insight as an instructor, and I need that. What about two weeks from Saturday?"

"That could work."

"Okay, great, is there a particular airline you prefer to fly?"

"Nope, I'm pretty laid back."

"Wow, most people typically jump at the opportunity to tell me what they prefer. I'll send you your flight tickets along with your hotel information, which is walking distance from my studio in Manhattan. Be on the lookout for that. Serenity, if you can do me a favor and email me your information so I can make the arrangements, that would be great."

"Okay, I sure will. Thank you for the opportunity to interview with you."

"No, thank *you*. I'll be in touch soon."

We hung up the phone, and I couldn't believe I was even considering. Cynthia was going to flip when she heard about this. The opportunity was something new. I never would've thought in a million years I would consider living back in New York. The cost of living was certainly more expensive, but it would be nice to be closer to friends and family again, and I did miss the culture of the city. There was so much to consider.

I wondered, if Imani and I would've worked out, would I even consider this opportunity? Who knew? I didn't know why I was even thinking about that. We were in two different places in our lives. Imani was still trying to figure herself out. She never had the opportunity to explore her relationship with Iris and that would always eat away at her. She definitely had a great life with Alex and the most beautiful little girl ever, but she was yearning for a deeper connection. I could tell because that was also what I wanted. I couldn't force her to end up with me, nor did I want to because I wanted it to be genuine.

I started surfing online for apartments in Manhattan, but I was still going to be a yoga instructor, so I didn't know how I was going to afford that. Maybe if I would've accepted that Director of Operations position, I could afford the cost of living. I was now having second thoughts. I loved New York, but I'd grown accustomed to the way of life here in Arizona. Nothing beat being able to wear shorts all year-round. I needed a sign, something that would point me in the direction of where to go. Even though being a yoga instructor in New York would probably pay more than what I was bringing in with my own business, it was still New York, and the expenses kind of made me feel like I was throwing money down the toilet.

Being in Arizona, I felt at ease. I felt like I could hear my own thoughts. Arizona had a calm vibe I'd grown accustomed to in comparison to the fast-paced lifestyle of New York. I would've loved to grow my business even more and maybe even open up a studio of my own someday. Even being considered for this opportunity helped me see what I could do for myself. I was really at a crossroads. I could do well either way, but I had to follow my heart.

I looked around my house and began thinking about the many memories created here. I remembered when Dave and I moved in. Mama was so excited and happy for us. I was at my happiest then. Dave's app was doing really well, and he was excited to purchase our first home together. It's crazy how time flew by and everything had changed since then. I had no clue I would be divorced and would no longer have my mother. Thinking about all of that made me sad and a tear fell from my eye. I was okay. I knew I was just reflecting on those times.

I decided to call Dave.

"Hello?"

"Hey, Dave, it's me."

"Hey, Serenity! How are you?"

"I'm alright. Did I catch you at a bad time?"

"No, not at all. I'm just looking over some business expenses. Why? What's up?"

"Nothing much. I just thought I'd give you a call. I was just sitting here in the living room going down memory lane, thinking about when we first moved into this house."

"Yeah, we were so excited when we moved there. You sound sad."

"I guess that's because I am."

"What's wrong? Thinking about your mom?"

"Yeah, and other things."

"Like what, if you don't mind my asking?"

"It's cool, Dave. I called you. And I do want to talk about what's going on with me. It's just this situation with Imani and Alex. We sort of broke up, I guess. And I'm sitting here thinking about a job opportunity that's come my way." I proceeded to tell Dave about Kevin's offer.

"Wow, did you say Manhattan? And I'm sorry to hear about you, Alex, and Imani. I didn't know much about Alex, but the day I met Imani, you two seemed to really be into each other."

"That's because we were. But I was more of their third, not a real partner within their relationship."

"Is that what they communicated to you, or is that what you assume?"

"Oh, trust me, I asked. Alex was fine with me just purely being there for entertainment, and I think he felt that's what Imani wanted from me too, but in actuality, Imani and I connected on a deeper level. We began sneaking around as well without his knowledge, and I just can't live like that. I want to be open about who I'm with, and Imani is just not in that same frame of mind. I can't force her."

"That's unfortunate. You tend to give everything you have in a relationship. I recognized that firsthand while we were married."

"Well, that didn't exactly stop you from leaving either." I blurted out the words before thinking about what I was saying. "Dave…"

"No, I get it, and I deserve what you just said. I benefitted from the love you gave me, but when things got rough, I decided to leave. Believe me, every day I recognize more and more what I did. It has taken me this time to really wrap my brain around that, but it is what it is. I seriously fucked up."

"I really can't do this right now."

"No, Serenity, I'm not saying that for you to feel sorry for me and take me back. I was just responding to what you were saying, that's all. I know how adamant you were and are about moving on." Dave sounded sincere. "I just know that sometimes people don't value someone so free and transparent as you. I guess we take advantage, thinking you'll always be there and understand."

"I still refuse to be a bitter person because that's not who I want to be. Clearly Alex, Imani and I had our time, but it appears this is the end, so I have to accept it."

"You also mentioned a job in Manhattan. What do you think you're going to do?"

"I really don't know. I think it could be a great opportunity, but I've just become so used to my faithful clients and my own business here. This is where my life has been for quite some time. I'm not afraid of switching things up, but I want to make sure I'm doing what makes me happy."

"I know you'll make the best decision for you. Of course, the selfish part of me would want you to stay, but I also know my opinion doesn't matter anymore. I want you to be happy as well."

"Thanks, I really appreciate that. I feel like over the past year, you're starting to understand me more. I don't know, but you're not trying to be the one that saves me."

"Well, I can't lie, a part of me wants to offer to give you the funds to open your own studio because I want to see that for you, but I'm holding back right now. I know it's not my place."

"Yeah, you're right, it's not your place." I chuckled a bit. "But I appreciate you being who you are."

"Hey, Serenity, let's forget all this talk right now. Let's just go catch a movie and grab something to eat. No strings attached."

"That sounds like a good idea. Let me freshen up, and I can be ready in about fifteen minutes."

"Alright, good. Can I pick you up in about thirty minutes? I need to tie up a few things here at the office."

"No problem. Take your time. And Dave, thank you."

"No problem. I'm glad I can be here for you. So go ahead and get ready. I'll see you soon."

"Okay. See you soon."

I was looking forward to this time out with Dave. I needed to get my mind off of everything. Hopefully by tomorrow, things would be a lot clearer.

*****

"*Bad Boys 3* was pretty good. Not as good as the first two in my opinion, but it was still entertaining," I said, chomping on some leftover popcorn while Dave and I walked out of the theater. It was a beautiful evening and hanging out with him was really doing me some good.

Dave and I had always been friends, even within our marriage, but tonight felt really good. I wasn't experiencing any romantic feelings for Dave, just genuine friendship. It was weird how that happened. Dave had always accepted all of me, which was why it hurt so badly when he decided to leave during one of the most vulnerable times in my life. I could sit around all day long and be mad at him or question him until I was blue in the face for that, but I chose not to. I just never understood where that would get me.

"Well, I liked it. Did you know at one time I wanted to be an actor?" said Dave.

"When? Like when you were twelve or something? I've known you pretty much your whole adult life and never heard you talk about that."

"It was in high school. I had a few headshots, went on a couple of auditions, but I bombed terribly."

"Why didn't you ever tell me that?" I laughed.

"I don't know. I guess the topic just never came up. Clearly tech is my thing."

"Yeah, it is, but you're also an extraordinary entrepreneur."

"Why, thank you." Dave was beaming from ear to ear.

"I say that because I didn't realize how much of an impact your entrepreneurial genius had on me until someone noticed how I handled a few things at the fest in Bali. I guess I never really paid attention to how much you influenced my own business practices."

"That's really cool to hear. Thanks for saying that. I love entrepreneurship, and I'm glad you've also chosen to work for yourself over the years. I can understand why you're hesitant about possibly taking that job in Manhattan. Ever since I've known you, you always struck me as the kind of person to be your own boss."

"Yeah, but maybe I have been thinking too small. I was looking at the website of the yoga studio opening out there and it looks amazing so far. Maybe it's time for me to grow. I don't know. I think I've been pretty comfortable with where I'm at, but I have been wanting to reach more people and touch more lives through yoga. The one woman in Bali I met almost made me cry when she shared her story and talked about how my session helped her. I want to contribute more like that to others."

"So, what's stopping you?"

"I guess nothing at this point. I wasn't thinking about this amount of growth, even in regards to opening my own studio, until that job offer presented itself, and I'm looking at this guy's studio and thinking I can do that too."

"But think about the yoga retreats you've led so far, including the one in Bali. I'm pretty sure you made some great contacts. Why not start there? Start calling some of those people back. I wouldn't necessarily forfeit that interview in Manhattan yet. Even if you still decide the job isn't for you, you could learn a lot just by meeting the owner and visiting the studio. Trust me, I think it'll be great for you to just see."

Dave was giving me a lot to think about. Why shouldn't I check things out? I had my work here, but I was my own boss, so I could leave anytime I wanted to. My home was paid off, I wasn't in a committed relationship, I had no kids, and dammit, I didn't even have a dog. The sky was the limit for me. I could do anything at this point.

"You've made some great points. I guess part of me, in the back of my mind, is holding out hope that maybe Imani will come back."

"Unless her husband has a total change of heart, that may not happen."

"You're right."

"So, Serenity, I was actually kind of surprised you were in a relationship with a woman. I know you've hooked up with a couple, and I remember that threesome we had once, but I never thought you had any interest in being in a relationship with a woman."

"What's your question?"

"I don't know. I guess I'm asking, are you gay now?"

"You've known me for a while now, Dave. I've never been one to label anything. I don't identify as gay. I enjoyed the experience of being with both Alex and Imani. I didn't expect to connect with Imani as deeply as I did. I just happened to be attracted to her both as a friend and romantically. I'm still very much attracted to men too."

"Well, if it's okay for me to say this, Imani was pretty hot. The two of you did seem happy together. And I'm not just saying that because I was imagining anything, even though that would've been nice. I saw the way you two looked at each other when I came over to your house that day, and I sensed it was a little bit more than just a hook up."

"Yeah, it was pretty nice while it lasted. On another note, what about you? Is there a special someone?"

"No, not really. You know Melissa and I were hanging out for a while, but the spark didn't last. I've been on a few dates, but nothing serious. I think I like being committed to someone rather than just random hookups. I was all for coming home to you every night, Serenity."

"I know you were. And I felt like you were an open-minded person, as well, which is why I was attracted to you. But you weren't ready for dealing with the level of grief I was experiencing. Our life for the most part was pure bliss. You had your career and I had mine. We did things together, had amazing sex, traveled, and lived well, but we also had our own lives. Things were great until shit got real and I lost my mom. My world literally crumbled after that, and we'd never experienced anything so difficult in our relationship before. No one ever knows what to expect in a long-term relationship."

"I get it. But did you see your relationship being long-term with Imani even though she was married?"

"Honestly, this is how I saw it: I was always attracted to both Imani and Alex, but at the beginning, I thought it wasn't even an option because I didn't know if they were into me in that way, so I rarely entertained the thought. The more I got to know them, I knew I was feeling something, but again, their family was already formed, including a baby. When they approached me, I was very open to the idea. Imani struck me as someone who really understood me and my pain and embraced it all. If Alex was fine with Imani and me still having that contact and connection, I think we could've been together for a while."

"Were you in love with her?"

"I believe I was, and I think I still am."

"I see why you're at a crossroads."

"Yeah, it sucks big time. I still want her in my life. I want to call her and talk to her, but I know how the two of us can be. She's my kryptonite, but I'm not comfortable sneaking around. I can't jeopardize my freedom, not even for Imani. I have to face the fear of not having her in my life."

"I didn't know you were going through all of this. I'm sorry, Serenity."

"No need to apologize. Believe it or not, you listening and talking with me helps a lot. I feel like you're asking questions because you're seeking to understand me, and I really appreciate that."

"Anytime. Well, the night is still young. Let's go bowling. I just want you to have some fun. I don't want you to worry about anything or try to figure out your career or Imani. Let's be carefree." By this time, we'd talked so much we walked around most of the outdoor mall where the movie theater was.

"I am definitely down for that. And Dave?"

"What's up?"

I smiled at him. "Thank you."

Dave grabbed me, held me close, and kissed me on the forehead. I liked this space we were in. I think we'd finally moved past what was once a marriage impacted by a huge loss and embraced our newfound friendship. Dave wasn't trying to reel me back in with nostalgia, and I wasn't trying to remind him why we were no longer an option romantically. We both understood where we were, and the acceptance of that was refreshing. It was amazing what time could do.

11

Being back in New York was amazing, nostalgic, but also pretty calm despite being infamously known as a fast-paced city. I hadn't visited New York since Dave and I first got together, and even then, it was a short New Year's Eve trip. I'd missed it, but from a distance. When Cynthia worked as a call girl, she loved going on Fifth Avenue where all the high-end shops were. She could afford any and everything there. I, on the other hand, was more the bohemian, gypsy-type, who rarely had a dollar to her name but was always able to survive.

Nothing compared to the culture of the city. It wasn't just the art and music, but the people. There was something about the people. They were the heartbeat and pulse of the city. Once you had an opportunity to live there, nothing really compared.

When Dave and I settled, I embraced a new way of life on the West Coast. I'd always been open to change, and even though I was a Baltimore girl turned New Yorker, I was game to embrace another environment when Dave and I committed our lives to one another. Now that I was here, it felt weird to be back.

I hadn't told Cynthia I was visiting. I knew she would kill me once she found out, but I really wanted to spend some quality time with New York by myself. I wanted to hear the music of the city, like the trains passing by, the waiters taking orders in the pizza joints, the beggars on every corner, and the sound of nighttime, equipped with honking horns and folks yelling. New York and I were reunited, and it felt so good.

As my Uber continued to get closer to my hotel, the city felt eerily different than I'd once known it to be. New York had evolved, not for better or for worse—just different. I had already accepted that in the thirty-minute ride from the airport. I checked into my hotel, settled in, and took a nice, long, hot shower. I put on my fluffy robe, walked over to the window, and basked in the sights of the city. I was on the tenth floor of the Langham Hotel, and the view was simply amazing.

I sipped some wine and contemplated calling Cynthia to tell her I was here but decided to call her tomorrow. Once Cynthia found out, she would want to go out, stay up, and talk all night, which I just wasn't in the mood for. Paradise Valley taught me how to appreciate quiet, and that was all I wanted right now. I was torn because I wanted the culture, music, and people, but also quiet and solitude.

I checked my email and noticed Kevin sent me a reminder regarding tomorrow's interview. His message was so warm and inviting. He definitely didn't have that New York swag about him. His southern hospitality was very apparent in his message, but I loved when people were still themselves no matter where they went.

I was pretty excited about the interview. Even if I decided not to take the job, it was nice being back in New York. I wouldn't be leaving until Monday. I would get some rest now, go to my interview tomorrow, and catch up with Cynthia later. Once I lied down, the bed engulfed me, and I watched the city from my window like it was a movie. Before I knew it, my eyes began to get heavy and I dozed off to sleep in the city that never slept.

*****

"Hi, my name is Serenity Hayes, and I'm here for a ten o'clock interview with Kevin Lattimore."

I arrived at Yoga Theory and was anxious yet excited at the same time. I was welcomed by warm-colored walls, soft lighting, beautiful hanging lanterns, plywood furniture, bamboo floors, and amazing artworks of various yoga poses that graced the walls. I thought our yoga studio in Scottsdale was a sight to see, but this one was a masterpiece. It was apparent the designers were meticulous and paid extreme attention to detail when this building was being conceptualized.

"Oh, yes, Kevin is expecting you and will be available shortly. Can I offer you some tea or water while you wait?" The receptionist's aura was delightful, professional, and inviting at the same time.

"Oh, no, I'm fine, but thank you." I smiled, as I was determined to return the energy she gave to me.

All of a sudden, I heard a male's voice approaching the lobby. It sounded like it was Kevin, but I'd only spoken to him a couple times on the phone, so I wasn't quite sure.

"Serenity?"

"Yes, that's me. Kevin?"

"Yes, it's such a pleasure to meet you. Come on back to my office." Kevin gave me a firm handshake followed by a pretty gorgeous smile.

I didn't know why, but I was caught off guard by how attractive he was. I guessed I wasn't expecting that because I was so focused on the interview. Kevin was dressed in a linen shirt, fitted chino pants that exposed his ankles, along with some penny loafers. I could tell he was professional but had a Feng Shui vibe about him.

He guided me to his office, and I noticed his bowlegged walk.

"Thanks so much for agreeing to meet with me on the weekend. I know this isn't how you normally do things, so thank you," I said.

"No need to thank me. Your experience and reputation speak for themselves, which is why I really wanted to make this happen."

"Well, thank you. I'm honored."

"Great, let's get down to business. I do have another meeting right after this, so I want to make sure I give you the full background of the studio and also allow you time to ask me any questions as well."

Kevin and I discussed his business, which was really intriguing to me. He had been a yoga instructor himself but was more attracted to business, which led him here. Kevin had attended Texas Southern University and even mentioned he was a drummer in the band at one point. Our conversation was pretty relaxed, but I appreciated him providing me with little nuggets about himself so I could understand him more as a person. I also shared my experience and background. At one point, I noticed Kevin seemed a little more smitten than he should be toward a potential hire, but he never veered from his professionalism. I really liked his style, his vision, and what he offered to the health and wellness industry. I felt like there was so much for me to learn from him.

"Kevin, can I be totally frank?"

"Sure, I encourage it."

"You're an entrepreneur, so for some reason, I think you will understand where I'm going with this. I haven't worked for anyone in a long time. My business isn't on as large a scale as yours, but it's mine, and I enjoy it. However, something about this place feels right. I get that you feel I have a lot to offer your business, but I also feel like I can learn a lot from you."

"I think whatever it is you're feeling, deep down inside, you already know which way you want to go." Kevin smiled, and dammit, his smile was captivating.

"Now that's something I would say to someone in class." I chuckled a bit.

"Serenity, you don't have to decide at this moment. I really want you to make the best decision for you. This will change your entire lifestyle, especially if you have family to consider."

"Nope, that's not the case." Kevin's face lightened a bit when I said that.

"Again, I want you to be totally sure. I do understand your point as it pertains to entrepreneurship, but honestly, I love working with other entrepreneurs because they just get it. I hired another entrepreneur for my Maryland location and wouldn't have it any other way. Entrepreneurs are already innovators, thinkers, problem solvers, and I value that because you all breathe life into my businesses. I need people around me who understand they're not just employees but also believe in the vision and are willing to be challenged and grow. I'm not intimidated at all by that. I crave that sense of community."

I really valued Kevin's mindset. He oozed a certain level of confidence that appeared to require no effort.

"I really like that, Kevin. I appreciate your forward thinking."

I found myself getting more and more excited about this opportunity, but I didn't want him to think he had me in the bag just yet.

"Well, like I said, sleep on it, and if you can give me an answer within the next week, that would be great. I want to give you enough time, as I know you probably have a lot of things to consider. If it's any consolation, just know I'm prepared to discuss things you need in order to consider this position. I take my business seriously and I have to ensure I have only the best people representing the Yoga Theory brand. I believe you would be a great fit."

"Thank you, and yes, I do have a lot to think about, so I'll be in touch soon."

"Great. Before I have to get out of here for this meeting, I would love to show you the entire studio, but be prepared: it's jaw-dropping."

"Well, if it's anything like the lobby, I know I'll be mesmerized."

Kevin grinned. "Then prepare to be mesmerized."

As Kevin gave me a tour of the studio, I could really feel his excitement and passion for Yoga Theory. He explained the history of the studio and the reasoning behind its design. There was a purpose to everything he did which was lovely to hear about.

"I'm amazed by this place. You have a true passion for yoga. I can tell."

"I feel like that's the only way to be. I'm definitely a go-getter at heart. I remember, as early as five years old, talking to my parents about how I wanted to teach people how to exercise because I was so fond of my gym teacher."

"Wow, at five years old? That's cool. I just remember always being seen as a hippie kind of girl growing up in the hood in Baltimore. I've always loved fitness as well, and I remember experimenting with different foods when my mom realized she had high blood pressure and diabetes."

"Yes, I can understand that. Does your mom do yoga as well?"

"My mom passed away almost four years ago."

"Oh, I'm so sorry. I didn't mean to come off insensitive."

"Please, no apologies at all. You didn't know. She wasn't exactly the yoga type, but she always encouraged me when it came to the path I chose to take. She never made fun or questioned my judgments with food choices or my career path. She did, however, start changing her diet when she noticed positive changes in how she felt and looked. I believe she would've gone fully vegetarian or vegan if she lived longer. She was amazing." I found myself slipping into that space where I would get lost in my thoughts about my mom.

"I can tell. You're exactly what Yoga Theory is about. I want people to understand the lifestyle we lead is not just about yoga, but it's a mindset, it's changing your diet, it's encouraging others no matter where they are in their journey, and it's about truly living. Thank you for sharing that about your mom. I'm always appreciative when people allow themselves to be vulnerable."

"Thank you for allowing me the space to feel comfortable enough to share."

There was a long pause where we found ourselves staring at each other.

"Serenity, I'm so glad you decided to participate in this interview. I'm hoping to hear from you soon with some great news, but no matter which decision you make, please know I support you in your endeavors. I really believe you're a huge asset to the wellness industry, and I want to continue to support your journey."

"That's so nice of you to say. Thank you."

"Seriously, I mean that." Kevin reached for a hug. It wasn't a typical salutation after an interview, but I enjoyed his embrace. It felt genuine and comforting.

His scent lingered, and his energy alleviated any stress and nervousness I had been feeling. I wasn't expecting that, and even though I found myself attracted to him, it was something about his soul that seemed familiar. Just like when I stepped off the plane and arrived in New York, I felt like I was home.

"I can tell."

"Well, please be safe returning to Arizona. I really enjoyed meeting you, and I hope to hear from you soon."

"Thank you, and you will."

As I began walking out of the door, I happened to turn back around, thinking I left my sunglasses. I didn't; they were actually on my head, but Kevin was still standing there looking at me. Part of me wanted to go back in there and ask if maybe he and I could have dinner later, but I thought that was too forward and inappropriate. I was never the one to disregard how I was feeling, especially if I was feeling a significant attraction to someone, but I decided to just leave it be. This was a job interview, so I remained focused on that. I really wanted one last encounter with Kevin before my flight back to Arizona, but if that were to happen, I wouldn't force it. I would just allow it to come.

I continued to walk toward my hotel on the busy streets of New York when, all of a sudden, my phone rang. It was Imani. I contemplated not even answering it. I just couldn't imagine what there was to talk about. But my curiosity got the better of me, and I answered.

"Hello," I answered formally.

"Hey, Serenity."

"Hey, Imani. How are you?"

"I guess I deserve that distant greeting. I'm okay."

I was silent. I didn't feel the need to force this conversation. "I'm not being distant. I'm just being polite," I finally said.

"I can hear the disappointment in your voice, Serenity, and I really just wanted to call to say I'm sorry."

"I appreciate your apology, and you're forgiven."

"So, you're not upset with me anymore?"

"No, I'm not upset. In order for me to move on, I have to release the anger I had about the situation and the anger I felt toward you. There have been some days that were hard because I genuinely love you, Imani. I care about your well-being. I care about who you are as a person. I enjoyed every minute I spent with you. You brought something new and fresh to my life, and I will always be grateful for that."

"Oh my God, thank you, Serenity. I thought you were still angry with me. I thought you'd never would want to speak to me again. It was tearing me up inside."

"So, how are Alex and Yaya?"

I could feel Imani trying to possibly slide her way back in because I felt like I knew enough to know her style. I didn't think she was being deceitful, but I knew how she was when she wanted something.

"They're fine. Yaya is getting bigger by the minute, getting into everything. But she's the light of my life."

"That's good to hear. And Alex?"

"I guess he's fine. Things have gotten pretty busy at work lately, so he's been gone more often. I don't know. I've been getting the sense that he's seeing someone. I can't prove it, but his demeanor is different, his later nights are a lot later than usual, and I stumbled across a receipt from a restaurant that clearly looked like it was dinner for two. When I asked him that evening why he had gotten home so late, he mentioned he had to work late at the office because of a client. He didn't provide much detail and I didn't want to upset him by appearing jealous, so I dropped it."

I felt like Imani was preluding to something, but I didn't assume, so I just let her talk.

"I'm sorry to hear that, Imani. Alex seems to be a standup guy. I'm pretty sure if you're calm and just tell him how you feel, he'll put your worries to rest. He really loves you." I was keeping things very direct with Imani. I didn't want to go down that road with her.

"I love how you always choose to see the bright side of things. You're always so optimistic."

"Well, I think it's only fair to give people the benefit of the doubt until they prove themselves otherwise." That was sort of a dig, not a huge one, but I don't think Imani even picked up on that.

"Yeah, you're right. So, I actually just put Yaya down for a nap. Are you free to come over? Maybe we can talk more in person?"

"Unfortunately, I won't be able to. I'm sorry."

"It's okay. Did I catch you at a bad time? Are you busy?" I could tell Imani was intrigued with what I was doing and wanted to know why I was turning down her invitation, but I didn't feel I owed her an explanation.

"I'm sort of in the middle of something right now."

"Oh, okay, maybe later this evening? Alex is working later."

"I won't be able to make it later either because I'm in New York right now."

"Oh, wow, New York? Visiting Cynthia?" Imani was digging for answers.

"I'm not visiting her right now. I will before I head back home, though."

"So, if you don't mind my asking, why are you there?" Imani was really pushing it now, and I must admit hearing her voice did something to me.

"Imani, I'll be honest with you. You know I care about you, but you've given up that right to question what's going on in my life. I promise I'm not upset with you, but I'm pretty sure Alex wouldn't like it if he knew you were contacting me right now."

"Seriously, Serenity? Don't do that."

"Don't do what? Be honest? Or would you rather I pretend we still have something and do all this cake shit over the phone so when I get back, I come over when Alex isn't home and make love to you? I mean, I could do that, and you know I do it well, but that's not what I want for myself. I want full transparency. I've accepted that's not the kind of relationship you and Alex have, so I don't want to interfere with that."

"You're not being fair."

"You know, there was a time when I felt like we understood each other without words, but now that feels lost. If you knew me at all, you would know how much I cared about you. I care about you so much that I'm willing to let you go. You want to keep sneaking around, and I'm not interested."

"Please, Serenity, just give me some time to work this out with Alex. I miss you!"

"Work what out? Imani, be honest, you love him because he's the father of your child, y'all have history, and he takes care of you financially. Please don't take offense to this. You're a good actress. You serve your man very well. But the look in your eyes when I'm serving you is what I don't see when you're with him. You're missing that, and I'm not here to tell you to leave or stay with Alex, but I know what I know, and I don't want to get caught up in that. You're not ready for the level of authenticity I want."

"Babe, please don't shut me out like this. I've been missing our talks, our quality time, your hands on my body, and I need you." I could hear Imani crying over the phone.

"Listen, Imani, please don't cry. It sounds like you have a lot to think about. I can be your acquaintance, but I can't get wrapped up with you right now. That's not fair to me. I love you, and I always will, but I have to go." I hung up the phone without even saying goodbye.

It hurt, but I had to do it because I also loved myself, and I felt like there was more for me than waiting on Imani to figure her shit out. I didn't want to hurt her, but I just couldn't get wrapped up in her world right now. I was ready to move on. My phone began to ring again, but I just couldn't keep talking to Imani right now. When I looked down, it was Kevin. Why would he be calling right now?

"Hello?"

"Hey, Serenity. Did I catch you at a bad time?"

"No, I guess you probably just hear the surprise in my voice."

"It's okay. My meeting was cancelled. The person I was scheduled to meet with had a family emergency and had to reschedule."

"Oh, I'm sorry to hear that."

"I'm pretty sure he would appreciate that. The reason I was calling was because I know you mentioned you weren't heading back to Arizona until Monday, and I was wondering if you had some time to maybe meet for dinner?"

"Oh, okay. Was there something else you wanted to discuss regarding the interview?" I kind of sensed it wasn't that, but I didn't want to assume anything.

"Serenity, in all transparency, I'm asking you out on a date. I kind of went back and forth after the interview, wondering if you would be completely turned off by my forwardness. Just let me know if this makes you uncomfortable and you can totally disregard my advance. This will not affect the interview process." Kevin was so straightforward, which I thought was extremely attractive.

"I would actually love that."

"Okay, great! I was hoping you'd say yes. I can stop by your hotel and pick you up at eight. Do you have a preference regarding what you eat, or are you pretty laid back like you were when I was booking your travel arrangements?" Kevin chuckled.

"Well, I'm a vegetarian, so…"

"Your wish is my command, Ms. Hayes. I'll see you at eight o'clock then."

"I'm looking forward to it." I couldn't help but smile as I returned to my hotel room.

Kevin appeared to be very interested in me, but I also got the impression he wasn't necessarily looking for a relationship. After all, he was willing to shoot his shot and would be okay even if for some reason I wasn't interested. There was freedom in that, I believed.

When I met Kevin, I saw someone who was healthy not only physically but mentally. Growing up, all I saw was abuse. I constantly saw my mom in pain, whether it was from my dad, her job, or her family disowning her because she married a black man, even though she was biracial herself. James turned to the streets for survival, and Ellis moved as far away as possible to escape the hellhole we were in at the time.

Dave was amazing in a lot of ways, but he too struggled with his demons of abuse growing up. I thought Imani was a breath of fresh air because we instantly hit it off and seemed to connect so deeply, but for whatever reason, she was also struggling with who she really was and what she wanted for her life. I preferred honesty, and she was acting like that was a foreign concept.

I had been on a long journey of personal development and was no longer interested in attaching myself to things or people who didn't serve my higher purpose. I felt like everything Mama went through was for me to learn that I deserved more. I believed Mama actually wanted me to be the person I'd become. She always encouraged me to stand out, be my own person, and not succumb to what others wanted for me. Even when people said I was weird, different, and wondered why I couldn't do what everyone else was doing, she made me feel like I could do anything. When I saw Kevin, I saw someone who matched that same energy, someone who's happy with who he is. I wanted that in my life.

I sent Cynthia a text finally letting her know I was here. There was no way I could be in New York and not let her know. She would want to see me. While I waited for her response, I grabbed one of the hotel pens on my desk, pulled out my notebook from my luggage at the foot of my bed and began journaling. I started writing about when I first met Dr. Wilson. Journaling helped me deal with the pain and agony I felt after Mama's death, but I found myself writing more these days to just reflect on how far I'd come since then.

I was excited about tonight. For some reason, I felt like something really great was going to come from dinner. The more I entertained the job in my mind, the more I could feel myself leaning toward accepting the offer. I was starting to feel an evolution taking place within myself. Before I came on this trip, I was finding things to hold me back from this job like the weather, my clients, and the change in lifestyle, but what if this was my something new? What if everything that had happened in my life up until this point had been leading me here? I felt in my gut it was time to find out.

I lay in bed and continued to write, taking in the sounds of New York, which felt like the soundtrack to my new life. I felt, deep down inside, I had already made my decision and immediately felt a sense of calmness come over me. This was going to be my new life. I didn't want to tell anyone yet because I wanted to sit with the thought for a while by myself. I wanted to bask in what was on the horizon for me.

*****

"Wow, Serenity, you look absolutely beautiful."

Kevin and I met in my hotel lobby. Even though we could've met at the restaurant, he insisted on meeting at my hotel and taking an Uber. He said he asked me out on a date, so he wanted it to feel like a real date from beginning to end. I was always a pretty laid-back person who was fine with just meeting up, splitting the tab, and making my own way back home, but this felt different. I felt like Kevin was going to pull out all of the stops tonight.

"Thank you. You look extremely handsome yourself."

Even though Kevin was a Southern dude, and his Southern drawl was apparent when he spoke, he assimilated to the East Coast vibe. While he adapted the fast-paced energy needed for New York, something about him put me at ease. He wore his collared shirt with the sleeves rolled up, exposing his hairy chest, and chino shorts with Chuck Taylor's. On his strong and manly arms, he wore a chakra healing bracelet.

"Aw, you don't have to say that just because I commented on how beautiful you looked."

We both smiled at each other, and I chuckled. "Whatever."

"You really have a gorgeous smile, Serenity."

"Well, I have a great dentist."

"Actually, your teeth are nice too, but I was speaking of the aura that's bouncing off of you right now. You just seem really happy."

If the start of this date was any indication, I was in for an amazing evening.

"Well, I am pretty happy. You know how you have this feeling, like some things are changing in your life? You don't know how any of it's going to unfold, but you embrace change. Sorry, I guess I'm getting a little too deep." I chuckled a bit and glanced away. I could feel myself getting a little nervous around Kevin.

"I know exactly what you mean."

By the way he looked into my eyes, I could tell he was interested in getting to know more about me. He even seemed excited to learn more about what was behind my smile.

"I'm really excited about checking out this vegan restaurant you're raving about." I changed the subject. I didn't want to give off too much sexual energy too soon, even though I didn't know if that could even be avoided.

"Oh, yeah, I hope you like it. I'm a Southern dude that happens to live in New York, so I love soul food. Whenever I have a taste for it, I hit up this spot. It being vegan helps me to not feel as guilty about indulging."

"Ha! I like that."

"Yeah, and here's our stop."

I was happy how well he treated the driver, giving him a large tip, and I couldn't help the smile tugging at the corners of my lips as he jumped out of the car to open the door for me. Kevin opened my door, took my hand, and escorted me out of the car. It was funny because Dave and I saw each other as equals, so he didn't really cater to the chivalry idea, but this was really nice. I liked his Southern hospitality, but I liked how attentive he was to me even more.

We walked into the restaurant, and Kevin appeared to know everyone who worked there as if he'd returned home. Everyone was giving him hugs and pounds. They smiled at me like he was bringing home his girl to meet Mom.

"Wow, you know a lot of people here."

"Brooklyn is one of my favorite places in New York. I come here all the time. I just like feeling connected to my people, you know?"

"Trust me, I understand. I felt like that when I went to NYU, and that's exactly how I felt when I saw black neighbors for the first time in Paradise Valley."

"See, you already know what time it is."

"What's up, black man!" One of the workers called, a bright grin on his face.

"Man, just hanging out for a quick bite to eat. Yo, this is Serenity."

"Well, how are you, beautiful young lady?" I was greeted by an older man who appeared to be in his mid-sixties, who also might have been the owner seeing as he wasn't wearing an apron like everyone else and appeared to be in charge.

"I'm well. It smells amazing in here."

"And I guarantee it tastes amazing! Let me seat you guys and have someone bring you over some menus."

"Aight, Nipsey."

Nipsey darted his eyes between the two of us, smiling as if Kevin hit the jackpot. It was kind of cute. Kevin pulled out my chair, and even though we were in a very causal spot, he was still the ultimate gentleman.

"I can't wait to dive into this food. It smells so good! How long has this place been around?"

"I think it's been about five years now. That's right. You went to school in New York. Where did you like spending a lot of your time?"

"Oh, I loved going to Harlem. It was just one of those areas where I felt like I could totally be myself, and it was always so welcoming of all kinds of black people. With me being biracial and pretty eclectic, I always appreciated that."

"I can totally understand that. When I talk to you, I feel like there's so much more than meets the eye. I can't remember, did you say you were from New York?"

"No, I don't think I ever said where I was from." I smiled at Kevin because I could tell he wanted to get to know more about me. "I actually grew up in Baltimore, still the East Coast."

"Oh, okay, cool. How did you end up in Arizona of all places?"

"Well, when I met my ex-husband, he was living in Silicon Valley at the time, then we ended up moving to Arizona after he started a few businesses there."

"Okay, gotcha. I didn't realize you were divorced."

"Yeah, it's been about two years now. We're still friends, though." I wanted Kevin to understand that, yes, I still kept in contact with my ex, and even though I wasn't interested in rekindling our relationship, I was definitely not interested in someone dictating who I could and could not speak to. The sooner he realized that, the better.

"I can understand that. I'm still friends with my ex-girlfriend. She's married now and has a toddler and baby on the way, but we're still good."

Good, I could dig that about Kevin. I didn't sense any weirdness on his part about me still having a friendship with my ex, and I was fine with the fact that he did the same thing.

"That's wonderful to hear. It's always a good thing if people can still remain cordial, and even friends, after a breakup."

"You seem to be a free-thinker, Serenity. I like that."

"Well, it depends on how much freedom you're comfortable with." I laughed to myself.

"What do you mean by that?" Kevin questioned.

"So, I know this is a first date and all, and I'm totally fine with sharing more about myself, so…"

"Hey, Serenity, you don't have to premise anything with me. You can say whatever is on your mind. It's best for us to show each other who we really are anyway."

I really liked Kevin so far. The aroma of vegan mac and cheese and greens was putting me in a great mood as well.

"So, the reason my husband and I divorced was because when my mom died, the grief really took a toll on me. It affected me more than I expected, and he had a hard time dealing with it. I mean, don't get me wrong, I grieved for a long time, and he struggled with that, but I didn't think it was grounds for divorce. Throughout the five years we were married, we really didn't deal with a lot of stress in our marriage. I mean, everyone has disagreements, but I can't say a lot rocked our marriage except for my mom's death. I lost my appetite, I lost my desire for sex, I had a hard time teaching my yoga classes that he eventually took over. I barely said anything to him. Fast forward to my life within the past year, I was feeling better. I had a couple of panic attacks, but I was seeing my therapist and then eventually I got involved in another relationship. I was dating a husband and a wife, but the wife and I started connecting a lot more than her and her husband. So, needless to say, that didn't work out."

"Wow."

"See, I asked you first how much freedom you were comfortable with. So let's just enjoy this food, and if I'm a bit much, I totally understand." I knew Kevin was going to head straight for the door.

"I'm saying wow because I don't think I've ever met a woman who is so confident but so cool to be around. Your transparency is attractive."

My eyes blinked in surprise. "Are you serious?"

"Yeah, everything you said was so unguarded. You don't know me at all, but you chose to share that, even though you probably thought this date would end after that. But you still exposed yourself. Why?"

"Honestly, because I accept every part of my journey. When my mom died, I felt like I went to hell and back. I don't want to waste a moment not embracing who I truly am and what I've been through. I am who I am, and there's nothing wrong with that. You'll either embrace who I am or not. I would never force anyone to think how I think, or like what I like. But I am me. And that's more than enough."

"Damn! Where the hell did you come from?"

"What do you mean?"

"You are so beautiful. Your energy right now is seriously radiating this room!"

"So, you mean to tell me you're cool with everything I said?"

"It's not about being cool with anything. I just respect your viewpoint. The way you think and feel is drawing me in. I want to learn more about you."

"Listen, you think that's some shit. If I told you how I grew up…"

"Well, that's what I'm saying; I can tell you have an easy-going demeanor, but you have a fire in you as well. I really like that. Damn, is all I can say." Kevin started laughing and shaking his head while glancing at the menu. It was kind of funny because he seemed to really appreciate who I was but was amazed to meet someone like me.

"You're funny, Kevin."

"And dammit, you're fine. I could tell there was something about you when I met you at the interview. I didn't realize it was gonna be all of this."

"Speaking of the interview…"

"Girl, hold on, let's order this food. You've messed me up for a minute—in a good way, of course." His Southern drawl popped out a little bit.

"Okay, I know what I want."

"Yeah, me too." Kevin signaled for the waitress to come over and take our orders. Once we relayed what we wanted, he said, "Okay, so lay it on me. You wanted to talk about the interview."

"There's not much to talk about. I just wanted to let you know I'm accepting the offer."

"Okay let me put on my professional hat for a minute. Thank you so much for coming on board. I'm excited for you to join the company. I know you're going to do amazing things. I'll be sure to connect you with HR next week to start the paperwork, and then we can work out a timeline for when you'll start based on your move from Arizona."

"Okay, great. I'm excited!"

"Okay, now I'm going to take that hat off again and tell you that you made my entire evening. Only a few hours after meeting you, I'm in awe of you. I really look forward to getting to know you more."

"Same here."

We both smiled at each other and enjoyed our meal. We continued to talk, and I continued to reflect on my life. I was taking life by the horns at that point and following my heart, and I was really excited about it.

CHAPTER

12

I swore, just when I thought my life was heading one way, it took a turn, but this time, it felt like it was for the best. I was nervous about this move but in a good way. I was excited about being so much closer to Cynthia and my brother again. It would be like old times. I'd have to wrap my brain around cold weather again, but I knew I could do it. I was devising a plan with my yoga students and connecting with my colleagues in the industry in order to ensure my students were in good hands. I was really going to miss seeing Dr. Wilson too. I knew I hadn't been going to her office consistently for a while, but it was nice to talk to her on the phone, which wouldn't have to change, but going to her house wouldn't be as easy anymore.

I was debating if I should tell Imani. I didn't feel like I owed her anything, but even in that short amount of time, I felt like her and I shared something pretty special, and I didn't want to just leave her hanging like that. I'd probably just reach out to her and Alex together.

As I walked around my house and reflected upon my trip to New York, about what was ahead for me, I couldn't help thinking about all of the memories here. This was where Dave and I made a house a home, but this was also the place I lived when Mama died. Maybe this move would be good for me. Maybe it was finally time to fully move on. I didn't have much time to sell the house before moving. I thought about either making it a rental property or preparing it to become an Airbnb. There were plenty of possibilities, especially because it was paid off and I owned it.

I wondered how Dave would feel about my move, not that it was a determining factor in my decision, but he had been a huge part of my life for a while now. Even though he encouraged me to take that trip to New York, now everything was really happening, and I was heading out of here.

Kevin and I really hit it off. I really liked him and was interested in exploring a friendship with him at the very least. I wasn't quite sure of anything more just yet because I was focused on this new career path, but if something blossomed between us, I didn't think I'd deny it. I wasn't making it a priority, though. I got the sense he would understand that.

Kevin was nice enough to connect me with some of his favorite realtors who could assist me in my apartment hunt. I was going to also take some time in the afternoon to go through those. I had already been saying to myself I wanted to downsize.

It was fun to go with the flow because I was so open to embracing this new chapter of my life. On the first day of classes after my return from New York, it felt different driving into work knowing I only had a few more weeks before moving on. When I told Kevin I would take the job, he asked if I could start in a month, and I agreed. As soon as I got back from my trip, I began looking at my calendar and making a checklist of things that needed to get done from week to week, and slowly closing down my business was one of them.

I grabbed my car keys, walked out the door, hopped in my car and headed to work. When I pulled into the parking lot of the yoga studio, I had to do a double-take because it looked like Imani's white convertible BMW was parked in front of the studio. As I eased closer, the license plate was recognizable. I could tell the person sitting in the driver's seat was her. She must've seen me because her car door opened, and she walked toward the entrance of the studio as if to meet me there.

"Hey, Imani. What are you doing here?"

"I know you open up the studio on Thursday mornings by yourself, and I just really wanted to talk to you."

"Why didn't you just call me?" I asked while unlocking the door to the front entrance.

"Well, because the last time we talked, I tried explaining myself to you, but then you hung up on me." Imani's voice began to elevate a bit.

"Hey, Imani, do you think we can possibly talk about this after work? People are going to start heading in in about thirty minutes or so, and they don't need to be privy to our conversation." I tried to remain calm.

"Serenity, can we please just talk in your office? Please?" Imani insisted.

I signaled Imani to my desk. Something was obviously really pressing on her mind.

We walked into my office and Imani paced around the room, even though I signaled her to sit and try to calm down.

"Imani, what is it? You seem really bothered by something."

"Alex wants another baby!" Imani just blurted it out, and a tear fell from her eye. I could tell it wasn't what she wanted.

"So, what did you tell him?"

"I said I didn't think now was the right time, and he asked why not. We're financially stable, in good health, we've made some friends in Arizona, so our support system is growing. He said Yaya needs a sibling."

"Sounds like all good reasons to me to increase your family."

"Dammit, Serenity! I'm in love with you. You know damn well this isn't what I want, but you're acting so nonchalant, like you don't care!" Imani began yelling at this point.

"Okay, listen, Imani, I really need you to calm down at my place of work."

"I'm sorry, babe. I just can't do this anymore. I just can't. I think Alex really just wants to keep me barefoot and pregnant. What better way to keep me locked down than by having another baby?" Imani began crying again.

"Okay, let's backtrack for a minute. When I first met you and Alex, you seemed so into him. I mean, the way y'all looked at each other and held each other appeared so genuine. And when you invited me into your relationship, I honestly thought your bond was strong enough to handle having a third person. I really felt like we would hang out, then I would go home, and y'all would still have your tight-knit family. And, of course, we became more attracted to each other and more intimate, but I still thought it was something we could all maintain together. I like Alex. I think he's a great guy."

"C'mon, Serenity, you and I both know Alex is incredibly sexy, smart, and stable. But you and I are fire together. I can't get enough of you when I'm around you. I don't get that anymore from Alex."

"Babe, that's because I'm still new to you. Once the novelty wears off, you'll grow more comfortable with me too. Everything is not all about me eating your pussy all day long."

"Don't talk like that to me right now. It's doing something to me."

"I'm not trying to get you aroused, I'm really not. I'm just trying to get you to see the bigger picture. I would've totally been fine with still being with you but not if we had to lie about it."

"But Alex wouldn't go for that."

"Honestly, Imani, how do you know? Have you ever talked with him about it?"

"Look at how he's been! When we came back from Bali, he didn't even want me to see you!"

"Okay. He missed you. He just wanted some alone time with you. That wasn't too much to ask, now was it?"

"Are you serious right now, Serenity? Have you forgotten about how he wanted me to break it off with—"

"Right, Miss Iris Senegal. Yeah, thanks for the reminder," I said sarcastically.

"Don't do me like that."

"Do you like what? You're the one bringing up the chick that got away. See, this is why I said let's talk about this later. You're getting my chakras out of balance before I start this class."

"Babe, listen to me! I wasn't trying to upset you. I just don't want to have another baby with him."

"Well, then don't. Fuck it! Why are you telling me this?"

"Because I want to leave him, Serenity, and be with you! That's what I want. I want you, dammit!"

I couldn't believe Imani dropped this bomb on me right before work, right when I decided to take this job in New York. Imani sat on top of my desk looking as if she wanted nothing more than to just be with me. She looked so damn beautiful, too, with her floral mini dress that exposed her thighs. Could, for one moment, I throw caution to the wind and just make love to her on my desk and tell her we would figure it out together? I wanted to kiss her so badly and hold her and tell her it would be okay. But I didn't want to give her false hope. It just wouldn't be fair.

"Imani, I want to have more time to talk with you about this. Can we please finish this conversation tonight? Are you able to stop by my house?"

"Yeah, I guess," Imani said somberly.

"I know you're upset, but I really gotta get to work, babe. Let's connect tonight."

"Okay." Imani walked over to me and kissed me. I missed the feel of her body, the softness of her lips, and her sweet scent. "I'll see you tonight."

Imani left the studio, and I felt so lost at that moment. I knew where all this was headed if I gave in to Imani and allowed her to get what she wanted. She was at a crossroads in her life and needed to figure that shit out, but I couldn't say I was interested in waiting on her to decide. Of course, I could say what the hell and go with the flow, but everything had a cost, and I wasn't interested in paying the price on finding that one out.

I decided to really get lost in my classes today. I wanted to enjoy the space I was sharing with my students. I was so thankful to have a career that not only paid the bills but also provided an outlet for me. I really needed this today.

I often wondered, was I who Imani really wanted, or was she going through a phase in her life, or even trying to compensate for what she really wanted years ago? That was why I saw red flags with this. Alex had no clue what Imani truly desired, which was not a threesome where each party felt safe expressing their true wants. But why didn't she feel safe expressing that? Did Alex create that energy in their relationship, or was that Imani's personal hang up? I didn't want to diagnose Imani, but I just wanted to be with her and was open to a relationship with Alex as well.

It was clear Imani did not want that. She wanted me, and even though I was happy about that part, I couldn't get with someone who wasn't as comfortable being free and transparent as I was. I knew it would cause a lot of issues down the line.

I could hear people outside and knew it was time to unlock the doors and allow students to come in. When I opened the door, that hot Arizona heat grazed my face immediately. It took me some time to get used to the temperature when I first moved here, but eventually, I did. This had been home for a little over a decade now, and I felt a sense of nostalgia for the past. Memories of when Dave opened up the juice bar in this plaza and when

I held my first class here at the studio popped up in my mind. As I let the students in, I saw Melissa standing in front of the juice bar talking with what looked like a very handsome man, but I could only see the back of him. I tried to hurry up and close the door so she wouldn't see me. I would always appreciate her for connecting me with Lisa, but she was still annoying. Melissa looked a bit occupied anyway as her and the mystery guy started kissing. This was definitely a passionate kiss. They also hugged for a while, and before I knew it, the guy turned around.

It was Alex.

*****

Imani was on her way over to my house, and I felt this weirdness in the pit of my stomach. Seeing Alex with Melissa really threw me off. You would think I would be happy about this, as I could just tell Imani about Alex and that would make her decision easier, but I didn't think it was that cut and dry. This was her husband, the one she'd been sharing a home and a life with, along with having a child together. If anything, this was going to make her even more upset because she'd been denying herself what she wanted while he was out doing what he wanted to do without her knowledge.

I wrestled with what to do. Part of me wanted to call Alex and talk to him about it, but then another part of me thought I should just leave well enough alone and get ready to move on and start my new life. What was crazy was that Imani was just at my studio a little before him. I wish she could've seen that and just dealt with it herself.

All this time, Imani had known where I worked, my favorite place to eat, and so many other things about me, but Alex had never been to the studio, nor did he seem interested. What were the odds I would see him kissing another woman in the same plaza as my studio, and it would be Melissa of all people?

I started to cook dinner, but I didn't want her to stay any longer than she should, so I decided to eat after she left. I didn't even know what we needed to talk about. I felt so selfish thinking this way, but I didn't want to get caught up in any of their family problems. I needed to remind myself I was the third in their relationship, and whatever they chose to do from this point on was not my concern.

The doorbell rang, and when I opened the door, Imani was standing there in the same floral mini dress she wore earlier—a couple more buttons were unbuttoned—she clearly wanted to greet me with her breasts. I invited her in, and she hugged me tight and thanked me for allowing her to come over.

"I've really missed coming over here, Serenity. Thanks for meeting with me. I've been in a mood the entire day. I feel like Yaya can sense it too."

"Well, I was always in tune with my mom since I was a little girl. I could always tell when she was happy, upset, or worried. Kids really can pick up on these things."

"Yeah, that's why I gotta get myself together quick."

"Well, don't rush, but I think you owe it to yourself and Alex to talk about your real feelings about having another child."

"I can't do that."

"Seriously, you can't keep hiding from him. You're going to eventually have to talk about your true feelings. Does he even know you're here right now?"

"Of course not!"

"See, I can't do this right now."

"You can't do what?"

"This!" I waved my arms and hands between us.

"Serenity, I can only be myself with you!"

"Well, if you're that pressed about it, you need to tell him because I am not going to be running around, hiding and sneaking. You can seriously hang that up. I'm a grown-ass woman, and when I want to talk to you, see you, go out with you, make love to you, I'm not asking another grown person for permission. C'mon now!"

"I know, I know! I'm just so confused."

"You're not confused, honey, you're not ready to rearrange your world right now, and I have been telling you for the longest time that I get it. I'm not forcing your hand. I'm just letting you know what I can handle and this shit ain't it. I'm not going to get caught in the middle of y'all's lies."

"Serenity, what the hell are you talking about? *Y'all's* lies?"

When Imani said that, it hit me that I almost slipped up and gave away the fact that I knew more about Alex than she did. I had to figure out a way to clean up what I said.

"You know what I mean. I'm talking about you not feeling comfortable telling Alex how you feel about me. It's not my fault you came over here, looking like that and throwing off my thought process."

As soon as I said that, I realized I put my foot in my mouth again because now Imani was looking at me as if she wanted to say fuck this conversation and just have sex. And, of course, she had that look in her eyes, and she started walking over to me seductively after I made a point to stay at least six feet away from her.

"Babe, I know I have so much to sort out, so how about this? I will talk with Alex tomorrow, I promise. I will tell him about wanting to have you back in our lives."

"But that's not what you want. You want *me* back in your life, and you don't want Alex anymore, unless that's changed."

"I mean, maybe the three of us can work something out."

"There you go again, not being real with yourself."

"What do you expect me to do, Serenity? I can't rip my family apart."

"And I know that, and I don't expect you to. I just don't want to get caught up in the middle of all this when the shit hits the fan."

"But aren't you the one who said you were okay with it being the three of us? You said I should be honest."

"Listen, Imani, the three of us is not what you want, and if Alex decides he doesn't want me in the picture, you're going to appease him and leave me out but expect me to sneak around with you, and I ain't doing it."

"Oh my God, can we please just stop this? I want you, Serenity, and I need you right now. I need to feel your touch. I need to touch you, caress you, and kiss you."

As Imani was talking, she was trying to entice me. She started rubbing her thighs, allowing her dress to slide further upward. Then she started unbuttoning her dress even more, and it was just a matter of time before she was sitting on my lap and had the nerve to come over here with no panties on. She guided my hand between her legs while she whispered in my ear how much she loved me and needed me. I tried so hard to deny her, but she kept pushing her titties in my face, and I gave in.

We made love as if it were the last day on earth. Our love was literally imprinted across that whole house from the living room couch, to the kitchen, to the stairs, and the bedroom. I didn't even think it was possible to orgasm that much in one session, but we did. We landed in my bed, and as Imani continued to kiss my neck while we were lying there, I kept thinking about not only the fact that Alex was out in the open with another woman she knew nothing about, but now I was trying to figure out when I was going to drop the bomb that I was moving to New York. Cynthia told me I was going to run into some problems with Imani before I left, and I swore up and down I wouldn't.

"Hey, Imani, I have something I need to tell you."

"What's that, babe?" Imani was still kissing me, and I knew it was going to break her heart once I told her my news.

"I don't know how say this."

"You know you can tell me anything. That's what I love about you. You're always so honest with me, no matter what it is."

"I never told you why I was in New York."

"Were you with someone else? I mean, I understand you have your own life, and I'm pretty sure if you were in a whole other state you were probably getting some too. I mean, I know you have needs—"

"Imani, I don't mean to cut you off, but there's no one else."

"Okay, so what is it?"

"I was out there for a job opportunity."

"What do you mean a job opportunity? Are you talking about that job that you mentioned a while back when the three of us were out to dinner?" Imani quickly sat up and pulled the cover over herself, which was something she never did because she loved exposing her bare body to me, so I knew she was getting irritated.

"I made some amazing contacts while we were in Bali, and yes, Lisa called me about some new yoga studios opening up on the East Coast and the main studio is in New York. She recommended me to the owner, and so I was out there for a job interview, and I decided to take the job."

"What the fuck do you mean you took the job? I thought you said you weren't even interested? You're moving to New York?"

"Yeah, that's pretty much what I'm saying."

"So, you're just going to leave me like this? Are you fucking kidding me?"

"Babe, please don't yell."

"Don't tell me what to do. I can't believe this shit. You tell me this after we make love? Serenity, that's even a new low for you."

"What the hell are you talking about? I've been telling you for the longest time that I didn't think this was going to work. You're the one who keeps pushing your pussy in my face, acting as if I shouldn't do anything about it. What did you expect to happen? You're the one that showed up here with no panties on. You were already trying to get it in before you even walked through the door."

"You know what? Fuck you, Serenity! I can't believe you would do this to me!"

"I can't believe you're actually mad at me for a decision I made when we were not together. C'mon now."

"I can't with you right now. I'm so over this, and I'm over you."

"You've got a lot of nerve, Imani. I've always been straight up with you and Alex about myself and my feelings. I can't exactly say the same about you, though."

"Oh, so you gon' keep throwing that in my face? I'm trying to deal with all of this. I didn't know I was gonna meet you and fall in love. I really thought Alex and I were good, and we were just adding you to the mix for some excitement from time to time. But it became more than that for me, and I'm sorry I didn't exactly know how to handle that. Excuse the fuck outta me for not having all of life's answers like you, Serenity. I'm fucking trying, okay? I didn't really know how this poly shit was supposed to work."

"Believe it or not, me either, but I thought we were all mature enough to handle it."

"It's not just about maturity, Serenity. I didn't know I was going to feel the way I do about *you*. Dammit, I said I'm sorry." Imani just sat on the bed crying, and all I could do was hold her. At least she let me.

I didn't know what to do with all of this. For that moment, I didn't try to figure it out. We just laid in bed together. I rubbed Imani's hair and continued to hold her until she fell asleep. Before I knew it, I dozed off, too, until I woke up and glanced at the clock; it was three in the morning. I looked at my phone and had five missed calls from Alex. I knew if he had called me that many times, he had to have called Imani a dozen more times.

"Babe, wake up. It's three o'clock in the fucking morning! Check your phone. Alex called me, like, five times!"

"Oh shit! Oh my God, he called me too!" Imani began checking her voice messages.

The first time Alex left a message, he sounded calm but just inquiring where she was. The next few messages, we could hear the anger in his voice. But the last few messages, his voice changed to worry.

"Imani, you gotta head home. Do you want to call him first?"

"I better not. Maybe he'll be asleep when I get in."

"I don't know about that. I wonder if he tried coming by my house but we didn't hear the bell. Would you like me to follow you there? I don't have to get out of the car. I just want to make sure you're all good."

"You don't have to. You know I'm just a few blocks away, and I did drive so I won't be out late walking by myself."

"Okay, well, please text me once you get in."

"Okay, I will." Imani put on her dress and tried to toss her hair back to camouflage the look of sex all over her. "We still need to finish this conversation later."

"Okay, we will, but please head straight home."

"I will." Imani quickly ran to the door and let herself out.

I watched her as she hurried to her car and drove off. I could only imagine what that conversation would be like once she got home.

CHAPTER

13

What a difference a year made. It was my forty-first birthday, and I definitely didn't imagine it would be like this.

At this point last year, I was finally getting a grip on my life after Mama's death. And just when I thought I was embarking on so many great things in my career and a budding relationship, that all changed. There were a few times I could sense my panic attacks trying to return, but somehow, I was able to calm myself and work through it with the help of the calming techniques Dr. Wilson had shown me.

The sky was beautiful, and seeing people ride their bikes in front of my porch was relaxing for some reason. I'd always wanted to live in a brownstone when I was an undergrad at NYU, and now that was my reality. As soon as I put my home on the market, it sold in a matter of days. Ironically, I ended up attracting an investor from New York who was looking to buy single-family homes near Scottsdale. I knew that was a sign I was going to be okay, and moving to New York was the path I was supposed to take at the time.

"Hey, beautiful queen. You're glowing!" a bike-rider dressed in a dashiki said to me.

That was something I didn't see or hear in Paradise Valley, and I embraced every minute of it. It was so exciting to be immersed in such rich culture again. I loved hearing the various languages and dialects of people from all over and had missed hanging out in the numerous boroughs. Who would've thought I would be ecstatic to ride the subway again? I took more walks now that everything was in close proximity to each other. I enjoyed nightlife again and even gradually started eating meat again, which came as a shock to me. After being a vegetarian most of my adult life, I decided it was time to unlock myself from any one way of thinking or living. There was no reason to deny myself some of the best food on earth. This ass and these hips filled out a bit more because of it, but nothing too excessive.

I spent the morning of my birthday people-watching, thinking about Mama, and reflecting on my growth over the past year. Accepting the position as lead yoga instructor at Yoga Theory felt like the best decision I could've made. The night Imani left my home was the beginning of my new life. I worried about her after she left. I tried texting and calling her for days before she responded back to me. For a minute, my mind wandered, and I wondered if Alex snapped and hurt her, but I trusted she would return my call. Eventually she did and apologized for not getting back to me. She said she told Alex she was at one of the other mom's houses that Yaya has playdates with and they had a little too much to drink, so she didn't want to drive home and ended up falling asleep. I guessed he bought that story. She told me that since I was moving, she was just going to work on her marriage. So, in a nutshell, her and Alex were both lying to each other. Alex was doing God knew what with Melissa, and Imani was in a marriage she didn't really want to be in. That made my decision to move that much easier.

When I poured my heart out to Dr. Wilson about what had been going on in my life and that I was moving, she said she was so proud of me for the work I had done on myself and that I was following my life's path. She said, even though I had taken some hard hits over the past four years, she could tell I was facing life head on. She gushed like a proud mama, and I accepted her praise. She slipped up and called me Gigi, her daughter, a few times in our conversation and even made a statement to me that I figured was intended for Gigi and not me. That was hard to deal with because I knew that time would come; I just didn't know how soon. I didn't get too wrapped up in the inevitable and tried to maximize every moment and conversation we had.

Yoga Theory was amazing to me, though. Of course, my income was very nice, but the perks, exposure, and opportunities I gained were priceless. I started to feel like I was a part of a community again. Working for myself was great, and I'll never regret the experience it afforded me, but I just felt more connected to people since moving back to New York. As much as I enjoyed my solitude, I still felt pretty secluded in Arizona. Now, I was able to see Cynthia and my brother a lot more. I still wasn't looking forward to those winters, but I figured I'd make it.

"One time for the birthday bish?" Cynthia had called and started singing to me before I could even say hello.

"Aw, thanks, hun. I'm almost positive you've always been the first person to call me on my birthday since Mama passed."

"You know it, Poodah! And that'll never change. What're you doing?"

"Just sitting on my porch, relaxing."

"Only you can find relaxation anywhere you go, even on the busy streets of New York."

"Well, that's me."

"Still taking it all in?"

"Pretty much. It's crazy. I've only been here three months, and I've done and experienced so much already."

"C'mon, you know that's New York. This city don't sleep for shit. There's always something going on."

"Clearly."

"So, look, I know you said you just wanted to chill for your birthday, but at least let me take you out to dinner. You know how crazy my schedule can be at times, and I have the next few days off which is so rare, so let me do something nice for you."

"Hmm…"

"Don't *hmm* me. I want you to wear a hot dress and do your makeup. No yoga pants today, honey."

"Listen, Cynthia, I ain't in the mood for no club scene tonight."

"Girl, hush. I ain't talking about no club. I was just thinking a really nice restaurant at least. C'mon, please?"

"Okay, okay. I know you, and you're not going to let up, so yeah, count me in. Where are we going?"

"Can you let me surprise you a little bit? Damn, I ain't telling you. But now that I know you eating meat again, I ain't gotta be all vigilant about taking you to a vegan spot."

"But that vegan soul food joint Kevin took me to—"

"Girl, if you don't quit…We ain't going to Brooklyn to some hood spot. We doing it big tonight."

"Cynthia!"

"What did I say? It's your birthday, you got that new job, you moved back to New York. Girl, there's a lot to celebrate, and that's all I'm gon' say about that."

"Okay, I got it. And I'll be there."

"And I'm picking you up because I want you to be on time."

I rolled my eyes. "Cynthia, I'm not five."

"It don't matter. I'm picking you up. Better yet, stop by my house first."

"Aight. Love you."

"I love you too, Poodah."

I guessed this year I'd be celebrating my birthday in style.

*****

I couldn't remember the last time I straightened my hair, but I decided my birthday dinner was as good a time as any. I had forgotten how long my hair was simply because I'd always worn my natural curls. I didn't know what it was, but I felt confident and happy. My red strapless dress hugged me in all the right places. I had played around with a makeup tutorial I found on YouTube, so my face was flawlessly done up, and I couldn't help but throw on Mama's black heels. I felt really good, and I didn't want anything to spoil the moment.

I twirled a couple of times in the mirror to do one last full-length body check. I even took a selfie and posted it on Instagram for once. Social media still wasn't my thing, but in the last few years, I tried to get acclimated more to it due to running my own business. The likes and comments started rolling in about how beautiful everyone thought I looked, as well as birthday wishes. Then, of course, there were the comments from the men I grew up with, saying things like, "You getting thick, ma." My old yoga students from Scottsdale were telling me how much they missed me, and they wished me happiness and success in New York.

All of a sudden, I noticed Imani liked my picture, but there was no comment. I waited for a while just to see if she would post anything, but she didn't. No hard feelings; it was just a reminder that we were both moving on.

When my phone vibrated, I thought maybe it was her. Strangely, most times I would think about a person, they would call seconds later. But when I looked at the screen, it was Kevin. There was a slight disappointment it wasn't Imani, but I was still happy to hear from him, nonetheless.

"Good evening, beautiful, and happy birthday." Kevin's voice was so rich and smooth like caramel.

"Hey, thank you! I really appreciate you reaching out to me."

"No problem at all. I would've loved to take you out today, but I wanted to respect your space. I know you said you really wanted to just chill tonight, and I totally understand that. By any chance, are you free for lunch or dinner tomorrow, seeing that it's Sunday and you don't have to work?"

"Of course, boss." We both laughed. "My friend Cynthia convinced me to get up and get dressed. She wants to at least take me to dinner tonight."

"And she's right. I'm glad you're spending time with a loved one. Your friend seems really cool. I hope I get to meet her soon." I agreed, then he continued. "Well, I'll be thinking of something we can get into, and I'll let you know before the night ends. You can let me know if that works for you or not. How does that sound?"

"Sounds perfect. And again, Kevin, thank you so much for the birthday wishes and this opportunity. I wouldn't be back here if it weren't for you."

"Well, I'm not sure if I can take the credit for all of that. You're amazing all by yourself, but I'm glad you've invited me on your journey. I look forward to more time spent with you— outside of work, of course."

I smiled to myself because Kevin often said such beautiful things to me that always felt genuine. Kevin and I had been out on a few dates together since I'd moved back to New York. We'd kissed a few times, and with the way he kissed, I was actually surprised we hadn't made love yet. We were both extremely tempted to, but I wanted to be sure Imani was fully out of my system. Even though I knew I needed to let Imani go, it didn't mean I wasn't still in love with her. But every day I was getting closer to fully closing that chapter of my life.

"That sounds very good to me."

"Okay, enjoy your evening, and I'll talk with you soon."

After I said goodbye and hung up the phone, I turned on one of Mama's favorite songs again, "Nights Over Egypt," as I put the finishing touches on my hair and makeup. I felt really good for some reason. I scheduled my Uber, and while I waited, I looked around my beautiful brownstone and was just so thankful of where I was in my life. I felt fulfilled, like there was so much in store for me. Even at forty-one, with no life partner and no children, I was satisfied with my life. I knew, in time, if there was someone I was supposed to share my life with, it would come, and there was no need to rush that. I was enjoying this moment in time.

As I walked down the steps of my building to enter my Uber driver's car, I couldn't help but notice the license plate read MRSJUDY. I couldn't believe my eyes—Mama's name was Judy. Tears of joy swelled in my eyes, and I tried to hold them back, but I couldn't. I felt like Mama was telling me everything was going to be just fine and she was, and always would be, with me.

"Good evening," my Uber driver said from the front seat, then turned around to see me blotting my eyes with a tissue and sniffling. "Oh, Miss, are you okay?"

"I'm fine. It's just when you pulled up, I noticed your license plate. My mom's name was Judy and today is the four-year anniversary of her death."

"Oh, honey. May God be with you today. But just know this: it's no coincidence this happened. Your Mama is truly smiling down on you. I can see the glow all around you." My driver appeared to be around the same age my mom would've been. Her car smelled like fresh fruit, and the gray ringlets in her hair gave me comfort for some reason, as if I were in the presence of wisdom.

"Thank you so much for that." I continued to blot my eyes as to not smear my makeup.

"Anytime, honey. You look so beautiful. Going somewhere special?" she asked curiously.

"I'm meeting a friend for dinner. I'm heading to her house first."

"That sounds wonderful. Is it a special occasion?"

"Actually, there's a lot to celebrate. I just got a new job and moved back to New York a few months ago. And today is my birthday." I smiled.

"Oh sweetie, that *is* a lot to celebrate! By the looks of it, I'm pretty sure your mom would be proud of you. You look young, my dear. How old are you?"

"I'm forty-one."

"Oh, beautiful! Well, they say black don't crack, and you're proof of that. I thought you were in your twenties!"

"Aw, thanks for the compliment." Mrs. Judy was definitely putting a smile on my face.

"No need to say thank you at all. You're the one looking like a bright light."

Mrs. Judy's laugh reminded me of those grandmas in the movies—the ones always cooking and sharing stories from the past. I never knew any of my grandparents, so I didn't have first-hand knowledge.

"Mrs. Judy…can I call you Mrs. Judy?"

"Everyone does, love."

"I miss my mama so much. I think about her all the time. I started having panic attacks after she passed. I've only had three, but sometimes they come out during times when everything seems fine—more than fine. I'm actually really excited about tonight. I just feel my mama's presence, but I've been excited about something before and then I'll have a panic attack. I don't get that. I've gone to a therapist for some time, and she's taught me how to cope with it, but I'm so curious as to why I have them even when I seem to be in a good mood."

For some reason, I got the sense I could talk to this woman who I'd never met before but seemed to have the wisdom necessary for me to get over this hump.

"Oh, baby, those panic things don't care if you're happy or sad. They just come if you're overwhelmed. You see how you cried when you saw your mama's name on my car? Sure, you were happy to feel like she's with you right now, but that too can be overwhelming. I used to have those panic things when I was young, but there wasn't a word for it then. I would get so scared, thinking I was gonna die, and my mama would make light of it and just act like I was being dramatic. But my grandma used to sit me on her lap and rock me back and forth and sing a hymn to me, and that always calmed me down. I was never diagnosed with anything, but I knew it was real, and so did my grandma. She said I had to be a little more observant than others when I felt really happy or sad so I could balance my reaction to it. She told me to pretend she was rocking me while singing that song, and do you know it worked every time?

"See, all this medicine and diagnosis stuff is fine and all, but people need to get back to just loving each other and being in the company of good people who will comfort you. When you said your friend was taking you out for your birthday, that made me smile because we need good friends, family, and loving neighbors around us. That's why we're so on edge and anxious these days because we're trying to do so much alone, and we got stress on us. When I was a little girl, my daddy would drink a lot and hit my mama, so I really believe that's where my anxiety came from."

"Wow, Mrs. Judy, you're saying so much to me right now. My daddy was the same way, and he used to hit my mama too!"

"Well, baby, that's probably where those panic attacks started coming from. And then it all started happening when your mama died. Listen, baby girl, I can tell you're a fighter. If you went through all of that and you're still here to tell it, you gon' be alright."

"Oh my God, thank you, Mrs. Judy!"

"No problem, baby. That's what I'm here for."

"If you don't mind me asking, what made you start driving for Uber?"

"Because of moments like these."

That statement alone said enough. I needed to have that moment with her. I looked up and thought to myself, *thank you, Mama.*

"Thank you so much, Mrs. Judy. I appreciate you."

"God bless you, honey. I see this is your stop. Enjoy your special day, and be safe, you hear?"

"I sure will."

As I was on the steps of Cynthia's house, she called me, asking where I was. I told her I was literally at the door. When Cynthia opened the door, she was breathing a bit hard.

"What the hell were you doing?" I chuckled.

"Girl, nothing, just trying to fix the button on the back of my dress."

"Why is your house so dark?"

"Because we're about to go out, duh?"

"Whatever, I just know you. You still leave the light on above the stove. I never understood why people do that."

"Girl, would you just come in? I don't need a whole bunch of people trying to look into my house."

When I closed the door behind me, Cynthia realized she had forgotten something in the kitchen and asked me to turn on the light, so she could see. Amused, I shook my head, but went to do as she asked. I felt along the side and flicked the switch, then—

"Surprise!"

I almost fell when all of the people popped out of every corner of Cynthia's house.

"Surprise, beautiful! It's your birthday and your welcome back to New York party!" Cynthia screamed as if it was the new year.

I couldn't believe the décor. There were balloons, a big sign that read, "Welcome back Serenity and happy birthday," with a very beautiful picture of myself on it. Cynthia even had DJ Tam spinning. I couldn't believe it. Kevin was even here and both of my brothers, along with my nieces and nephews, who I hadn't seen in a long time. Quite a few of my college buddies showed up, and even Jeanette did too. No one could separate Cynthia, Jeanette, and myself with a crowbar back in the day. Also, some people from the yoga studio came.

"Cynthia, how did you do all of this?"

"Trust me, I have my ways." Cynthia winked and instructed everyone to move to the rooftop. Cynthia lived in a beautiful brownstone as well, a couple of thousand square feet larger than mine, but she also had a beautiful rooftop where the party was going to take place. There were hanging lights, catered food, banquet-style seating, space for a makeshift dance floor, and amazing music.

"Happy birthday, gorgeous." Kevin approached me and gave me the longest, most endearing hug, like he hadn't seen me in a long time.

"Thank you, Kev. So, you knew about this the whole time?"

"Yeah, I did. You'd talked about your friend Cynthia quite a few times, so I could tell how close y'all were. She stopped by the studio one day when you were teaching a class and told me about her plans to surprise you. She said you mentioned me to her a number of times and said how enamored you were by me." Kevin winked.

"See, now I know you're lying because Cynthia doesn't say shit like *enamored.*"

He laughed. "I know, it's all good. I'm just messing with you. But for real, she did mention you were kind of digging me a bit and thought it would be cool if I came. So, are you okay with me being here?"

"I'm more than okay with you being here." I smiled seductively.

"That's what I like to hear." Kevin kissed me passionately.

"Okay, break this shit up for a minute. We're about to play the birthday song for you."

Cynthia grabbed my arm and took me over to the floor, and everyone followed. We were all dancing to the music, and I felt Kevin come behind me and slowly grind on me. It felt like we were at an old-school basement party.

"This is amazing. I thought I didn't want all the bells and whistles for my birthday, but this is so cool." I just kept admiring the décor and all the people who showed up for me.

"You deserve all of this and more. I am so fucking happy to have you back in New York!" Cynthia yelled from across the rooftop.

She was drinking and kissing her man. Kevin kept dancing with me, and we had our moment on the dance floor. He looked happy to have me in New York as well.

"You look so fucking good tonight, Serenity," he said while staring at me.

I twirled and smiled. "Why, thank you."

"But you know what looks most beautiful? Your happiness."

"I appreciate that because I really am happy."

"I can tell."

We were interrupted by my phone vibrating. My heart sank. It was Imani. I struggled for those few seconds if I should answer or not then decided to.

"Can you excuse me, Kevin? I need to take this."

"Go right ahead. I'll be waiting for you."

I zoomed past the crowd back inside Cynthia's building so I could hear.

When I picked up, Imani's beautiful voice immediately overtook the speaker as she sang happy birthday to me. Moments like these, I was reminded of how talented she was. "Thank you. I really appreciate that."

"No problem. I'm just glad you picked up the phone. I figured you were probably busy celebrating."

"Well, believe it or not, I was just going to chill tonight, but Cynthia actually threw me a surprise party. I can't believe my brothers and my nieces and nephews are actually here."

"That's great. You sound really happy."

"I am."

"Well, I don't know anyone who deserves it more." Imani sounded a bit melancholy. I really didn't know what to say.

"Are you okay?"

"Yep, why do you ask?"

"Imani, I know you. I can tell in your voice something is wrong."

"I don't want to be a downer on your birthday."

"I wouldn't have asked if I didn't want to know, so tell me what's up."

"Alex is cheating, and I'm leaving him, Serenity." Imani gave absolutely no warning at all that she was about to say something like that.

"How do you know?"

"I saw him out with some chick when I was running errands. Honestly, I don't even care. I was ready to be done with this marriage, anyway. I guess it was just a sign."

"So, did you confront him about it?"

"No, not yet, and I'm not going to. He won't know until I file the divorce papers."

"Are you sure you just want to end it like that? You do have Yaya to think about."

"Whose side are you on, Serenity?" She paused, and I could imagine her shaking her head. "Okay, my bad, it's your birthday, and I don't want to ruin it for you. Just have a nice life."

This time, Imani hung up on me. I could tell she was frustrated and angry, but I didn't really think her anger was toward me. I think she was finally starting to see everything she'd compromised for Alex, only to find out he was still thinking about himself at the end of the day. I could tell she was resentful. As much as I wanted to call her back and soothe her pain, I knew it wasn't my place.

I took a deep breath and thought about what Mrs. Judy said about feeling overwhelmed. I pretended I had a grandmother to rock me back and forth to calm my worries and sing to me. It really helped. I returned to my party and allowed everyone there to express their love to me. I needed it a lot. Dave even sent me a text message telling me happy birthday and that he was thrilled for where I was at in my life. Dave was the one who convinced me to even come out here and inquire about my new job. It was funny, out of all people, he would've been the one to do that. I could only imagine what was to come of my new life. I knew one thing—I wasn't afraid of something new.